THE GREAT REVOLT

A Selection of Titles from Paul Doherty

The Canterbury Tales Mysteries
A TOURNAMENT OF MURDERS
GHOSTLY MURDERS
THE HANGMAN'S HYMN
A HAUNT OF MURDER
THE MIDNIGHT MAN *

The Brother Athelstan Mysteries
THE HOUSE OF CROWS
THE ASSASSIN'S RIDDLE
THE DEVIL'S DOMAIN
THE FIELD OF BLOOD
THE HOUSE OF SHADOWS
BLOODSTONE *
THE STRAW MEN *
CANDLE FLAME *
THE BOOK OF FIRES *
THE HERALD OF HELL *
THE GREAT REVOLT *

* *available from Severn House*

THE GREAT REVOLT

Paul Doherty

Severn House Large Print
London & New York

This first large print edition published 2017
in Great Britain and the USA by
SEVERN HOUSE PUBLISHERS LTD of
19 Cedar Road, Sutton, Surrey, England, SM2 5DA.
First world regular print edition published 2016 by
Crème de la Crime Ltd, an imprint of
Severn House Publishers Ltd.

British Library Cataloguing in Publication Data
A CIP catalogue record for this title is available from the British Library.

ISBN-13: 9780727895134

Typeset by Palimpsest Book Production Ltd.,
Falkirk, Stirlingshire, Scotland.
Printed and bound in Great Britain by
T J International, Padstow, Cornwall.

Historical Note

England's royal family has endured a bloody and twisted history. In 1326 Edward II of England was deposed and allegedly murdered in Berkeley Castle on the orders of his wife Queen Isabella and her lover Roger Mortimer. Edward II was buried at Gloucester, where his splendid tomb can still be visited. However, this magnificent monument masks one of the most tangled mysteries in the history of the English crown, a mystery which continued to surface long after the hurling days of 1326 had come and gone. Edward II was succeeded by his warlike son Edward III, whose successor, Richard II, became immersed in the tragic and violent fate of his great-grandfather, Edward II . . .

Part One

Athelstan, Dominican friar and parish priest of St Erconwald's in Southwark, moved restlessly. He breathed a prayer for help against the horrors he half-suspected lurked behind the door, now being forced, on the upper gallery of the guest-house at Blackfriars. Athelstan swallowed hard and stared at the wall painting to the right side of the door. In the circumstances, the painting was most appropriate. The artist, whoever it was, had certainly caught the present times. The wall fresco depicted the fall of Sodom and Gomorrah, cities of the plain, which tumbled from God's grace into the deepest destruction. The painting presented a vivid scene of divine wrath: all the elements of nature running riot, the black-horizoned landscape glowing with flame. Strife held sway over raging hordes of warriors bristling with weapons. Fiery furnaces and hellish volcanoes burnt fiercely, the blackness beyond them constantly pricked with globes of light which illuminated fang-faced demons armed for war.

'Do you fear the worst, Brother Athelstan?'

'Certainly, Procurator General.'

1

Matteo Fieschi, Procurator General of the Dominican Order, was deeply agitated. He was a small tub of a man, with a smooth Italianate face, round, expressive eyes, snub nose and the soft, pursed lips of a lady, an individual most delicate in his gestures and movements. Procurator Matteo had now been joined by his two assistants, Brothers Cassian and Isidore, young Dominicans, tall and slender, with clean-shaven, intelligent faces and sharp, hawk-like eyes. Athelstan had quickly learnt how their master's mood and every whim governed their conduct. Now was no different.

Prior Anselm's guests were clearly agitated on this morning of 12 June, the year of Our Lord 1381, the Feast of St Sempronius. They had good cause to be: their colleague and comrade Brother Alberic, secretary to the Procurator General, had failed to attend Divine Office in the main church or gather with the rest to break his fast on honeyed oatmeal in the refectory below. Anselm, Prior of Blackfriars, had been summoned, Athelstan too. He now watched his superior direct lay brothers hammering at the heavy, elmwood door with their mallets, aiming at the leather hinges as the door appeared to be securely locked and bolted from within. Knocking and shouting had failed to arouse Alberic. The door was to be forced and Athelstan steeled himself against what might lie beyond. On so many occasions the friar had waited for this chamber or that room to be forced to reveal some gruesome murder. Was this about to happen now? But why? The delegation from Italy had arrived in the city ten days ago, ostensibly to meet with King Richard on '*Coronae secreta negotia* – Secret business of the Crown', only to be swept up in the Great Revolt which now threatened to engulf London.

Athelstan closed his eyes and prayed earnestly for help. He sighed and opened his eyes, then stared again at the wall painting of Sodom and Gomorrah being consumed by fire. London was facing the same fate. Two peasant armies now massed outside London; the men of Essex to the north at Smithfield, and Kentish men to the south at Greenwich. It was only a matter of days before they united. They would then sweep through Southwark where they would be joined by Athelstan's parishioners, led by Watkin the dung-collector, Pike the ditcher, Ranulf the rat-catcher and all their cunning coven. These miscreants now openly proclaimed they were Upright Men, stalwart supporters of the Great Community of the Realm, that mysterious, almost invisible organisation dedicated to violent revolution; the overturning of both crown and church, the toppling of prince and prelate, the destruction of the great Whore of Babylon, namely London, and the setting up of a new Jerusalem. A new commonwealth would be created where land and property were held in common and all were equal before God and the law.

Athelstan scraped his sandalled foot in frustration. He did not care for such make-believe, ale-fumed dreams which, he feared, would end in hangings and disembowellings on execution platforms dripping with gore, beneath gaunt

3

scaffold branches and gallow ladders black against the sky. The head-severing block, the axe, the tumbril and all the horrid impedimenta of brutal, judicial death carried out to the bitter, anguished cries of widows and orphans, would be the order of the day.

'Satan sets up banquets at such times and in such places . . .'

'I beg your pardon, Brother Athelstan?'

The friar smiled his apologies at Prior Anselm.

'Father, my apologies,' Athelstan whispered, 'but I am so deeply worried. You summoned me here six days ago and I am now anxious about my parishioners . . .' Athelstan was momentarily distracted by a clatter on the stairs and the sudden appearance on the top step of the royal courier. Master Luke was staying at Blackfriars on the orders of the King, so he could take messages to and from Procurator Matteo. In the end, however, the King's messenger had also been caught up by the turmoil in the city and forced to shelter in Blackfriars. The messenger, his handsome face framed by blonde hair, stared quickly around, grimaced and promptly disappeared down the stairs.

There was a sudden crack. The door was buckling. The top hinge had snapped. The lay brothers were now battering at the bottom one, which abruptly broke loose. The door was forced back. Prior Anselm hurried to go around it, followed by the Procurator General and his escort. Athelstan heard their cries and exclamations and hastened to join them, stepping around the door into the cavernous guest room: a gaunt, stark chamber with only the narrowest lancet window providing light, a few meagre sticks of furniture, a simple cot-bed, a table, two stools and a chair. The lanternhorn on its rest was extinguished and the candles on their spigots had long guttered out. Brother Alberic lay twisted on the floor, head slightly back, eyes eerily glassy in their soulless stare. The cause of death was a deep dagger wound to the chest, close to the heart. The weapon itself, its blade stained with dried blood, lay next to the dead man's half-curled, stiffened fingers.

'This is your domain, Athelstan,' Prior Anselm whispered. 'You are most skilled in such matters.'

'In such matters?' the Procurator General snapped.

'I shall explain later,' Anselm retorted. 'Brother Athelstan, please . . .?'

'All of you,' Athelstan gestured gently with his hands, 'stay back. Do not touch anything, I beg you.'

Reluctantly, Fieschi obeyed. The prior also ordered the lay brothers who'd forced the door to stand outside. They would keep other members of the community at bay and curb their curiosity about the abomination which had occurred in their friary. Athelstan asked for a candle to be lit, waiting until the flame glowed beneath its cap.

'Very well.' Athelstan crouched down, placing the candle on the floor beside the corpse. 'First the rite.' The friar blessed the corpse. He whispered the 'Absolvo te' giving absolution, followed by the swift anointing of Alberic's forehead, eyes, lips, hands, chest and feet.

'Good,' Athelstan breathed. 'So first. The corpse is cold and rigid, yet in places . . .' He touched the dead man's right hand, 'beginning to soften again. The face is shocked and livid, eyes staring, mouth agape. Bloodstains to the lips and chin but this is dried as, in the main, is the heart's blood on his chest. Brother Alberic is dressed in the black and white robe of our order with no ornamentation. He wears outside sandals on his feet. When did you see him last?' Athelstan glanced up at Fieschi.

'Last night, an hour after Compline. We all shared a jug of your mead along with chopped bread and meat in the refectory.'

'And he seemed well?'

'Very well.'

'And how old was Brother Alberic?'

'Just past his thirty-fifth year.'

'Young, vigorous,' Athelstan murmured. He felt the hard muscle of the dead man's right arm. 'A former swordsman?'

'Very much so,' Fieschi replied. 'A former knight in the service of the Visconti of Milan. A soldier of fortune who experienced a road to Damascus vision. He saw the error of his ways, converted and became a Dominican priest.'

'Faithful in his vows?'

'*Usque ad mortem*,' Brother Cassian declared lugubriously. 'Faithful even until death. Alberic was a true friar, a chaste priest, a loyal son of S. Dominic.'

Athelstan rose to his feet and asked for more candles to be brought, lit and placed in a circle on the table. Conscious of the others watching him, he picked up the dagger and scrupulously examined it in the flaring light of the candles. An old weapon, he observed, its long double blade encrusted with blood from top to hilt.

'What is this?' Athelstan gestured to the others to draw closer and inspect the dagger.

'I don't know,' Prior Anselm declared. 'I have never seen the likes before.' His remark was echoed by the others. Athelstan placed the dagger on the table, took the candle and crouched down to scrutinise the floor. He detected traces of blood on the rope matting stretched across the polished open boards, though no blood on the door. Ignoring the growing murmur of whispered conversation around him, he studied the heavy door. He noted how the bolts at the top and the bottom had been ruptured, along with the simple but heavy locking device, the key still twisted within. The chamber door could also be opened on a chain, so the person within could first check any visitor; this too had been in place when Alberic was mysteriously killed, the chain obviously snapped when the door was forced.

'Did anyone visit Brother Alberic?' Athelstan asked, staring down at the harsh, raw-boned face of the dead man. 'I mean, after you left the refectory yesterday evening?' Murmured denials greeted his question.

'Prior Anselm,' Fieschi protested. 'Must we be questioned like this?'

'Yes!' Athelstan did not wait for his prior's response. 'Yes, you must! A human being has been foully murdered. I had little to do with poor Alberic but I respect him for what he was, not just for what he did. He was a comrade, a brother in our order, a priest with the power to absolve sin and to change bread and wine into the body of our Risen Christ. So yes, you must, I must, we must, all be questioned. Is that clear?' Athelstan caught himself and decided to say no more. He was aware of how tired he was. Worries nagged at him about the safety of his parishioners, his good friend the widow Benedicta and, above all, his bosom comrade Sir John Cranston, one of only a few crown officials who had not abandoned his post and fled. Outside a violent storm was swiftly gathering, threatening to engulf those Athelstan loved and cared for.

'*Pax et bonum.*' Fieschi held up a hand. 'Athelstan, my apologies, I am just distraught.' He and Athelstan exchanged the kiss of peace. The clamour from outside had grown. Prior Anselm stepped around the door and the noisy chatter immediately subsided.

'Continue, Athelstan,' Anselm instructed as he re-entered the chamber.

'Very well. Brother Alberic was a former soldier,' Athelstan declared, 'vigorous and strong. He apparently left the guesthouse refectory last night and came up here, where he locked, bolted and chained the chamber door. He should have been secure, safe from danger, but he certainly was not. He was brutally stabbed to the heart with an ancient-looking dagger which no one recognises. More mysterious is that this murderous assault was perpetrated in a locked room with no sign of any other entrance, no secret passageway, and there is more.'

8

Athelstan knelt beside the corpse and pulled back the robe to examine the dead man's legs. He then folded back the sleeves, scrutinising the arms, wrists and hands of the cadaver most diligently. 'Strange, most strange,' he murmured, 'no sign, not even a scratch of any struggle or challenge.' Athelstan glanced up. 'A vigorous man, as I have said, a former soldier. Surely he would have resisted and there would be some evidence of this?' He got to his feet. 'Are we to believe that this experienced fighter allowed someone to approach him with a naked dagger and thrust it deep inside him, but not react? No evidence of a struggle, nothing overturned. Of course, that prompts the most pressing question: why?' He paused as Procurator Fieschi walked across to the far wall where cloaks and robes hung from the pegs; boots, sandals and a leather chancery satchel rested beneath. 'Procurator?' Athelstan called out.

Fieschi lifted a hand in acknowledgement; he knelt, picked up the chancery satchel, opened it and swiftly searched its contents. He rose as Athelstan walked over to him.

'Brother,' Fieschi murmured, 'nothing is out of place, except . . .' He opened the chancery satchel to reveal a roll of parchment, an ink horn, pumice stone, sander and a collection of quill pens. 'Something is missing.'

'What?' Athelstan asked.

'A leather schedule fashioned out of the purest Moroccan; it should be here. It contained certain documents in Alberic's care. Now they have gone.'

'What were they?' Athelstan demanded.

'At the moment,' Fieschi glanced over his shoulder at his two companions, 'I cannot say. No, I cannot say any more.'

'And neither can I,' Athelstan retorted. 'Prior Anselm, Alberic's corpse should be removed to the death house.'

Anselm left the room. Athelstan stared round. Fieschi was correct, he reflected: nothing was out of place. The bed was undisturbed, made up and neat, the candle-stool beside it hadn't been moved, the three-branched spigot and psalter were placed orderly together. Athelstan walked over and picked up the psalter, but it was only a copy borrowed from the friary chapel and contained nothing significant. He carefully examined the stoppered jar of fresh water on its tray along with two pewter cups, but he could detect nothing amiss. Everything was as it should be except for that corpse sprawled gruesomely on the floor.

'But how can it be?' Athelstan whispered hoarsely. He paused as three Dominicans came in unannounced. Athelstan smiled as he recognised two of the priory's most senior friars – Brother Hugh, the infirmarian, and Matthias, chief clerk and scribe – and their usual shadow, the gatekeeper, lay brother John. Old men, but wiry and alert. John was the shortest of the three: almost bald, with a ruddy face, his nose broken and twisted, a relict, so he boasted, of his turbulent youth. Hugh and Matthias looked alike: tall and slender with close-cropped white hair, their faces lined and furrowed but their eyes sharp, bright with life. Each man had a dimple in his chin, which offset the rather severe cast of the firm mouth and high cheekbones.

'We heard.' Hugh crouched beside the corpse, studying it carefully. He peered up at Athelstan. 'Did you examine the corpse as I taught you?'

'As you taught me, Magister.' Athelstan smiled at his former mentor. 'How in God's name can I ever forget my months of scrupulous work with you?' Athelstan nodded at Matthias. 'Or with you, the most skilled of scribes and master of novices, or Brother John, gatekeeper and constant helpmate to you both? However,' he gestured at the corpse, 'as you can see, our comrade is beyond all physical help.'

'Shall we remove him now?'

'Yes, you can,' Athelstan replied. 'In fact, I shall help you.'

Brother John left and returned with a stretcher, a piece of canvas pulled tight across two ash poles. Athelstan hid his smile: he remembered carrying this battered, stained bier so many times during his novitiate at Blackfriars. He helped the others to lift the corpse on to it. All four then carried the stretcher along the gallery, down the stairs and into the great cobbled yard which stretched outside the guesthouse. The other three sides of the bailey were taken up by the two-storied accommodation of the community, along with spacious chambers for honoured guests such as the Procurator General. The area was heavily shaded but Athelstan still marvelled at the brilliant blue sky and the warm, balmy fragrance. A truly beautiful day was

11

promised, one with more than a touch of late spring freshness.

'Brother Athelstan, Brother Athelstan!' The friar turned as a young girl, no more than nine summers, slipped her hand free from her severe-looking nurse and raced across the cobbles so swiftly her long, blonde hair broke free from its jewelled hairnet, her gown of silk-edged sarcenet billowing out all about her. Athelstan excused himself from the others, ensuring the blanket over Alberic's corpse covered everything, and hastened to meet her. He dropped to one knee as she literally threw herself into his arms.

'Brother, Brother,' she gasped, 'I have missed you! Haven't we, Katrina?'

She turned and shouted at her nurse, still standing as forbidding as a Cistercian nun. The woman nodded and lifted a hand.

'I see you mix with the midnight clover?' The young girl pointed at the other three Dominicans.

'Pardon?' Athelstan held her out at arm's-length.

'The midnight clover.' The girl leaned forward, eager for Athelstan to embrace her, which he did.

'So you know about herbs?' he teased.

'Father told me. I call them that because they are always together.'

'Yes, they are!' Athelstan agreed. 'It's been the same since I was not much older than you, Isabella.'

'Who are they?'

'Dominican friars. Hugh Biscop is our infirmarian, one of the best in London, and his bosom comrade Matthias Damoy is a skilled clerk, and

12

the third man is their life-long helpmate John Guisborough, otherwise known as Brother John the gatekeeper. I believe all three were born in the shadow of Warwick Castle.' Athelstan stared at the group of Dominicans, who stood patiently waiting for him to return. He indicated that they move on but Hugh grinned, sketched a blessing in Athelstan's direction and turned back to his comrades deep in conversation.

'That's what happens in our order, Isabella.' Athelstan smiled and gently touched her ivory skin, stroking her cheek as she stared wide-eyed at him. 'We leave our families for a life of prayer but that doesn't stop us from making friends or indeed creating a new family: those three Dominicans are more brothers than men who share the same womb.'

'They frighten me a little.'

'Oh, that's because they became wise as they have grown old.' Athelstan glanced swiftly over. Hugh and Matthias did look severe, with their deep-set sharp eyes and hooked noses. They had the look of the falcon, with minds just as sharp. Both were skilled in physic, the diagnosis of disease and the potions to combat it. Brother John was also a skilled herbalist. The three of them had been Athelstan's faithful mentors and, if possible, he was determined to use them to resolve Alberic's murder.

'Who is the dead man?' Isabella whispered. 'I know he is dead. I have seen men like that before. Bodies hidden under a cloth, taken up from the cellars in my father's house long after the midnight hour. I have peered through the shutters to the street below and seen the corpses put on a death cart. Father always thinks I am asleep but I am not.' She smiled impishly. 'I love to get up and watch at the witching hour.'

Athelstan gently held the girl away and stared into her angelic blue eyes. She leaned closer.

'It doesn't frighten me, Brother.' She crossed herself swiftly.

'Nor should it,' Athelstan declared. 'Now I must go.'

He kissed her on both cheeks, rose and rejoined the rest.

'Thibault's daughter,' Hugh whispered.

'Master Thibault, Gaunt's creature,' Matthias echoed. 'Athelstan, I thought you had no time for him?'

'I don't, but come,' Athelstan urged. 'Not here. Isabella, like her father, is very sharp of mind, wit and ear.' He helped the brothers carry the bier across the cobbles and into the cavernous, sprawling corridors and passageways of Blackfriars.

The mother house was busier than usual due to the growing troubles in the city and surrounding shires. Many Dominicans had decided to withdraw from their pastoral work and take refuge behind the fortified gates and battlemented walls of Blackfriars. They crossed yards and baileys, hurrying through the petty cloisters and the great cloisters where the clerks and scribes from the library sat busy in their carrels, poring over their sloping desks, copying and illuminating different manuscripts. The scholars were taking full advantage of the brilliant sunshine, impervious to the

14

storm gathering beyond their walls. Now and again a brother would place a hand on the bier. Athelstan and his companions would pause so a blessing could be sketched over the corpse, then they'd continue along stone-hollowed passage-ways smelling fragrantly of vellum, ink, paints and the pervasive odours of candle smoke and incense. It was a striking contrast to Athelstan's tumultuous parish life in the nave of St Erconwald's, which could become as noisy and smelly as any market place.

On they went under the watchful, stony gaze of demons, gargoyles and babewyns carved on the top of pillars, or the sightless smile of saintly statues, their stone hands raised in perpetual blessing. They skirted the great church. The words of a cantor rehearsing the Divine Office for later in the day drifted out on the morning air, a plea from the Book of Proverbs: 'The house of the wicked will be destroyed . . .'

'God's anger certainly hangs over our city,' Brother Matthias murmured, 'and God knows where it will end. Athelstan, I am so glad you are sheltering here.'

'The city will be swept by a whirlwind of fire,' Brother Hugh declared.

'Refugees are already gathering outside our gate,' Brother John added. 'What is more fright-ening, I have also glimpsed some of the Earthworms dressed like fiends fit for battle.'

'And I am worried about my parishioners,' Athelstan replied. 'Brother John, we have received no message from them or my good friend Sir John Cranston?'

The gatekeeper shook his head. They continued on into the great garden of the monastery, an exquisitely fragrant sea of grass, herb plots, flower beds and small orchards of apple, pear and plum tree. Raised parterres, cultivated shrubs, rose bushes and neatly clipped box hedges pleased the eye whilst flower-covered arbours and trellises offered shade against the summer sun. At the far end of this, down a shadow-dappled pathway, rose the great death house of the friary, a soaring barn-like structure.

A lay brother ushered them into the Chapel of Waiting, a long, gaunt room, its lime-washed walls draped with purple and gold cloths depicting the Five Wounds of Christ and the Seven Sorrows of the Virgin. At the far end hung a crudely carved rood screen. According to tradition, this had been hewn out of the wood used for the execution platform when the Scottish rebel, William Wallace, had been barbarously torn to pieces at Smithfield. Athelstan always thought the room was gloomy enough without such stories. The Chapel of Waiting had small chambers or enclaves leading off from the main room where ointments, oils and potions were stored. The rest of the chapel was used to hold rows of death tables, slightly sloped, so fluids from the corpses being prepared for burial could run off into the funnels dug into the hard-packed earthen floor. Athelstan was given a pomander as some protection against the foul odours of corruption and the heavy stench of pine juice used to clean the cadavers. Four of the tables were in use, covered by black canvas sheeting.

Athelstan noticed how a vein-streaked arm and hand had slipped from beneath one of the sheets as if to touch the reddish water which swirled in pools beneath the table. He sketched a blessing and turned away. Alberic's corpse was swiftly stripped, except for the linen loin cloth, and laid out on a table beneath the great crucifix. In the poor light lancing through the roundel windows high in the wall and the flickering lanternhorns which stood on the corner of each mortuary table, the dead friar's corpse looked truly grotesque. Bone-white flesh contrasting with the sunburnt chest, neck and face and, of course, the gruesome purple-red death wound close to the heart. Under Brother Hugh's careful direction, as if they had journeyed back down the years, Athelstan, assisted by Matthias and John, once again scrutinised the corpse.

'Muscular and strong,' Athelstan murmured. 'No other marks and strangely no sign of violence apart from the death wound.'

'And?' Hugh asked.

'First mystery,' Athelstan retorted, 'as I have said before. How could someone draw close to Alberic, a strong, capable man with considerable military experience, and plunge a dagger deep into his chest without leaving any other sign of violence, either on Alberic's corpse or in his chamber? Nothing to signify even the lightest token of resistance?'

'And secondly?'

'Alberic was stabbed in a sealed chamber, locked and bolted, with no indication whatsoever of how the assassin entered or left. There are no secret entrances, no window large enough to climb through.'

Athelstan paused and smiled at these three teachers from his youth. Hugh and Matthias' harsh faces were all intent under their wiry hair, cut neatly to form the tonsure, whilst Brother John sat head half-turned, listening carefully to what was being said.

'And thirdly?' Hugh demanded.

'Oh, and fourthly and so on!' Athelstan replied, staring down at the corpse. 'Why kill poor Alberic? Why steal his manuscripts? Why such murderous mystery?' He rubbed his brow. 'I have been in Blackfriars now for six days. Prior Anselm says he needs me here. Why, do you know?' All three shook their heads.

'And what is the Procurator General doing here with his party?' Athelstan asked.

'Something about a dead king,' Matthias murmured, pulling up the death sheet to cover the corpse. 'We do not know any details. Father Prior will surely inform us all in good time. But there is another mystery, Athelstan.' Matthias' stern face relaxed. 'What on earth are you doing with young Isabella, daughter of your enemy Thibault?'

'He is not my enemy,' Athelstan retorted. 'He is a man steeped in politics and intrigue, and the leading henchman of Lord Gaunt.'

'And Gaunt is now absent in the north?'

'True, Brother Hugh. God knows why Gaunt chose to leave his nephew and the city at a time like this.' It was a question that many were asking, though Athelstan and Sir John Cranston, Lord

18

High Coroner of the City, had their own private theories about Gaunt's devious machinations. They had discussed it in places where no one could eavesdrop, sharing their suspicions that the self-styled regent and uncle of the boy king Richard II had left his nephew, the court, the city and the kingdom to face the storm. Once the tempest was over, he would return to seize what juicy morsels he could, and if that included the crown, then so be it.

'And Master Thibault?' Matthias snapped his fingers to catch Athelstan's attention.

'Thibault is allegedly sheltering with others of the royal council in the Tower.' Athelstan shrugged. 'They think they are safe there.'

'Are they?'

'I don't really know. I don't think so. The Tower has many postern gates and doors, and I am sure the Upright Men have sympathisers amongst the Tower garrison.'

'So why,' Brother Hugh asked, 'is Thibault's daughter Isabella here?'

'As you may know, the rebels have marked down Gaunt and his coven for brutal death, and that includes members of their families and households. Thibault's only family is young Isabella. I gave Thibault my word, my sworn, solemn word, to look after his daughter; that is why she is here. Master Thibault may be steeped in all forms of wickedness but she is only an innocent child.'

'So she has taken refuge—'

'Sanctuary, Matthias,' Athelstan interjected. 'Isabella has sought sanctuary with me, you and all the good brothers here in Blackfriars, as others have. They want our protection against the cruel storm being whipped up outside.'

'*Pax et bonum*.' The infirmarian lifted a hand placatingly. 'Athelstan, there are rumours that London Bridge is being stormed. Is your friend Sir John safe?'

'God knows!' Athelstan stared at the door. Deep in his heart he wished to go. Prior Anselm had kept him dancing from foot to foot with this excuse or that. Athelstan secretly suspected that the prior wished to keep him out of harm's way and hoped that he might possibly help with the Procurator General's mission to England . . .

'Perhaps he committed suicide?' Brother John broke into Athelstan's thoughts, his weather-beaten face screwed up in concentration, light-blue eyes blinking furiously. 'Alberic, I mean. I have heard of—'

'I doubt it very much.' Athelstan smiled. 'I truly do. There's a tangled tale of murder here, so the truth of it, as always, may take some time to emerge. If Father Prior wishes, I will help. Perhaps it's time I spoke to him bluntly.' He bade all three companions farewell and left the Chapel of Waiting.

Athelstan wanted to be alone. He made his way through a copse of trees into the great meadow, a beautiful stretch of grassland to the east of Blackfriars. The meadow's long grass was lush and peppered with clumps of wild flowers. The cattle which browsed there had already been herded into the milking sheds, their lowing carrying faintly on the river breeze which rippled the grass and whispered amongst the clumps of ancient trees, pools of shade against the strengthening sun. Athelstan was glad to sit out of the sunlight. He stopped and stared at the beacon tower built in the very centre of the meadow, a soaring, drum-like edifice, crenellated and fortified at the top with narrow, arrow-slit windows. Built at least one hundred and fifty years ago, the tower had once served as a refuge for the community against the depredations of river pirates, as well as a defence against the incursions of French galleys during the Season of Winter, the early years of King Henry III's reign when the Capetian kings in Paris nursed secret dreams of reducing England to another province of the French crown. The building was reminiscent of the Peel Towers Athelstan had seen in Ireland along the Pale outside Dublin, or on the Northern March, that desolate wasteland which stretched into Scotland. The tower was designed for defence; its door, built high in the wall, could only be entered by a platform of wooden steps. Athelstan recalled the legends told him as a novice about this eerie, haunted place, of how it was still polluted by the vicious ghosts of river pirates hung on the great gibbet further down the riverbank.

The tower also reminded Athelstan of the rumours sweeping Blackfriars, about the growing threat to the city and the massing of rebel armies. Prior Anselm had intimated that Blackfriars could well be stormed. The Dominican mother house possessed riches and had offered sanctuary to individuals whom the rebels wished to seize.

Athelstan wondered how Sir John Cranston was faring and murmured a prayer for the coroner's safety as well as that of his parishioners, though God knows what mischief they were now involved in! Athelstan shaded his eyes and stared up at the top of the tower. Heights frightened him, but when he was a novice, he was used to climbing this tower to feed the beacon flame to guide river craft when those thick sea mists rolled in to shroud both London and the Thames in their thick, grey fug. Athelstan drew a deep breath. On a lovely summer morning like this the tower would provide a clear view of the river and the far bank, so perhaps he might learn something.

He walked on and climbed the steps. The heavy, weather-beaten door was off its latch. Inside the stairwell, cobwebbed and dirty, reeked of fox, badger and the other wild animals which sheltered there. Athelstan climbed the crumbling steps. Now and again he paused to gaze through the lancet windows. The staircase was spiral, the steps sharp edged. The higher he climbed, the more Athelstan could feel the strengthening breeze. He paused on a stairwell which also housed a narrow jake's chute behind a battered door kept shut by bags of sand. He strained his ears, certain that he had heard a sound from below, but there was nothing, so he continued on.

At the top Athelstan pushed open the trap door. The breeze was warm and vigorous, buffeting him gently as he carefully climbed on to the tower top. Thankfully the ground underneath was covered with thick shale to provide a good secure grip. He stared around. The rest of the tower top looked derelict. Athelstan carefully picked his way across to grip the iron bar fixed on to the inside of the crenellations. He steadied himself and got his bearings, staring out across the river. This was strangely deserted except for a few barges scurrying like water beetles along the Thames. Athelstan looked to his left, and his heart skipped a beat. Thick, black columns of smoke were beginning to rise either side of London Bridge. Had the rebels finally broken into the city? If so, would they carry out their threat to lay waste with fire and sword? Were his parishioners now part of a violent mob swarming around the Tower? And Sir John? Would Cranston fight even if the odds were heavily against him? Athelstan reined in his panic. As if to reflect his mood, clouds drifted across the sun sending dark shadows racing over the meadow land below. He leaned against the fortified parapet and murmured a prayer for those in his love, then crossed himself and made to leave.

Athelstan pulled back the trap door and went carefully down the steps. The silence seemed oppressive, even baleful, but Athelstan put this down to what he had glimpsed from the tower. A scraping sound echoed up the stairwell; he paused. He heard it again as if the door at the bottom had opened and shut. He caught his breath and strained his hearing but he could detect nothing untoward. He continued on down; his feet slipped. He grabbed the guide rope and saw that the steps were now glimmering with oil. Athelstan hastily retreated just in time as a lighted taper followed by another was tossed to land on the step he had just left.

He needed no second urging, but swiftly retreated back up the stairwell as the steps below erupted into flame. Athelstan realised the fire was deliberate yet his assailant had failed. The flames could not go any higher whilst at the same time they blocked the mysterious attacker from drawing any closer. Moreover, there was no wood on the stone spiral staircase, nothing combustible except the hard, cord guide rope. Athelstan glimpsed the bags of sand. He grabbed one and shook the sack empty, cascading the sand over the now dying flames, smothering the fire until there was nothing but tendrils of black smoke. Carefully, he resumed his descent. The sand had deadened the flames and cooled the heat. He reached the bottom and went out through the half-open door. He could see no one. The meadow stretched empty. The only sign of what had happened was the thinning tendrils of smoke. For the rest, nothing but this rolling sea of greenery, the call of birds swooping and diving and the faded lowing of the cattle. Athelstan's gaze swept the great meadow but there was no trace of his attacker.

'Why?' Athelstan shouted at a dark copse of trees as if his mysterious assailant lurked in its shadows. 'Why me?' he yelled. Only the cry of a bird answered him. A wave of sheer weariness swept over him. Athelstan sat down on the bottom step. He recognised the trap he had so fortunately avoided; the splashing, fiery oil could so easily have caught his sandals and robe. In other circumstances he might have panicked, slipped and so made a bad situation infinitely worse.

'So it begins,' Athelstan murmured. He crossed himself as he recalled the words of an ancient Celtic poem: 'Be thou my armour, my sword for the fight, be thou my shield, be thou my might.' He rose to his feet. The great meadow stretched so peaceful, so glorious in the full glow of an English summer's day, yet murder had set up its tent here, unfurled all its baleful banners and sinister standards.

'Protect me as the apple of your eye,' Athelstan whispered. 'Hide me in the shadow of your wing. So let us begin.'

He returned to the guesthouse to find a lay brother hopping from foot to foot with a message that Father Prior wanted to meet him immediately in the parlour or chancery chamber. Athelstan hurried there to find Anselm, the Procurator General and Brothers Cassian and Isidore seated around the oval council table. A bowl of freshly crushed herbs exuded a most delightful fragrance to mingle with the delicious smells of wax, vellum and polished leather. Despite the sunlight lancing the stained-glass windows, the chamber was rather dark, so candles had also been lit. Prior Anselm welcomed him and gestured at Athelstan to take a seat. A servant brought in small pewter goblets of hippocras and thin honey wafers. Once he'd withdrawn, Anselm tapped the table and was about to begin when the door opened and Brother Roger Desaures, chief librarian and chronicler of Blackfriars, hurried in muttering his apologies. He pulled back a leather quilted chair and placed a chancery satchel on the table before him.

'My fault, my fault, my fault,' he gabbled, 'but I was busy.' He nodded at the Procurator General and his companions then beamed at Athelstan, whom he always called 'my favourite scholar'. Athelstan grinned back. Brother Roger always reminded him of a furtive rabbit, with his small round face, pointed ears, protuberant front teeth and constantly twitching nose. Brother Roger himself confessed he suffered from the 'rheums' brought on, he believed, by the dust from old manuscripts. He waggled ink-stained fingers at Athelstan then became all attentive as Prior Anselm coughed to attract everyone's attention.

'Brother Athelstan,' Anselm began. 'You have examined the corpse?'

'Yes, Father, most thoroughly. I found no other mark of violence except for the death wound. Tell me,' Athelstan gestured at the Italians, 'do you occupy a chamber on the same gallery as Alberic?'

'I do,' Brother Cassian replied. 'My two brothers here have rooms below.'

'And you saw or heard nothing untoward last night?'

'Nothing.'

'Then, Father Prior,' Athelstan declared, 'how, why and when brother Alberic was murdered remains a mystery. As does the identity of his assassin.'

'What will happen to his corpse?' Brother Roger demanded. 'It is summer, should we not—'

'He will be buried here,' the Procurator General

murmured. 'We cannot take Alberic's remains back to Italy. My brothers and I will sing the requiem . . .'

For a while funeral arrangements were discussed until Prior Anselm brought matters to order.

'Athelstan,' he began, 'you have been summoned back to Blackfriars for your own protection. St Erconwald's may be your parish but it is also a hotbed of agitation, conspiracy and revolt.' He smiled thinly. 'We cannot afford to have you exposed to such danger. No,' he held a hand up to still Athelstan's protests, 'you must remain here. Brother, that is a command which I impose on you out of love but also in the expectation of strict obedience.' He waited for Athelstan to murmur his agreement. 'Very well.' The prior breathed in sharply. 'We also need your keen wits and sharp mind not only to resolve the brutal murder of Brother Alberic but other matters which have brought our brothers here in the first place.' Prior Anselm paused to gather his thoughts.

'Four years ago,' he continued, 'our noble King Richard went on pilgrimage to St Peter's Abbey in Gloucester, where he visited the tomb of his great-grandfather Edward II, who,' the prior gave a small smile, 'allegedly lies buried there beneath the most exquisitely carved tomb of Purbeck marble. They claim it is the finest royal sarcophagus in all of Europe. You have seen it, Athelstan?'

'Yes. I am from the West Country. My father often took me to the great fair in Gloucester, and of course we visited St Peter's Abbey. I remember it well. The tomb is a magnificent monument dominated by a life-size effigy of the dead king.'

'Slain king!' Fieschi interrupted. 'Edward II was murdered by his wife and her paramour Roger Mortimer.'

'Brother Matteo is correct,' the prior hastily intervened, 'Edward II's murder is a royal scandal which few, if any, like to mention even today.'

'Killed at Berkeley or so they say,' Brother Roger murmured, 'imprisoned in the castle there, confined to a pestilential pit.'

'Brother Roger, perhaps you can tell us more?' Prior Anselm smiled. 'I did ask you to become knowledgeable in this matter, as you are,' he added drily, 'in so many others.'

'And so I have,' the chronicler blithely replied. He half closed his eyes as he began to recite what he had learnt. 'Edward II, or Edward of Caernarvon as he was popularly called, was the heir of Edward I, the great warrior king who battled in Scotland. Now,' he opened the satchel on the table before him and took out a folio of pure vellum which he smoothed out before him, 'Edward II succeeded his father in 1307. The following year he married Princess Isabella, daughter of the French King Philip IV—'

'The one who crushed the Temple Order?' Athelstan asked, trying to shake off a growing unease, as if sinister shadows were gathering all about him.

'Philip IV did many things,' Brother Roger retorted. 'Marrying his daughter to the English heir was one of his greatest achievements. At first the marriage seemed happy enough. Isabella bore her husband four healthy children. However, Edward II's rule was dominated by vicious

28

in-fighting between the King and his nobles. There was trouble with a royal favourite, Peter Gaveston, whom Edward made Earl of Cornwall. Edward was certainly obsessed with him. He and Gaveston may have been lovers—'

'There is no evidence for that.' Fieschi's voice was sharp.

'Anyway,' Brother Roger shrugged, 'Gaveston was executed by the earls, only to be replaced by a new favourite, Hugh Despenser. He and Edward united to destroy the great barons led by Thomas of Lancaster. A bloodbath ensued. Great lords were either executed or, like Roger Mortimer of Wigmore, imprisoned before fleeing abroad. Despenser then turned on Isabella. However, she managed to escape to her relatives in France, where she and Mortimer became secret lovers and public allies. They gathered others about them and invaded England. Edward and Despenser suffered a devastating defeat. Despenser was dragged into Hereford. He was disembowelled, his innards burnt before him, then he was hanged, castrated, beheaded and quartered. Edward II was also captured. He was eventually deposed as king and imprisoned, first at Kenilworth and then in Berkeley Castle.

'Now,' Brother Roger spread his hands, 'what I say comes from the chronicles of the time; I cannot verify it. Anyway, according to reports, Isabella wanted her husband killed. She refused to meet the imprisoned king or allow their children to visit him. Isabella of course continued to play the role of estranged wife. According to rumour, Edward is said to have sworn that he

29

would kill Isabella with his own teeth. Consequently, he was judged too dangerous to be freed. Some chroniclers say he was thrown into a pit along with the rotting carcasses of animals in the hope that he would catch some contagion and die. Edward was strong and robust, he survived. Meanwhile, popular sympathy for him deepened. Conspiracies were formed to free him. Sir John Maltravers, Sir Thomas Berkeley and a knight called Gurney, all keepers of the royal prisoner, pleaded with Mortimer for "*un tiele remedie*".'

'A suitable remedy?' Athelstan interjected. 'You mean the King's death?'

'Yes. According to popular rumour, this was carried out on the Feast of St Matthew, on the twenty-first of September 1327. Gurney and a group of assassins burst into the former king's cell. They seized him, turned him on his stomach and thrust a red-hot spindle or poker up his anus into his bowels, thus killing him.' Brother Roger sighed noisily. 'Some say this is just a gruesome story which reflects the former king's allegedly sodomite practices. According to other reports, Edward suffered a "*fatalis casus*" or fatal accident. Others argue that he was smothered or suffocated to death.'

'Suffice to say that Edward II died in tragic circumstances,' Fieschi declared. 'His wife and Mortimer refused to have him buried at Westminster Abbey, the Plantagenet mausoleum. Instead they arranged a lavish funeral at Gloucester, hence that gorgeous tomb.'

'And what happened next?'

30

'Oh, three years later Mortimer and Isabella fell from power. Isabella, as Queen Mother of the young Edward III, was sent into honourable retirement. She died at Castle Rising twenty-eight years later and lies buried beneath the flag-stones of Greyfriars near St Paul's. Mortimer was not so fortunate. He was judged a traitor and a regicide. He was gagged throughout his trial, found guilty and hanged at the Forks over Tyburn stream . . .'

'And how does this concern me?' Athelstan demanded. 'Brothers, you have come here for a purpose?' He was tempted to give vent to the frustration curdling within him. He was certain that somehow the recent attack on him was connected with the mission of these three Italian friars.

'Brother Athelstan, what is the matter?' Fieschi had sensed his bad temper.

'I asked a question!'

'And I shall answer it,' Prior Anselm retorted. 'Four years ago, as I have said, our young King Richard, much taken with the story of his great-grandfather's life and tragic death, visited Gloucester. He saw it as a pilgrimage and stayed for some time, venerating Edward II's tomb. So immersed did he become in the account of his ancestor's death that he ordered his own personal emblem or insignia, the White Hart, to be carved on the royal shrine. Richard never forgot the experience. He came to firmly believe that Edward II was a saint, a royal martyr who, by his death, transformed his life and reign. A true martyr king in succession to other saintly monarchs such as St Edward, St Edmund, St Oswald and others stretching back into the misty history of the English crown.'

'And no doubt our young King Richard sees himself cast from the same mould?' Athelstan enquired.

'Very much so,' Fieschi replied. 'He has petitioned the Holy Father for the formal opening of the process for the beatification and canonisation of Edward II.'

'But his private life,' Athelstan interposed, 'it was hardly—'

'Thomas Becket,' Fieschi said swiftly. 'Your Thomas Becket, did he not love luxury and ostentation before his conversion? People change, Brother Athelstan, they make reparation for their faults. In my view, the martyrdom of Edward II, like charity, covers a multitude of sins.'

'You seem convinced already?'

'I certainly am,' Fieschi replied.

'Brother Matteo,' Anselm intervened tactfully, 'is promoter of the cause. He may well insist that the tomb at Gloucester be opened so the royal corpse can be inspected. As you know, there are occasions when a martyr's body does not decompose.'

'In this I support the Procurator General,' Brother Cassian declared.

'Whilst I and poor Alberic,' Isidore crossed himself, 'were supposed to act the role of *advocati diaboli*.'

'The Devil's Advocates,' Athelstan translated. 'You would search for evidence which would nullify any attempt to sanctify the dead king.' He pulled a face. 'In the circumstances, that might not be difficult.'

'The Holy Father thinks otherwise.'

'Well, he would . . .'

Athelstan paused abruptly. He did not wish to condemn himself out of his own mouth. He rose to his feet, walked to the narrow window and knelt on the quilted bench beneath, staring out through the mullioned glass. In the courtyard below, brothers were busy around the washtub where the sacred cloths were being cleansed. They sang as they worked, powerful male voices intoning the words of the *Magnificat*, 'My soul doth magnify the Lord . . .'

'Athelstan . . .' Prior Anselm had come close up beside him. 'I did fear for you being left alone in Southwark but I also brought you back to help with this matter. I need you to stay because of it. No Dominican I have ever met can rival you as an inquisitor.' He grasped Athelstan's shoulder. 'You are also a benevolent and just one. Our king,' the prior continued in a sibilant whisper, 'has appealed to the Pope.'

Athelstan turned to face the prior, working out the implications for himself. 'And our Holy Father in Rome, Urban VI, has a rival, an anti-pope styling himself Clement VII residing in Avignon. Urban does not wish to alienate the English crown, to drive this kingdom into Clement's camp, so he has agreed to our king's request.'

'And the Dominicans, Athelstan, are a natural choice. First, the Holy Inquisition in Rome is under the authority of our Minister General.'

'And secondly?'

'Come back to the table, Athelstan, and I will continue.'

'As I was about to explain,' the prior continued as they retook their seats, 'Edward II of blessed memory was a generous patron of our order: his confessors, advisors and soul counsellors were always Dominicans.'

'But why have you come to Blackfriars, Brother Matteo?' Athelstan still felt discommoded. 'What can we offer you?'

'You know full well,' Fieschi lisped quietly. 'Blackfriars is the mother house of our English province. The Holy Father and our Minister General wish it, as do I, Procurator General of our order. Finally, Prior Anselm who, in all truth, is your divinely appointed superior with authority over you—'

'Saving my conscience,' Athelstan interrupted abruptly. 'And the teaching of Christ.'

'Very good, Brother.' Fieschi shrugged.

'Brother Athelstan will help,' Prior Anselm swiftly intervened. 'Brother Roger will also assist. Our library and archives possess a great deal about Edward II, especially his last days. I also asked – thanks be to God in good time before these present troubles – for the records of the Exchequer, Chancery, King's Bench and the Justices of Oyer and Terminer to be thoroughly searched and copies of all relevant documents to be made available. The King himself ordered this, and Master Thibault, your—'

'Adversary?' Athelstan interjected. 'Master

Thibault and I have crossed swords, Sir John Cranston likewise, on a number of occasions.'

'Master Thibault has generously supplied us with documentation,' Fieschi explained, 'King Richard petitioned the Holy Father a year ago. Preparations were completed before the rebellious commons made their presence felt.'

'And the manuscripts stolen from Alberic's chamber?' Athelstan demanded.

'Certain information from our Minister General and the archives of our Curia in Rome.'

'What, exactly?'

'I cannot say.'

'Important enough however for Alberic to be murdered and the documents stolen?'

'Brother Alberic was *advocatus diaboli*, so he would collect evidence against the dead king's reputation. Alberic was a man of integrity. What he collected he would not share with me; I did the same with him. There would be a time and place for Alberic to plead his case but I do not know what he actually held, so I cannot comment.'

'Yet someone at Blackfriars was determined enough to murder him and seize those documents?'

'Brother Alberic may have had enemies here.'

'So soon?' Athelstan queried. 'A visitor from Italy?'

'Oh, Alberic made his presence felt.' Fieschi looked away. Athelstan quickly recalled the handsome young messenger who came clattering up the stairs and disappeared just as they forced the door to Alberic's chamber.

'There is more to this than the sanctity or not of a long-dead king, surely?'

'Athelstan.' The prior chose his words carefully. 'Edward II was a man of contention. His life still divides our order; his reign, particularly his captivity and death, raises matters of deep concern. The past can and does haunt us. Isn't that true, Brother Roger?'

The chronicler, half-hiding his face behind his hands, simply nodded. Athelstan glanced at Brother Roger: the reference to the theft of manuscripts from Alberic's chamber seemed to have agitated him. Athelstan had caught the worried look he had thrown Anselm and the prior's reply, a slight shake of the head as if warning the chronicler to remain silent.

'Athelstan?'

'Father Prior, you were talking about the past haunting us?'

'It certainly does. My family name,' Anselm declared, 'is Mortimer. I am a distant kinsman of Roger Mortimer of Wigmore, the lover of Queen Isabella and the moving spirit behind Edward II's deposition and destruction. Brother Roger is related to the Despenser family, Edward II's favourites at the time of his fall. We have old retainers in Blackfriars, men who served in the royal households of Edward and Isabella: they have earned the right of a corrody – a pension – here, comfortable bed and board for years of loyal service.' The prior waved a hand. 'For all I know, there may be old Dominicans who were once caught up in those hurling, violent years when Edward II fell from power. Some members of our order disappeared and then re-emerged years later.' He caught the disbelief in Athelstan's eyes. 'Brother, walk around Blackfriars now. There are Dominicans who have come in to shelter, some of whom I have never met before. Look at you. You spend more time at St Erconwald's than you do here.'

The prior pulled a face. 'Memories run deep. What is mere history to one person is a living, enduring reality to another. Brother Roger will tell you how Blackfriars became a hotbed of intrigue and conspiracy during the turbulent years of Mortimer, in support of the imprisoned king.' Athelstan glanced at the chronicler, who nodded in agreement. 'So,' Anselm crossed himself, 'what we must do is help our brothers here move matters swiftly on. You, Athelstan, aren't needed at St Erconwald's, so it's best if you stay at Blackfriars out of harm's way and assist us.' The prior broke off at the powerful wailing of a hunting horn, followed by the clanging of the tocsin bell sounding the alarm. The raucous noise stilled all conversation. Again the hunting horn brayed.

'The water-gate!' Prior Anselm gasped. 'Some danger at the water-gate!'

Athelstan followed the prior and the others out of the chancery chamber. The priory was in a ferment. Armed retainers, lay brothers and old soldiers lodged at Blackfriars were busy arming themselves. The barbican tower had been opened, the weapons' chests unlocked. The sacristan in charge of defence, a tall, burly, bold-faced Dominican, was organising the distribution of crossbows, arrows and quivers, clubs and bill hooks. He called out to Prior Anselm but the prior just shook his head and hurried on, pausing only to beckon at Athelstan.

'I am sure the rebels are making their presence felt,' he whispered. 'They know of you, Athelstan, so they will treat with you, though God knows what they want.'

They left the main building and took a path which cut through bushes and grassy plots down towards the soaring, battlemented water-gate built into the great curtain wall overlooking the Thames. The guard tower was two storeys high and had three entrances: double gates which could be opened when the tide fell, with two portcullises on either side which could be raised on chains. The entrance and steps to the tower platforms thronged with armed retainers dressed in the black and white livery of the order. They stepped aside for Prior Anselm and Athelstan, who hastened up the steps and out on to the fighting platform which provided a clear view of the river. Athelstan leaned against the stonework and his heart sank at the sight. Six great war barges, all displaying huge banners black as soot or blood-red, now faced the water-gate. The barges were oared by professional watermen who skilfully kept their craft in one battle line, carefully spacing out their prows which were jutting towards the entrance to Blackfriars.

'The Guild of Bargemen must have joined the rebels,' Athelstan whispered. 'Although I suspect they were given little choice in the matter.' He pointed at the armed retainers now thronging up the steps, warbows and arbalests primed. 'We cannot afford a mistake.'

The prior nodded. The noise and clamour from below was rising. Many of the fighting men were deeply agitated. The serjeants were already bellowing for boiling oil and water to be prepared, whilst small war catapults were being dragged out of nearby sheds to be readied for deployment. The prior shouted for calm and, helped by Athelstan, cleared the fighting platform, telling the men to wait below, to do nothing without his order. At the same time, one of the servants was despatched to bring the prior's crozier, a long bronze pole surmounted by a jewelled cross, which arrived with an altar cloth. Athelstan tied this to the crozier and held it up so the cross glittered in the bright sunlight and the brilliant white linen fluttered and snapped in the river breeze. Silence descended. The hubbub and clamour from both the water-gate and the waiting barges died.

One of the barges crept forward, oars dipping slowly, the tillerman keeping it steady. The boat was crammed with archers, some dressed in pieces of armour, most wearing the green, black and brown jerkin and hose they had donned before leaving their ploughlands in Essex and Kent. Several of the men had strung their bows. Athelstan hid his nervousness. Some of these rebels, indeed many of them, had served in royal arrays and chevauchées in northern France and Spain, master bowmen who could loose one deadly shaft after another in the twinkling of an eye.

'*Pax et bonum!*' Grasping his crozier, Prior Anselm stood up on the fighting step in clear view of the men in the leading barge, which was still edging closer. Breathing a prayer for help, Athelstan stepped up beside his prior.

'*Pax et bonum!*' Athelstan repeated. 'Peace and goodness to you all!'

'You are?' A man had climbed on to the prow.

'Prior Anselm of Blackfriars and Brother Athelstan, Dominican priest of St Erconwald's in Southwark.'

'And I am Wat Tyler,' the man shouted back. 'Chief amongst the Upright Men, the one who sits high in the council of the Great Community of the Realm, the commonwealth of free peasants.'

'I know who you are . . .' Athelstan hurled back. 'We have met. I know what you plot.'

'Athelstan,' Prior Anselm hissed, 'what is this?'

'*Alea iacta,*' Athelstan murmured. 'The die is cast. I know this reprobate, a true villain out of Kent.'

Tyler was now conferring with his comrades. Athelstan stared up at the blue sky. The breeze had shifted, bringing in the stench of the nearby Fleet river which, as usual at the height of summer, would be clogged with all the filth and refuse of the city. The corpses of cats, dogs and horses mingled with the leavings of the great dung carts which emptied their swill into the mud-encrusted waters of that open sewer. Athelstan wondered idly if London would be cleaned or if that too would collapse and the stench he smelt now would creep across the entire city. He thought of his own little house with its kitchen, bed-loft, scullery and storeroom; he hoped all would be safe. Would Benedicta and the rest look after Philomel, his old warhorse? Would Bonaventure, that wily, one-eyed great tomcat, have the cunning to go into hiding? He hoped no one would hurt Hubert the hedgehog in his little house, the hermitage which Crispin the carpenter had built. The friar shook himself free of such distractions.

'Brother Athelstan?' Tyler's voice echoed across the water. 'Are you loyal to King Richard and the True Commons?'

'Is the Holy Father a Catholic?' Athelstan yelled back, provoking laughter amongst the men on the barge.

'What do you want?' Prior Anselm intervened. 'Why are you here? This is the mother house of the Dominican order who work amongst Christ's poor and dispossessed.'

'We know you shelter people,' Tyler bellowed back. 'Individuals who the true Commons wish to question. We insist on a thorough search of the friary precincts.'

'Refused,' Anselm shouted back. 'This is a place of hallowed sanctuary, consecrated ground, protected by Holy Mother Church.'

Tyler climbed down from the prow platform to engage in deep discussion with the others. Two of the barges pulled closer, packed with men all bristling with weapons. Athelstan glimpsed a small moveable catapult. However, though he could not make out individual faces or hear even a word of what was being said, he

41

sensed there was little desire amongst the fighting men for a confrontation with Blackfriars. He suspected the war barges had moved along the north bank of the Thames to test the defences of different places, from the quaysides of the Wine Wharf and the Duke of Norfolk's Inn to the formidable fortifications of nearby Castle Baynard. The rebels were simply unfurling their standards and making their authority felt. Both he and the prior gave a deep sigh of relief as the barges started to pull away, but then the leading one came darting back, aiming like an arrow towards the water-gate. Orders rang out, oars were lifted. Tyler – Athelstan was sure it was he – stepped back on to the prow platform.

'Brother Athelstan?' he yelled. The friar raised his hand and Tyler leaned forward. 'We know your allegiance is to the King and the True Commons, as is mine . . .'

'Liar!' Athelstan whispered.

'Brother, I assure you, you have nothing to fear from us, but I should tell you this. Your parishioners, the loyal Upright Men of St Erconwald's and their Earthworms, have disappeared, vanished.'

'What do you mean, vanished?' Athelstan called.

'Disappeared,' Tyler repeated. 'Gone like thieves in the night. Are you sheltering them? Do they lie imprisoned in your priory dungeon?'

'No one lies in my dungeons,' Anselm shouted, 'on my solemn oath over the Eucharist, the Body and Blood of Christ whose feast we celebrate tomorrow. God be my witness, I have no knowledge of what you say.'

Tyler stepped down off the platform and the barge withdrew.

'What does he mean?' Athelstan fought the panic bubbling within him and grasped Anselm's arm. 'Father Prior, I must go to Southwark. I must find out what is happening. I promise, just one visit, then I shall return.'

Anselm stared into the anxious eyes of this little friar who meant so much to him. A true priest, Anselm considered, an honest son of the soil who loyally followed Christ the ploughman, Christ the ditcher, Christ the harvester. A priest who truly cared for his flock and not just its fleece. He patted Athelstan on the shoulder.

'You may go, but be back by the morrow. We need you here.'

Athelstan thanked him. They left the water-gate fortifications and returned to the main building. Fieschi stood in the hallway gossiping with Cassian, Isidore and Brother Roger. They were apparently deep in discussion over the issue of Edward II's love for his Gascon favourite, Peter Gaveston. Athelstan was invited to join them but he excused himself, adding that Prior Anselm would inform them about the confrontation at the water-gate. He wanted to be away, to hide his confusion over what he had just learnt. According to Tyler, his parishioners had simply disappeared. Watkin the dung-collector, Pike the ditcher, Moleskin the bargeman and all the rest were Upright Men. They should have been on those barges, yet, according to the rebel leader Tyler, there had been no sight or sound of them.

Agitated, Athelstan wandered into the main church, now deserted after the high Mass and the recitation of Divine Office. A ghostly, shadow-filled, incense-perfumed place; the long nave stretched before him with shafts of light pouring like coloured moonbeams through the stained-glass windows high on either side. At the far end a red sanctuary lamp glowed through a gap in the heavy, exquisitely carved rood screen. Athelstan could make out the aisle leading to the choir, the gleam of candlelight on the oaken stalls where he had stood so many times to sing Matins, Lauds, Vespers and Compline. He walked slowly along the nave then paused. He felt a cold prickling between his shoulder blades. He was not alone, he was sure of that. He turned quickly, staring at the sunlight pouring through the half-opened main door. Nothing! Yet he was sure he heard the scuff of a sandal, a quick intake of breath. Was he being followed, and if so, why? Blackfriars, like so many religious houses in London, had become a sanctuary, but what else might be happening here? This investigation into a long dead king, what was the relevance of all of that?

Again, Athelstan heard a sound. He whirled round, staring to the left and right at the dark-filled transepts. He walked back to the entrance porch and stood near the baptismal font, close to St Christopher's pillar where a picture of the saint, a hairy, burly figure, moustache and beard all bedraggled, carried the Christ Child on his shoulder. Athelstan murmured the St Christopher prayer which his mother had taught him when he was knee-high to a buttercup, a special plea that the great saint would protect him against sudden, violent death.

He walked around the pillar, his gaze caught by glimpses of the different wall paintings. One in particular was quite startling: a devil with a salamander-like face and body, was using another demon as an ink horn to write out the offences of a sinner kneeling before him. Next to the salamander, a rat-headed fiend pierced a usurer's head with a pointed candlestick. The usurer was blindfolded with an execution sword buried deep in the back of his neck. A devil with a bloated belly and a grape as a navel waited close by with a dish to receive the usurer's severed head. Another demon, with a gaping toad-mouth and whip-like tongue, grasped a piece of parchment covered with warnings against fornicators, jugglers, dancers, gorgers and guzzlers. Nevertheless, the demonic preacher advocated lechery without shame and gluttony without blame to a group of ribalds, drunkards, pimps and ladies of the night. Athelstan smiled. He was always fascinated at how sin seemed to attract artists. Giles of Sempringham, for example, the Hangman of Rochester, when he wasn't busy around the scaffolds of Tyburn and Smithfield, loved nothing better than to decorate the walls of St Erconwald's with dramatic paintings. Where was the Hangman of Rochester now, and his companions?

Athelstan walked up into the north transept

45

where the chantry chapels, each separated by a trellised oaken screen, stretched the full length as they did along the south transept, small altar shrines, each carefully enclosed and dedicated to this saint or that. Athelstan realised it was years since he had visited any of these: his gaze was caught by the lighted candles flickering on one of them further up the transept close to the Lady Altar. Curious, he walked towards it and entered the altar shrine dedicated to St Edward the Confessor, whom the Plantagenet royal family regarded as the founder of their dynasty. He found a comfortable, well-furnished chantry, the floor carpeted with thick, soft turkey rugs. The walls proclaimed different scenes from the Confessor's life, all executed in the Plantagenet colours of scarlet, blue and gold. The roundel window high in the outside wall was filled with painted glass depicting the saintly king's head circled with a shining blue and gold halo, whilst the table altar was covered in costly cloths of scarlet trimmed with silver.

Candles glowed in their gilt spigots. Apparently Mass had recently been celebrated here: the air was sweet with incense smoke and the rich tang of altar wine. The sacristan had failed to douse the candles. Athelstan stepped on to the dais and, wetting his fingers, extinguished each of the dancing flames. His gaze was caught by the reredos, the wooden decorated screen behind the altar, cleverly carved out of polished elmwood with small, lozenge-shaped enclaves, each boasting an insignia repeated time and again, either a double-headed eagle or a crown in chains. Athelstan wondered about the symbolism behind the emblems. This was a chantry chapel, consecrated to the Confessor, yet Athelstan could not recall these heraldic insignia being associated with that saintly Saxon king.

Mystified, he moved to the door of the chantry chapel and stood there, thoughts teeming like wheels, then he sat down on the altar server's stool and tried to marshal his own thinking. First, Prior Anselm had summoned him from his parish and kept him kicking his heels here at Blackfriars. Secondly, a papal delegation led by Fieschi had arrived in England because of King Richard's determination to hallow the memory of his unfortunate ancestor, Edward II, deposed, detained and barbarously executed at Berkeley Castle. Fieschi and Cassian were promoters of the cause. Isidore and Alberic were to act as Devil's Advocates. Thirdly, they had come, not just because the Dominicans were responsible for the Inquisition, but also because Edward II had a deep devotion to the friars, hence the Pope entrusting this task to the Order. Blackfriars had been chosen because it was the mother house of the Dominicans in England: it also possessed extensive records and archives and was close to the royal muniments of the Exchequer, Chancery and the different courts. Apparently, relevant records had already been despatched by the Crown for the papal envoys residing at Blackfriars.

'So far, so good,' Athelstan whispered to himself. To all intents and purposes, a scholarly exercise, an investigation into a murder, albeit a royal one, which had apparently occurred some fifty-four years ago. Nevertheless – and fourthly – this royal death still played a part in the lives of others. It apparently held its own dangers, and these had surfaced last night, or early this morning, when Alberic had been cruelly stabbed to death in his chamber – but how, why and by whom? The chamber was sealed, the only entrance being through a door which was strongly hinged, bolted and locked. Nevertheless, someone had gained entrance to that chamber, murdered a vigorous former soldier without any sign or noise, cruelly stabbing him with a dagger. The assassin had also stolen some documents and slipped into the dark. Yet how could that be? How did the murderer get in and get out?

Fifthly, it now seemed that Athelstan, aided by the garrulous chronicler Brother Roger, was to assist Fieschi's investigation assuming the role of Devil's Advocate now that Alberic had gone to his eternal reward. Sixthly, Athelstan was puzzled about how deeply people's feelings ran about a king who'd been murdered – or martyred, according to your perception – over fifty years ago. Prior Anselm had pointed out how different Dominicans, including himself, were related to families caught up in the hurling times of Edward II's deposition, imprisonment and death. But how and why should that matter so much now? Why should it lead to Alberic's murder as well as that savage attack upon himself in the beacon tower? Athelstan was certain this violence was linked to Fieschi's mission. What danger did he himself pose?

Athelstan put his face in his hands as he

recalled those ominous war barges. Did he have it wrong? Perhaps the attack on him was nothing to do with Alberic's death but was linked to the general disturbance throughout the city. Or it might be because of who Athelstan was and what he knew – because he and Sir John Cranston truly believed the rebel Leader Wat Tyler was Gaunt's creature suborned to kill the young king. Once Richard was gone, leaving no heir, the crown would pass to Gaunt and the House of Lancaster. Gaunt's behaviour was certainly suspicious, leading an army to Scotland when the King, the city and the kingdom lay under serious and bloody threat from rebel armies. Athelstan recalled his earlier confrontation with Tyler. Why had he come here? It was possible that he'd hoped to seize Isabella, Thibault's daughter, with some madcap notion of using her against her father, to gain entrance to the Tower and access to the young king. And where was Sir John Cranston in all of this?

Athelstan sighed, rose to his feet and left the chantry chapel. The nave stretched before him, a place of dappled, shifting light. Dust motes danced in the lance-like rays of sunshine across which trails of fading incense and candle smoke drifted. The twisted, leering faces of gargoyles and babewyns stared down at him. He caught the stony gaze of statues and glimpsed the faint glow of candlelight in the Lady Chapel. Again that sound. There was a faint scuffling, an ominous click. Athelstan recognised it immediately. He fell to his knees, head bowed, to crawl back into the chantry chapel as the crossbow bolt whirled above him. Another one followed immediately afterwards, smacking into the wooden trellised screen. Athelstan gabbled a prayer for protection. Ever since his days in the royal array he had never forgotten the distinctive sinister click of a crossbow loosing its bolt, a danger Cranston had, time and again, alerted him to. He wiped the sweat from his brow.

'*Pax et bonum!*' he called. 'This is God's house, the gate of heaven, not some slaughter shed!' Again the click but this time the mysterious archer must have fumbled. A bolt whirled but only to clatter along the paving stones. Athelstan edged his way across the chantry floor. He relaxed as the devil door further up the church crashed open.

'Brother Athelstan?' Isabella's young, carrying voice echoed down the nave. 'Brother Athelstan, you have visitors.' The friar rose to his feet. He heard a soft patter followed by a creak which came from the side door to the main entrance. He left the chantry chapel, peering through the smoky murk. The would-be assassin had fled. Athelstan turned and crouched as Isabella raced towards him.

'Brother, Brother,' she gasped, 'you have visitors! A very pretty woman, olive-skinned, kind-eyed, with hair as black as night. She is with a man as large as a horse with a white bristling beard and moustache and fierce blue eyes. He swears by . . .' Isabella pulled herself away, fingers to her lips as she tried to recall Sir John Cranston, Lord High Coroner of London's favourite curse. 'Oh yes, by Satan's pits!'

50

'You mean Satan's tits!' Despite the danger, Athelstan laughed. He rose and clasped her hand. 'Come.'

'Brother, what is wrong?' Isabella pulled his fingers. 'Your hands are always warm. Now they are cold. What is the matter? Why were you hiding?'

'Nothing, my pearl of great price,' Athelstan assured her. 'You are,' he whispered to himself, 'as sharp and keen as your father. I just pray you have all of his wit and none of his vices.'

Sir John Cranston and Benedicta the widow woman were waiting in the Chamber of Penitence close to the prior's parlour. A lay brother gave a whispered explanation as to how the other chambers were being used for this and that. Athelstan nodded, kissed Isabella on the head and asked the lay brother to take her back to her nurse, who must be beside herself with worry. Once they had gone Athelstan opened the door.

'Good morrow!' he called out. '*Benedico vos*, I bless you both.' Cranston and Benedicta spun round from looking at one of the wall paintings. Athelstan exchanged the kiss of peace even as he noticed how tired and drawn both his visitors looked. Cranston, despite the early summer warmth, was swathed in his usual bottle-green cloak which he used to cover his bulky warbelt as well as the light coat of Milanese steel beneath his jerkin. The coroner was unshaven and unkempt, his eyes bloodshot, his breath reeking of Bordeaux from the many sips he had taken from the miraculous wineskin concealed beneath his coat. Benedicta was garbed like a nun in dark blue with an old-fashioned wimple which framed her face though it did not completely conceal her glossy black hair. Athelstan stepped back. 'So good to meet you.' He half smiled. 'I heard—'

'Brother,' Benedicta gripped his hand, 'you must come back with us to Southwark. Something terrible . . .' Her voice faltered. Athelstan's heart skipped a beat.

'Your parishioners,' Cranston took a generous mouthful of wine and offered it to both but they refused. 'In a word, Athelstan,' Cranston declared, 'all the men in your parish, all those who are Earthworms or Upright Men, have disappeared.'

'Disappeared?' Athelstan exclaimed. 'I heard the same.' He waved a hand. 'I will tell you later but . . .' He sat down on a stool, gesturing at Cranston and Benedicta to take the two high-backed chairs. The door opened and a lay brother brought in a tray, a jug of ale, three tankards and a plate of spiced chicken which he passed around the guests. Athelstan stared at the painting to the right of the small, stained-glass window. This was the Chamber of Penitence where those who wished to be urgently and secretly shriven from their sins would be told to wait for absolution from a priest. The wall frescoes identified the Seven Deadly Sins, or rather their punishments, especially Avarice. The artist had depicted this vice in lurid colours. The picture showed a tavern room where the door had been ripped off its hinges to serve as a gambling table. Around this were grouped rat-headed fiends, a demonic pig dressed in the robes of an abbess and a slimy salamander with a human face, half-masked by a war helmet. These and other grotesques had assembled to divide the spoils of damned souls, mice with human heads who sat clustered in abject terror watching an ape-like animal devour one soul between his filthy lips even as his scaly claws searched for the next.

'Brother?'

Athelstan looked around. The server had gone. Benedicta and Cranston were sipping at their tankards, napkins on their laps used as platters for their strips of spiced chicken. Athelstan, his mouth dry, his stomach agitated, refused any food.

'What actually happened?' he asked.

Benedicta began to explain: 'Yesterday evening Pike, Watkin and all their coven received a message, allegedly from you. No, listen. We now know it wasn't you. Anyway, they were to assemble in the nave of St Erconwald's around the hour of the Vespers bell. Of course they all did, armed and ready to move off to meet the rebels at Mile End and elsewhere. I joined them—'

'Of course you did,' Athelstan interjected, leaning forward and grasping Benedicta's hands. 'My friend,' he smiled, 'now is the time for truth and plain speaking. You know, I know and perhaps Sir John here even suspects, that you, Benedicta, belong to their coven. You sit high in the councils of the Upright Men. You may even be one of their captains, recognised as such by the Great Community of the Realm.' Athelstan squeezed Benedicta's hand, holding her gaze. He glanced swiftly at Sir John, but if the coroner was surprised, he hid it well behind raised eyebrows and a wry smile.

'I say this, Benedicta,' Athelstan explained, 'because I know that all this great tumult is going to end in hideous slaughter. True, the Lords of the Soil have been caught unawares. Troops are leaving for both France and Scotland but there are others who will watch and wait. The revolt has begun, there is no longer need for secrecy.' He let go of her hand. 'Do continue.'

Benedicta swallowed hard. 'We assembled in the nave. Pike and Watkin had even brought their banners, broadcloths dyed scarlet and black fastened to poles. They trooped into St Erconwald's and piled their weapons around the statue of St Christopher, then waited. We thought you would come out of the sacristy, but even then I was mystified, as I had not seen you return. Someone had lit candles in the sanctuary. We wondered if you would bless us. Suddenly the corpse and devil doors were flung open, then, a few heart-beats later, the main door. Ranulf the rat-catcher was guarding it, but he was knocked aside. Some of the company tried to hurry over to their weapons, but it was futile.' She paused to wipe her mouth on the back of her hand. 'Like a vision from Hell,' she whispered, 'armed, masked men, mailed coifs up over their chins, conical helmets with broad nose-guards hiding their faces.'

'How many?'

'About two dozen under a serjeant similarly dressed. They carried arbalests primed and ready; sword and dagger in sheaths. They pushed in front of them some of the parish children: Crim, Eleanor, Matilda and the rest. They had apparently visited the houses and dwelling places of parishioners and seized these hostages. From outside we could hear the wails of mothers and sisters. Watkin tried to resist and received a blow to the face which drew blood like wine from a cracked cask. The serjeant was foreign. He spoke in a thick, guttural accent, perhaps from Flanders or Hainault.'

'Mercenaries,' Sir John interjected. 'I do not like the sound of this.'

'The serjeant threatened the men, saying he would kill any who resisted and take their children as hostages. Pike and Crispin the carpenter both objected, shouting, "What do you strangers want?" The serjeant replied that the children would not be harmed as long as the assembled men promised to offer no violence, that they were his prisoners and must go with him.' Benedicta played with a brooch on her cloak. 'They agreed. They had no choice. The serjeant ordered them to be bound.'

'How many?'

'Ten or eleven. All of them Upright Men. Watkin, Pike, Ranulf, Joycelyn, Merrylegs and his eldest son, Crispin, Hig the pigman.' She waved a hand. 'Once they were secured, they were hustled out of the church and loaded into a caged prison cart. Their womenfolk surged all around them but the serjeant was most thorough. He and his retinue mounted and, in a short while, they left the concourse, two of them staying behind to ensure no one followed.'

'Was the Hangman there?'

'No, I don't think he was.' Benedicta shrugged. 'He was busy on the gibbets at Smithfield and London Bridge.'

'Good Lord,' Athelstan breathed. 'Sir John, what do you think?'

Cranston, his face twisted in anxiety, took a generous gulp from the miraculous wineskin, then whispered a prayer as he pushed the stopper in.

'Sir John?'

'Mercenaries,' he murmured. '*Condottieri* – licensed brigands hired by this lord or that, to protect themselves. The rebels have begun to execute those they have proscribed; John Ewell, Escheator of Essex, had his head severed at Coggishall. Three more officials at Canterbury were just dragged into the High Street and decapitated. Others followed. They say blood swirled in the streets of Canterbury, mixing with the sparks and cinders from burning property. Tyler, the Kentish leader, has prophesised the same for London.'

Athelstan glanced away, sick with fear. Where had his parishioners been taken? By whom? And why?

'Brother?'

'Wat Tyler,' Athelstan replied without thinking. 'Wat Tyler came here this morning.'

'So I heard from Brother John, your gatekeeper. War barges filled with rebels. What did he want?'

'Entrance to Blackfriars, which, of course, was refused. Tyler is looking for those who have taken sanctuary here, including Isabella, Thibault's daughter which,' Athelstan crossed himself, 'will

56

be another case of children being held to hostage. I am sure Tyler would love to use her to make demands. He is a wicked malefactor.'

'But a leader amongst the Upright Men,' Benedicta declared sharply. 'A captain most feared and respected.'

'A true villain,' Athelstan retorted. 'Sir John, this mischief has begun. One sin hurls after another. We should tell Benedicta what we suspect.'

'What?'

Athelstan held his hand up as if taking a solemn oath. 'What we say, Benedicta, I swear to be the truth. Tyler is one of your captains. Sir John and I, not to mention another rebel leader, Simon Grindcobbe, believe that in truth he is Gaunt's man . . .' He stared at Benedicta who sat frozen, still and distant as a statue. 'Gaunt,' Athelstan continued, 'has left for the northern march taking much needed troops with him. Our king is left vulnerable. We suspect Tyler will entice Richard into a meeting where he will kill the King and those with him. Richard has no heir, so the crown will immediately pass to his uncle, John of Gaunt, head of the House of Lancaster and next in line to the throne. The threat is real and imminent, which is why Sir John and others of the King's council have insisted that Gaunt leave his own son and heir Henry of Derby in London along with the King. So, if our beloved prince suffers, so will Gaunt and his family. Few people know this. At the behest of the Queen Mother, Joan of Kent, Sir John and other knights of the body are sworn to protect her son with their lives.'

Benedicta now sat with her arms crossed, rocking slightly backwards and forwards, lips moving soundlessly. 'Divisions,' she declared. 'Deep divisions have appeared amongst the Upright Men about what this revolt intends to achieve. Some talk of sweeping away the old order, its total destruction, as well as the death or exiling of every prince or prelate. Others, like Grindcobbe, argue just for a reform, the calling of a supreme parliament, a new Magna Carta, a Great Charter of Deliverance; but other voices whisper about treachery and treason within our ranks. So yes, Brother, what you say is possible. The revolt has begun.' She shrugged. 'Already I sense it is not what we planned. We sowed the harvest but the reaping may not be to our liking. As for our brethren in the parish,' she looked questioningly at Sir John, 'what could have happened to them?'

Cranston sat with his legs apart and his head down as he threaded his beaver hat between gauntleted hands. Athelstan noticed the small, sharp studs which decorated the mailed gloves; Cranston was probably wearing them because he feared hand-to-hand combat with sword and dagger.

Cranston lifted his head. 'I have heard stories, hideous tales about the Lords of the Soil taking vengeance already. But, Brother, I don't want to alarm you.'

'I am alarmed already. I feel as if I am entering a land of deep shadow.' Athelstan wetted his dry, cracked lips. 'Sir John, I am desperate. Tell me you have no knowledge of this abduction.'

58

The coroner smiled wanly. 'Athelstan, my friend, two great armies now threaten London. The King and his council are locked up in the Tower with no troops at their bidding. Much as I grieve for your parishioners, there is little I can do about them.'

'You said you'd heard stories?'

'Some of the Lords of the Soil have hired mercenaries. Remember, the menfolk from the shires are now in London. There are many villages left exposed. Anyway, I have heard of landings along the east coast, hired killers from across the Narrow Seas. These men are ruthless. One lord, along with his Brabantine cohort, ambushed a small party of rebels on a lonely road somewhere near Walton in Essex. They herded their prisoners into a tithe barn, sealed the windows and doors and set the place alight . . .'

Athelstan put his face in his hands, fighting back the tears. He glanced up. 'I must go to Southwark. I must visit my church.' He grasped Benedicta's hand. 'Sir John, Benedicta, you must come with me.' The coroner nodded. Benedicta, eyes brimming with tears, excused herself and fled the chamber. For a while Athelstan and Cranston sat in silence.

'Little monk?'

'Friar, Sir John.'

'What are you actually doing here in Blackfriars?'

Athelstan, eager to distract himself, told the coroner briefly about Fieschi's visit, the reason for it and his role in the proceedings. He then, at Cranston's insistence, gave more details about the two attacks on him earlier in the day and the mysterious murder of Alberic. Once he had finished, Cranston, whispering under his breath, leaned back in his chair and stared up at the rafters.

'Edward II,' he murmured, 'allegedly a sodomite, an incompetent prince who blundered from one disaster to another in his lifelong journey, only to be murdered in a filthy pit in Berkeley Castle. It was a time of great intrigue.'

'Sir John, did you ever have dealings with those involved?'

'Yes, I did. When I was a young squire I met Berkeley, the king's jailor. I also had dealings with Sir John Maltravers, who was also accused of being involved in the regicide. Surly men from a different age with little to say. When they did speak about the old king's death, they stoutly maintained they were not involved. They pointed the finger of suspicion at a third individual, a Somerset knight called Sir Thomas Gurney. When Isabella and Mortimer fell from power, Gurney fled to Castile and then on to the kingdom of the two Sicilies. Edward III, then a young man of eighteen, fastened on Gurney as the real regicide. He despatched agents to hunt him down the length and breadth of Christendom.'

'And did they find him?'

'Oh, they caught him, then he escaped only to be recaptured. In the end little came of it. Gurney died on the sea journey back to England.'

'That was fortuitous. Gurney may have confessed and implicated others higher in the tree of state.'

'So many thought at the time.' Cranston took a mouthful of wine. 'A strange, eerie business, Athelstan. My advice would be to let sleeping dogs lie. But our king wants to have saints in his pedigree and the Papacy is malleable. I promise you, as I do with your parishioners, I shall do what I can to help.'

Part Two

'Falseness Does Reign In Every Flock.'
(The Letters of John Ball)

Athelstan, accompanied by Cranston and Benedicta, persuaded the friary bargemen to take them across the river to the Southwark side. The coroner believed the city on the north bank was too dangerous to travel through, whilst the bridge had already become a battleground between those in the city who welcomed the rebels and others such as Mayor Walworth, who had decided to resist. Thankfully their crossing was uneventful. The river seemed very quiet: wherries, fishing craft, herring ships and all the small boats which usually scurried backwards and forwards appeared to have vanished. Little moved along the Thames except for a solitary fighting cog making its way down to the estuary, and the occasional prowling war barge, packed with fighting men, pennants and banners now furled to conceal their true identity. Athelstan noticed how the dark smudges above London Bridge, shifting clouds against the light blue sky, had turned more lowering and threatening. Plumes of smoke rose fast on either side of the Thames, sinister curling heralds of more mayhem and murder.

They landed near the Stews on the Southwark

side and made their way up from the filth-strewn quayside. They hurried along the gloomy runnels which served as streets, cutting through the darkness created by the rotting, dilapidated buildings four to five stories high, held up by crutches pushed under the gables yet still leaning close together as if conspiring to block out both light and air. Rotting shells of former glory, the windows of these houses were all boarded up, their reinforced doors slammed shut. Athelstan could almost taste and breathe the gathering tension. The dark ones, the shadow shifters, the brotherhood of the knife and the garrotte, the night-walkers and the gloom-men had all heard the news. The rebel armies were about to invade the city!

Already trickles of armed men were threading the crooked lanes. Unaccustomed to the city, they stumbled and slipped on the unclean cobbles glistening beneath a coat of bloated, swollen matter oozing from the piles of animal waste as well as the decaying midden heaps. Faces masked against the hideous stench, mounted men also gathered, horsemen from Hell under their fluttering, soot-coloured banners. More terrifying still, the dreaded Earthworms, the street warriors of the Upright Men, garbed in dyed cow-skin, hair all spiked with grease, faces covered with hideous masks, made their presence felt. They emerged out of the blackness as if slipping from another world where they had been watching and waiting. The Earthworms mingled with master bowmen, their loose-fitting, quilted jerkins belted around the waist, tight patched hose pushed into scuffed boots, quick-eyed archers who could hit an oyster at the centre of a butt. They had their longbows ready, quivers crammed with feathered shafts across their back or hanging from their waist.

Athelstan, in his black and white robes, was not troubled but Benedicta and Cranston were stopped. The dark-faced, hooded captain of the Earthworms hastily stepped back, however, after Benedicta whispered in his ear and produced the Upright Men's insignia: a wax seal bearing the all-seeing eye. All three hurried on. Life in Southwark had not ceased but subtly changed. It was always a hotbed of unrest with its legion of pimps, whores, cunning men, nips and foists, but Athelstan sensed that the usual turbulence had been charged with a fresh menace which would swiftly descend into violence. Pillaging and arson had begun. Groups of rioters had already attacked a brothel housing Flemish prostitutes. Foreigners and lawyers, as Cranston whispered, were high on the attainder list drawn up by the Earthworms.

The brothel had stood at the gallows crossroad, one of the few open spaces between the cramped, crumbling houses. Earthworms were busy piling plunder on to a cart as others began to torch the brothel, the flames dancing in the window and along the main passageway. Rough, cruel justice had been meted out to the whores, who had been dragged out, stripped and summarily hanged from rusting iron wall brackets on the houses over-looking the crossroads. Athelstan glimpsed the choked, red faces, the dirty white corpses swaying as if in some macabre dance. Two lawyers, who'd crossed the river for a day's revelry, had also been caught, dragged from the brothel, abused and decapitated, their torn, bloodied heads placed alongside their naked torsos.

Athelstan whispered a requiem as well as a prayer against the gathering evil. They were walking the thoroughfares of Hell. No sunlight, only billowing smoke, foul smells and hideous scenes. Athelstan wished he could stop and administer the last rites, do something to challenge the gathering darkness, but he dare not. Cranston was recognised and, despite Athelstan's presence and that of Benedicta, the coroner was truly vulnerable. The bloodletting had begun. The devil was beating his drum. The demons piped their tunes. The calls were going out, the cry for the hunt and the prospect of villainy growing more real by the hour. The dwellers of the dark, the scavengers and polluters, were swarming from their tunnels, dungeons and fetid cellars. They would pour out in their hordes, eyes glittering sharp for the vulnerable, the weak, the defenceless, all in the pursuit of easy profit.

The Earthworms, terrifying as they were, could not fully control what Cranston called the 'Legions of the Damned'. Southwark and London would descend into chaos. Some of the rioters were already dressed in the discarded, bloodied clothes that had been stripped from the Flemish prostitutes. The dyed orange horsehair wigs of the whores were pulled drunkenly over shaven heads to make the filthy, pock-marked, weather-whipped faces of the rifflers even more grotesque. Smoke billowed across the crossroads. Athelstan glimpsed fiery glows against the narrow strip of blue sky. Somewhere bagpipes wailed and a kettledrum began to beat and then was answered by the bray of hunting horns. Voices shouted curses and slogans whilst the Earthworms declaimed the names of fresh victims, the most wanted being Richard Imworth, Keeper of Prisons and one of the most hated royal officials in Southwark.

'Let his bones be affrighted!' an Earthworm shouted hoarsely. 'Let the hair of his flesh stand up in terror!' He broke off as a pack of half-wild dogs burst out of a gate and raced forward to lap the curdling blood of the executed lawyers. One of the mastiffs snatched a severed head as if it was a ball, dragging it away. Athelstan turned to retch even as Benedicta pushed him on. They broke away from the milling crowd, hurrying down lanes where the violence was spreading like some red, murderous mist seeping along the runnels of Southwark. They passed corpses knifed and garrotted as people settled private scores or attacked the vulnerable. Corpses dangled from shop and tavern signs. Gangs of rifflers from the city were pillaging an ironmonger's shop whilst flames licked greedily at a clothing stall opposite. Benedicta led them on. Occasionally they would be stopped but the seal she carried and her assertion that she was 'loyal to the True Commons and King Richard' gained them swift passage.

'We should be gone from here,' Cranston said grimly. 'I have been in cities like this. Bloodletting begets bloodletting.' Athelstan could only nod his agreement and cross himself. Southwark

67

seemed to be caught up in a fevered dream of slaughter and savagery. Yet, at the same time, it might seem as if nothing was happening. They passed Simeon the shoemaker's shop and, as if impervious to the violence erupting around him, the cobbler was busy shaping leather footwear with a sharp knife and leather blackened with dye, sewing shoes together using pig's bristles for thread. Next to him before a narrow front door, a blood-letter was busy with a patient. Both men gazed blearily at Athelstan as he passed. Others too were busy within their trade as if oblivious to the gathering storm. Bridles and spurs continued to be made; metals fashioned; fabrics pricked; cups, drinking vessels, rings, thimbles and pins were still on sale. William the wax seller and Peter the pepper merchant along with Oliver the oil man, all stood at the doors of their shops, heads cocked as if listening keenly to the growing tumult.

Athelstan could never understand the human condition. People were being brutally murdered, yet, as they turned into Balsam Lane where the herbalists did business, he glimpsed Adam the apothecary treating a patient's wound with a bowl of egg white and a finger of calamine. Nevertheless, the violence was creeping closer like some malignant spirit summoning up its retainers: these now crept out of their filthy kennels, sores on their faces, naked arms and legs covered in scabs, grotesque and misshapen in their fluttering rags, monsters from a nightmare.

At last they rounded a corner into St Erconwald's parish, hurrying down the lane past the Piebald

68

Tavern and Merrylegs' pie shop, both boarded up and eerily silent. The same was true of the concourse stretching up to the parish church, empty, deserted of all the usual life and colour. Dust swirled in the breeze. The song of crickets echoed from God's Acre, the ancient, sprawling cemetery behind its high grey-stone wall. The heavy lychgate was closed and when he peered through the bars, Athelstan could see nothing out of the ordinary. The grass, weeds and summer flowers sprang long, lovely and lush, bending under a stiffening breeze. The old death house in the centre, converted into a cottage for the beggar Godbless and his constant companion, the evil-smelling, omnivorous goat Thaddeus, seemed deserted. But then Athelstan caught a glimpse of colour amongst two of the ancient yew trees close to the cottage. He glanced quickly over his shoulder at the church: the main door was closed and locked. Benedicta had assured him that she had secured both church and priest house; these would have to wait.

Athelstan strode through the lychgate, Benedicta and Cranston hurrying behind as the friar made his way up the coffin path, past the ancient hummocks, rotting headboards and crumbling crosses. The thick grass and the clusters of wild flowers were a magnet for a host of dazzling butterflies and buzzing bees. A serene place, yet Athelstan was determined to discover who was hiding in the graveyard. He reached the ancient yew trees, their branches stretched and bent to form a natural cave. Inside, Godbless the beggar, with Thaddeus standing beside him, was sharing

69

a pot of ale with Ursula the pig woman whose enormous sow stretched on the ground, its plump, glistening flanks billowing with every snort.

'God bless you, Father!' the beggar man shouted drunkenly. 'God bless you too, Sir John and whatever is in your codpiece.' He caught sight of the widow woman standing outside the branches. 'Oh dear, Benedicta. Heaven protect you all!'

'Godbless!' Athelstan warned. The beggar man was as mad as a March hare, and Ursula was no better. The friar gazed at the slumbering sow which had caused such devastation to his vegetable garden. Godbless, for all his moonstruck madness and the ale he had downed, sensed Athelstan's mood.

'Don't worry, Father,' he slurred, 'your garden is safe. Hubert the hedgehog is ensconced in the Hermitage whilst Philomel your old warhorse is asleep in his stable.'

'And Bonaventure?'

'The cat with nine lives,' Ursula exclaimed, 'and nine more. I have seen him prowling about.'

Athelstan nodded understandingly. Bonaventure had no love for Ursula or her sow.

'We were worried about you, Brother, weren't we, Godbless?' Ursula patted the sleeping sow. 'All is changed. The men have been taken away. We saw a caged cart rattling away, guarded by monsters in armour. All is now quiet. We lie with the dead here. Oh, truly Sion is deserted, Jerusalem a sea of ruins.'

Athelstan, despite the circumstances, smiled and shook his head in wonderment at the secrets of his parishioners. How on earth, he marvelled, did Ursula, a poor old pig woman, learn such biblical illusions?

'God bless you, Brother,' the beggar man exclaimed, 'but all had gone. So Ursula, Pernel the Fleming and myself held a council with Thaddeus and the sow in attendance. We couldn't find Benedicta, so we sat and thought.' He waved a hand. 'Then we sat and thought again. The men had been taken away. We couldn't find Benedicta but we knew Father had gone to Blackfriars, so Pernel said she would go and see you.' Godbless restrained Thaddeus from lunging at Athelstan's sleeve. 'She said she wanted to visit that place anyway.'

'When was this?'

'Yesterday, but she hasn't come back yet, Father. She went, I know she did. I accompanied her down to the Stews' quayside. Perhaps these present troubles have delayed her, or,' Godbless leaned closer like a conspirator, 'she has gone to get her hair dyed even redder. She said she might do that. A sign of the times. Blood will be spilt, Brother. Pernel said she wished she was back in her nunnery.'

'Her nunnery?'

'She made things up.' Ursula patted her still sleeping sow. 'Said she had been in love, said she had been a nun. Pernel's wits wandered. She seemed more interested in dyeing her hair than anything else.' Athelstan, however, was only half listening. He peered through the leafy branches and saw Cranston and Benedicta standing close together, talking softly. Beyond them, the sun bathed everything in its golden glory. Athelstan's

71

unease deepened. Something about this present conversation pricked his memory, but what? The friar stiffened as he recalled the death house, the mortuary at Blackfriars: those corpses sprawled on tables covered by stiffened cloths reeking of pine juice. A vein-streaked arm of one of the corpses had escaped from beneath a sheet, hanging down, fingers curled like a claw, whilst on the table and floor beneath swirled reddish-tinged pools of water.

'Oh, Lord have mercy,' Athelstan whispered.

'What, Father?'

'Nothing,' Athelstan murmured, getting to his feet. 'Godbless, Ursula,' he sketched a blessing in the air, 'may the Lord smile on you.'

He pushed his way through the cave of over-hanging branches, gesturing at Cranston and Benedicta to join him. He ignored their questions and led them up to the main door of the church. Benedicta fetched the keys from their secret hiding place. Athelstan unlocked the door and walked into the nave. St Erconwald's lay silent. Light poured through the lancet windows where the dust motes danced, but the rest of the church lay in deep shifting shadows. No candle flame flickered. No patter of prayer, scurrying of feet or whispered murmuring of people gathered here to gossip and do business. The nave was usually as busy as a market place with Watkin, Pike and their coven swaggering here and there. Now St Erconwald's lay gripped in the silence of the tomb, a shadow-filled house of ghosts.

'I've hidden all the sacred and precious objects,' Benedicta whispered, 'the pyx, ciborium, chalice and cruets are all hidden in the arca beneath the sacristy floor. Nothing to plunder here, Brother. The alms box has been emptied, the altar stripped; we have even hidden the sanctuary chair.'

Cranston, fingers playing on the hilt of his dagger, walked through the pools of light thrown by the windows. 'Athelstan, what is the . . .?' He paused, as they all did at a distant roar of hundreds of voices followed by the faint clatter of weaponry.

'Something is happening down at the bridge,' Athelstan murmured. 'All seems well here. Benedicta, it's best if Sir John stays hidden from view. Lock the church, take him to the priest's house. Allow no one in—'

'Brother, what do you—'

'No, Benedicta, please do as I say. Sir John, now is not the time for questions.'

Athelstan hurried out of the church. Everything seemed safe enough, yet a chilling premonition had seized his soul, a brooding sense of menace. Pernel was a garrulous ancient who sucked on her gums, constantly dyed her hair and wandered the parish, wide-eyed and curious. She would chatter like a magpie on a branch but she was gentle. Surely no one would hurt her? Yet that corpse in Blackfriars death house, the spindly vein-streaked arm and the pool of dyed water worried him deeply. He left the church precincts, and as if to echo his mood, the sombre sounds of conflict carried from the direction of the bridge, the roar of many voices, the clash and clatter of steel and the strident neighing of warhorses caught up in bloody conflict. Yet, at the same

73

time, the sun shone magnificently in a clear blue sky whilst a refreshing breeze cooled his sweaty skin.

Athelstan wished he did not feel so haunted and recalled his prayer asking for deliverance from the demon who had prowled after him at midday. Hell was undoubtedly casting its long shadow. The parish streets were eerily empty, doors and windows firmly shuttered, blind to the outside world. The occasional dog nosed among the rubbish piles. Rats scrabbled across the dried midden heaps, ever alert to the feral cats lurking like assassins in the shadows. Athelstan felt as if he was being closely watched, though no one came out to greet him. It was if he was walking along some deserted coffin path in the depths of the countryside rather than the streets of his parish. A furious billow of noise from the direction of the bridge made him pause and look back over his shoulder. The sky was not so blue now. Fresh, swift moving columns of black smoke were darkening this summer's day.

He hurried on until he reached Pernel's cottage, a grey ragstone box with a tiled roof and fire stack. The Fleming's house, like other cottages, had been built of stone after a furious storm which had swept the Thames a decade ago, destroying everything made of wood. The cottage stood in its own small garden ringed with a wicker fence, its battered gate hanging open. Athelstan went up the pebble path, mentally beating his breast at having been so judgemental about Pernel. The flower beds and herb plots either side of the path were well cultivated, the black soil newly turned,

74

the shrubs looked fresh and vigorous. The cottage door was on the latch but unlocked. Athelstan pushed it open and went into the warm, dark chamber which reminded him of his own priest's house, except the floor was of beaten earth. There was a small hearth with an oven either side; the mantelpiece above was decorated with statues and small crosses. The cottage also included a buttery and pantry, a bed-loft as well as closet chamber which housed a washtub, lavarium and jake's stool.

'So well kept,' Athelstan murmured staring around, his gaze caught by the polished brass candle spigot, the clean, swept hearth, the crushed herb powder strewn on the floor, and, in the bed-loft above, the white starched linen.

'This is a nun's cell,' Athelstan whispered. He stared at the crudely carved crucifix on the far wall. Above this hung an embroidered cloth displaying Christ's wounded face with a prie-dieu pushed firmly beneath it. Athelstan inspected the small buttery and kitchen and soon established that Pernel had not returned. The white manchet bread was turning hard in the bin; the meat and butter wrapped in linen cloths were stale and slightly rancid; the water in the jugs was laced with dust.

'Oh Lord, Pernel,' Athelstan prayed, 'where are you? What has happened?' He crossed to the coffer standing under the shuttered window. He opened it and took out the rugs and blankets; underneath lay packages wrapped in gauze and a small coffer. The latter contained Ave beads, a simple gold ring and several medals. The biggest of these was on a silver filigree chain, and Athelstan recognised it as one that would be worn by a nun of the Poor Clare Order. The other medals were a motley collection. One displayed the insignia of the Holy Blood at Hailes in Gloucestershire; a number were associated with St Peter's Abbey in that same shire; and the rest originated from churches in Hainault, Flanders and Zeeland. There was also one from the monastery of Sancto Alberto di Butrio. Athelstan's curiosity deepened when he untied the packages containing the brown robe, black veil, starched white wimple and waist rope of a Poor Clare nun. There was also a small psalter, its yellowing pages containing the horaria of each particular day as well as the holy seasons. In a blank folio at the front someone had written: 'This books belongs to Sister Agnes.'

'Is that who you really were?' Athelstan whispered, leafing through the psalter. 'A Poor Clare nun? And what is this?' The last page of the psalter was embossed with a seal displaying the title, '*Domus Sanctae Monicae*' – the house or convent of St Monica. Athelstan finished his searches, intrigued by what he had found.

'Lord forgive me,' he prayed. 'The cowl truly doesn't make the monk. I judge by appearances when I should wait for the truth.' He closed the chest and crouched beside it for a while. He'd always considered Pernel to be an eccentric old woman who babbled nonsense and was forever curling her crudely dyed hair. But now? Athelstan closed his eyes and a blizzard of thoughts swept his mind: Alberic's murder, the attacks on him, the disappearance of the men in his parish and the growing violence either side of the river. He must ignore the matters which he had no control over. He must get Sir John safely out of Southwark and return to Blackfriars to see if Pernel was safe. Athelstan recalled the prayer asking God for the energy to solve problems, the patience to accept those he couldn't and the wisdom to recognise the difference. Athelstan opened his eyes, crossed himself and glanced around. He had no right to be here, searching Pernel's pathetic belongings, yet he could not ignore the anxiety gnawing at his soul. Pernel was one of his parishioners and therefore his responsibility.

He got up and left, hurrying back down the silent streets. The occasional shutter and door opened and closed swiftly. Athelstan did not stop. Years ago he had served in the royal array. He recognised the tell-tale signs of a small community terrified into a watchful silence and frightful inertia. He reached the priest's house, where Cranston and Benedicta were sharing a blackjack of ale. The coroner's mood had changed. He was no longer the bon viveur, the merry soul and humourist. He sat silent, his unsheathed sword close to hand, his face drawn, his eyes watchful, betraying all the tension of a knight before battle. Athelstan beckoned both of them out of the house.

'Benedicta, we should lock up and get out of here as swiftly as possible. I . . .' He paused as the distant echo of conflict echoed around them. The black clouds of smoke above the bridge were thickening and spreading rapidly. 'I do not feel safe here any longer. The riverside is the only way out.'

They left the priest's house, Benedicta leading them along needle-thin runnels and alleyways lined with rotting houses. The ground, choked with all kinds of odours, reeked of filth and decay. Cranston called them the alleyways of Hell. Athelstan fully agreed with the coroner's description. They had entered Satan's kingdom, where the devils had set up banqueting tables to feast on human souls. Law and order, fragile at the best of times, were crumbling away. Fires had been started. Flames licked at windows. The billowing air reeked of blood, fire and the stench of unwashed bodies crammed into a seething mob hungry for mischief. Executions and slayings were commonplace now. Anyone associated with the law, officials and foreigners were all regarded as natural prey. Nevertheless, beneath the chaos, there was a moving spirit. The Earthworms had now emerged in force. The street fighters of the Upright Men directed the mob to this or that place to carry out grisly executions.

In the Penny Market close to the river, a group of Flemings had been decapitated, their torsos stripped of all raiment and left to be nudged and gnawed at by wandering dogs and pigs; their severed heads had been placed on poles, their gaping mouths stuffed with filthy straw. Athelstan had sensed when they first crossed earlier in the day that such executions were the exception. Now it appeared as if killing was a natural business and Southwark had become a slaughterhouse. Moveable gibbets had been seized and those found wanting swiftly hanged. The gallows were being pushed backwards and forwards by a cohort of Earthworms who chanted their doggerel hymns. Rivulets of blood streamed across the trackways curling into small pools and encrusting the dirt-laced puddles. Dense clouds of grey smoke stung the eye and clogged the mouth and nose. Arrow shafts whipped through the air, crossbow bolts smashed into crumbling walls and slingstones sang as citizens defended their houses and storerooms.

Prisons and compters had been stormed, their guardians brutally executed. The dungeons and cells had been opened to release a host of male-factors who clambered out to spread further chaos. Lunatics from the small hospital of St Sulpice wandered aimlessly dragging their chains, wide-eyed, haggard-faced, screaming and cursing as they traversed the bleak, jagged landscape of their own private Hell. They raised their hands, jumping up and down mouthing nonsense, until they were pushed or clubbed out of the way. Laystalls had collapsed or been pulled down, refuse carts overturned so the disturbed filth blocked paths and released the most rank, offensive smells. Taverns and alehouses had also been sacked and the mob were not so much angry as drunk. Mad, garish figures garbed in looted clothes, wearing tawdry jewellery and women's wigs, danced frenetically, shouting obscenities. The air was constantly riven with screams, yells and mocking laughter.

Athelstan felt he was crossing the landscape of Hades. He was also growing deeply concerned about Cranston. The coroner's great bulk and whiskered face had been recognised, though his drawn sword and dagger kept the nightmare figures away as they hurried down to the quay-side. Athelstan became particularly worried by one coven of malefactors led by two habitual criminals, Stocks and Pillory, their real names long since forgotten, as they had been punished so many times on the Southwark scaffold. When Athelstan first saw them they were forcing a beadle, his head decorated with a whore's blue and white wig, to jig to the reedy tune of a beggar boy's flute. They had caught sight of Athelstan and Cranston and were now following the coroner, collecting other ruffians on the way.

They reached the quayside, which reeked of fish as well as dried blood from the makeshift scaffold set up to decapitate foreign merchants and others trapped in the taverns and alehouses of Southwark. Earthworms, baleful figures in their grotesque attire, stood around, swords, clubs and maces at the ready. Alarmed now by how close Stocks and Pillory and their coterie were, Cranston shoved his way through. Mephistopheles, Master of the Minions and owner of the Tavern of Lost Souls, where most of the goods stolen in London ended up, was organising his own abrupt departure. A number of barges under the command of his brown-garbed minions were piled high with sacks, chests and coffers. Cranston, using his seal of office, commandeered one of these. Mephistopheles, bald-faced and glistening with sweat, did not protest but stared over Cranston's shoulder.

'You are the King's officer,' he murmured, 'but whether you remain a live one . . .'

Cranston and Athelstan whirled around, and Stocks, Pillory and their coven charged in. Cranston, sword and dagger out, went into the half-crouch of a fighting man. Athelstan seized a fallen club which Benedicta snatched from him. Immediately one of the minions thrust a fresh one into his hands.

'You will need that,' he hissed as the attackers swirled in. Mostly drunk, they were little match for Cranston, whilst Mephistopheles and his minions had no choice but to become involved. The fighting spread along the quayside. Athelstan, fearful of Benedicta being hurt, tried to pull her back as they edged towards the steps leading down to the waiting barge. Cranston was roaring his battle cry of 'St George! St George!' A grinning Pillory aimed a blow at Athelstan's head, but the friar caught it on his arm. The shooting pain and the malicious smirk on Pillory's unshaven, filthy face sent the furies throbbing through the little Dominican's body. All fear was forgotten as a red mist descended, a battle rage which threw him forward, impervious to the clamour and clatter of weaponry. Athelstan was swept up by a fury at the way things were, of being harassed and hounded when he thought no man, said no man and did no man any ill at all. He whirled the battle club either side as his beloved brother had taught him so expertly. Athelstan shouted with glee as the knotted wood crunched flesh and bone. He took a blow on his shoulder but this only infuriated him further. Time and again he whirled his club until he was pulled vigorously by the cowl. He swung round to face the new threat.

'Brother, for the love of God!' Benedicta stood behind the coroner staring at him open-mouthed. She came forward and eased the club from his fingers. Athelstan, sweat-soaked and breathing heavily, stared around: their attackers had vanished. The injured were crawling or hobbling away.

'Well, I never!' Cranston grinned as he ushered Athelstan on to the barge. 'Well, I never!' he repeated, taking a generous swig from the miraculous wineskin. 'A monk of war!'

'Friar, Sir John.' Athelstan grasped the wineskin, took a mouthful and clambered into the barge.

'They say you fought like a warrior, Brother Athelstan, but I find that difficult to accept.'

'Do you now?' Athelstan smiled down at Isabella, sitting next to him on a cushioned seat just to the right of the Lady Chapel in the main church of Blackfriars.

'Well, you are a priest, a friar, and you are always gentle with me.'

'Of course I am. Now, Isabella,' Athelstan pointed to the great candelabra, a candle on each of the many spigots, 'go on, light some. Remember, each burning taper is a prayer and as long as the flame lives, your prayer rises up to the Virgin. Pray for your father, pray for me.'

Isabella slid from the bench. Athelstan watched as she carefully lit a taper then knelt to slowly recite an Ave before beginning again. Athelstan stretched and crossed himself. He felt a strange tiredness since that affray on the quayside. They had left safely enough. Mephistopheles' minions were eager to take them across the river before hastening back to their master, who was fretting impatiently, eager to be away from Southwark. During their uneventful journey to Blackfriars quayside, Cranston and Benedicta had teased him mercilessly about being a berserker. The coroner declared that he had seen the likes before and mentioned the Black Prince, the present king's father, whose battle rage was a blinding red mist which numbed all fear. Once they had landed and been ushered into the guesthouse, the coroner had carried on exclaiming at the friar's martial prowess. Athelstan, growing increasingly embarrassed, had slipped away to the silence of the church whilst he waited for Brother Hugh and his shadow John the gatekeeper. Isabella, however, had heard the story about what was now being proclaimed as the 'Great Battle of Southwark' and rushed to pester Athelstan with a litany of questions. Athelstan couldn't answer these; as he had confessed to Cranston and Benedicta, it was just something which had happened. He recalled boyhood fights as well as his days serving abroad in the royal array. As always, he felt guilty about it, a part of his soul which had not been purged or even controlled, a slumbering fire which might erupt at any time. He'd fought so hard to control his temper, what he mockingly called 'the demon within'. He privately promised he would do some fresh penance, and he would pray that the red mist would evaporate and the fire which fed it be extinguished.

'Athelstan?' He glanced up at a smiling Brother John. 'Our infirmarian has returned. If you wish . . .'

Athelstan nodded, rose and took Isabella back to her nurse, who was sitting in the transept studying a vivid wall painting depicting the sorrows of Purgatory. He handed Isabella over, kissed her on the brow and followed Brother John out of the church along sun-washed passageways and across to the death house. Brother Hugh was working at the mortuary table with mortar and pestle. He greeted Athelstan and took off his thick butcher's apron.

'Brother?'

'I wish to study a corpse,' Athelstan replied. 'An old woman.' He stared round. 'She had reddish dyed hair.' The infirmarian shrugged, went to one of the tables and pulled back the corpse sheet. Athelstan's heart sank. 'Poor Pernel,' he whispered, 'poor, poor Pernel. Has she been anointed?'

'Of course. Absolution has been administered. She will be buried tomorrow morning in Poor Man's Acre, the same time we will be burying Alberic. Why, Brother, did you know her?'

'Yes, she was one of my parishioners – mad as a March hare, but,' Athelstan blessed the corpse, 'a good soul. Christ have mercy on her.'

'So what was she doing here?' Brother John came alongside, staring down at the waxen, white face.

'She came to see me,' Athelstan murmured.

'If she did, Brother, I never admitted her.' Brother John shook his head and his deep-set eyes crinkled in concern. 'No, I did not admit her. Neither at the water-gate nor through the gatehouse. You know I am responsible for all guests and visitors. A sentry manning the water-gate yesterday afternoon glimpsed her corpse being washed up against the quayside by the river tide. She was just bobbing there, hair and gown splayed out.' He shrugged. 'Of course we brought her in and,' he gestured, 'as you can see, that is all.'

Athelstan leaned over the corpse and pulled back the sheet. He searched for any head wound or blow beneath the matted, greasy hair but he could detect no contusion, bruise or blood.

'God knows,' Brother Hugh murmured. 'Did the poor soul fall from a barge or slip on a greasy quayside step? I examined her most rigorously, but I could detect no mark of violence.'

Athelstan stared into the kindly eyes, bright with a sharp mind which, Athelstan knew, loved to probe every effect and demonstrate true cause either in the physical or the metaphysical, be it examining a corpse or some syllogism in logic.

'She was full of water,' the infirmarian added. 'I suspect she fell and floundered for a while, swallowing deeply. Death would have been very swift.'

'Yes, I can see that,' Athelstan replied. 'But what caused that fall? There again,' he added bleakly, 'she was so fey and she did like her pottle of ale.'

'We have her clothes,' Brother John broke in,

'a few pathetic items.' Athelstan nodded, covered the corpse and collected the leather sack containing Pernel's paltry belongings. He was about to leave when Brother Matthias, face all flushed with excitement, burst into the death house.

'We have all been summoned.' He spread his hands. 'All of us. Our Italian brethren wish to discuss further why they have come here.'

'We know why they've come here,' Brother Hugh grumbled, 'and what a time to choose to talk about it. Why do you think they need us?' He tapped Athelstan's arm playfully. 'No doubt they will want to address certain, how can I put it, scientific or medical inquiries, especially when it comes to royal corpses, but why now?'

'I believe our beloved chronicler Roger has discovered something amiss,' Matthias declared.

'He would,' Brother Hugh murmured. 'So we will be busy enough, eh, Athelstan?'

The friar smiled as he stared at these three companions, his former teachers who had dominated his youth and training here as a Dominican priest. Sharp, witty, caustic, slightly sardonic and cynical, but good men. Now he could sense their excitement at being distracted from their usual daily routine, the ordinary tedium of friary life.

'We are to meet in the council chamber,' Matthias added, 'immediately after Compline.'

'So late?' Brother John protested.

'Time is passing.' Matthias shrugged. 'Our Italian brothers wish to finish here and return to Gloucester. Naturally, they are growing increasingly concerned by the deepening unrest in the city and elsewhere . . .'

'As they should be!' The door to the death house crashed back and Sir John Cranston, very much the Lord High Coroner, swaggered in.

'The news is not good,' he boomed, feet apart, cloak thrown back, thumbs pushed through his great leather warbelt. Athelstan was pleased to see the coroner return to his usual genial self, though he suspected as he made the introductions that the change in mood was due more to the miraculous wineskin than anything else.

'More trouble, Sir John?' he asked.

'Yes, according to my messenger Tiptoft, the rebels have crossed the bars and are now deep in the city. The Fleet prison has been stormed: all the lovelies housed there are now free to inflict whatever mischief they can wreak. They are attacking the houses of royal officials, ripping off roofs and setting buildings alight. They have sacked the Temple, hunting for lawyers. They entered the great round church there, the one built on the plan of the Holy Sepulchre in Jerusalem. They forced the treasury, seized all the records and used them to create a huge bonfire on the highway outside.' The coroner sat down on a stool, mopping his brow. 'Tiptoft believes they are going to march on Gaunt's palace of the Savoy.'

'It's well barricaded,' Athelstan intervened, 'with strong gates.'

'The Temple had the same,' Cranston retorted, 'or did have. But come, Brother. I need to discuss certain matters with you.'

'As I do with you,' Athelstan retorted.

Much to Cranston's surprise, 'the little ferret

of a friar' as he privately regarded Athelstan, did not take him to any chamber or garden to discuss matters, but back to the guesthouse and the room where Alberic had been so mysteriously killed. The door to the chamber still rested brokenly against the wall. Athelstan led the coroner around it and they both sat on a window bench from where Athelstan could keep a sharp eye on the gallery outside. He grasped the coroner's arm and felt the light chain mail beneath Sir John's doublet, a sure sign that even here, safe in Blackfriars, Cranston was deeply alarmed by the pressing danger.

'Sir John, my friend,' Athelstan began, 'you face a sea of troubles, as do I.' The friar then told the coroner about Pernel, and that the old woman's death seemed to be from natural causes, an unfortunate accident, but that in his heart he truly believed the poor woman had been murdered.

'And your suspicions are usually correct, Athelstan,' the coroner said heavily. 'We live in a wicked world and people do evil things for evil's sake – but why murder someone like Pernel? She was no more a threat than a butterfly!'

'I can't answer that, Sir John.' Athelstan stared around the chamber. 'What I do know is that Prior Anselm invited me back to Blackfriars to keep me out of trouble. I suspect you had a hand in that, Sir John?' Cranston glanced up sheepishly, shuffled his feet and then stared hard at the floor, as if seeing it for the first time. 'And my parishioners, my lord coroner? Did you have a hand in their arrest and abduction, as well?'

Cranston shook his head. 'Brother, I swear on

the lives of Lady Maude and my two sons the Poppets, whom I now miss more than ever, I have no knowledge about what happened to your parishioners. I have already told you of my fears about them. I cannot do any searches. London is sealed, the roads leading out are clogged with rebels.' The coroner fell silent and Athelstan leaned back against the wall. Cranston produced the miraculous wineskin and cradled it as a mother would a babe. 'Little friar, why have you brought me here? This must be where the Italian, Alberic, was murdered?'

Athelstan rose to his feet. 'Yes, another ploy by Prior Anselm. He wants to keep me out of harm's way. He also wants me to investigate Alberic's murder as well as assist Fieschi in the process of the canonisation of a long-dead king who perished in the most horrid circumstances. Since that event occurred over fifty years ago, it should be an academic exercise, dry as dust. Nevertheless, Alberic lies murdered. I have been attacked twice in Blackfriars, and Pernel, a parishioner who came looking for me, has also died in the most mysterious circumstances. What I first thought was a matter of academic debate – the death of a king over five decades ago – seems to have a malicious life of its own. In this matter, the past is very much alive.'

'And you want my help, little friar?' Cranston slurped from the miraculous wineskin.

'Well, you, like me, are trapped here. You have some knowledge about Edward II, and, above all,' Athelstan grinned, 'your razor-sharp wit is always appreciated.'

Cranston offered Athelstan the wineskin, which he refused. The coroner got to his feet and crossed to the door to ensure the gallery outside was empty before speaking. 'We have a great deal in common, Brother.'

'Such as?'

'Regicide. You are studying a king who died mysteriously some fifty-four years ago, whilst we know that out there, beyond the walls of Blackfriars, the rebel leaders are plotting another king's destruction. Wat Tyler, that mysterious will-o'-the-wisp who appeared from nowhere to lead the men from Kent, is, we are almost certain, Gaunt's man in peace and war. We suspect Tyler will try to draw our king into some dangerous meeting out in the open where he can be surrounded and slain.'

'And yet you have checked him,' Athelstan insisted. 'You insisted that Gaunt leave his own heir, Henry of Derby, who must go where our young king goes. No secret bowmen or clever assassin hired by Gaunt can strike, lest Gaunt's heir also be caught up in the bloody maelstrom.'

'Checked but not trapped,' Cranston retorted. 'Richard the King does not want Henry of Derby anywhere near him. The game is changing all the time, Athelstan. Gaunt has removed himself from public view, but so has Master Thibault. We have no knowledge or sight of our Master of Secrets or his shadow Albinus. They have disappeared like smoke in the air. Have they fled, or are they just lurking in the shadows?'

'Thibault must return,' Athelstan murmured.

90

'After all, as you know, he has left his daughter with me. He rode into St Erconwald's parish a few days before I was summoned here. Young Isabella is the apple of his eye. He made me swear that whatever I thought of him, I would protect her until he returns . . .'

'Well, he's disappeared,' Cranston declared. 'He should be with the rest of the royal council in the Tower, but he is not. This could mean two things. First, Thibault doesn't believe that fortress is as safe as others think it is. Secondly, I suspect Thibault is out of London, perhaps preparing for the revolt to fail. Now that's an interesting thought! Have Gaunt and his Master of Secrets decided to change the game? Perhaps they have come to realise that, in the long term, the revolt will collapse, the rebels will be defeated and their desired reforms discarded.' The coroner paused as a servant appeared in the doorway. He bowed and brought in a tray bearing a jug of white wine, two goblets and a dish of comfits coated in a hard, honey-shell with the letters 'B' and 'D' etched on them.

'What are these?' Cranston asked.

'We call them the "Blessing of Dominic".' Athelstan laughed. 'That's what the "B" and "D" stand for. It's a special comfit, baked hard, so you have to soak it for a little while. They are always given to those who visit any of our houses. A token of welcome. Taste one, Sir John, they are pleasing enough.' Cranston did so, muttering how hard they were but then adding how delicious to the taste. Athelstan refused one. Instead he walked slowly around the chamber recalling the events surrounding Alberic's corpse being discovered. He wondered about Luke the messenger who had clattered up to see what had happened and then left so swiftly.

'Brother Athelstan?' Prior Anselm stood in the doorway holding a leather sack. 'You forgot this, the belongings of one of your parishioners, the poor beggar woman in the death house.'

Athelstan thanked him and took it.

Anselm turned to face the coroner. 'Good morrow, Sir John. You will join our *concilium*, our council meeting after Compline? Roger, our chronicler, appears to be quite excited about something.'

'Yes, I will join you,' Cranston replied. 'I thank you once again for your courtesy and hospitality.'

Athelstan placed the sack on the floor. 'Father Prior, when we were waiting to gain entrance here and discover poor Alberic, that young man, came flitting up the stairs outside. He peered at what was happening then promptly disappeared. I believe his name is Luke. Is he a royal courier?'

'Master Luke,' Anselm replied, his tired eyes crinkling in amusement, 'claims to be our young king's favourite messenger. He journeys between Blackfriars and the court on this business of Edward II. Why do you ask?'

'I would like to speak to him.'

'Why?'

'Because I want to.'

The prior smiled, nodded and left. A short while later, Luke the messenger sauntered into the chamber. Cranston and Athelstan sat on the edge of the bed. Luke, who seemed unruffled at being summoned, slouched on a small three-legged stool before them. Athelstan sat there without speaking, as if listening keenly to the sounds of the friary, the ringing of bells, doors opening and closing, the faint strains of plain chant.

'Brother?'

'Master Luke.' Athelstan stared at the remarkably handsome young man. He could even be considered beautiful with his light-blue eyes in a smooth, soft face which glowed as if dusted with gold. The messenger's blonde hair had been recently cropped, his hands and fingers were elegant and he had a rather feminine way of turning and staring out of the corner of his eye as if flirting with the person he was talking to. An innocent? Athelstan wondered. Or a man who used his exquisite good looks to his own advantage, to pry, to discover information, to spy?

'Brother, you asked to speak to me and here I am.' He spread his hands. 'True, I am supposed to carry messages between Procurator Fieschi and His Grace the King, but matters have been rather hampered by the rioters, and I do have other tasks.'

'What of Brother Alberic? Did you meet him, talk to him?'

'Yes, I did.'

'About what?'

'His travels in Italy.'

'And why he was in England?'

'Alberic told me he was Devil's Advocate in the process of the canonisation of Edward II.'

'And?'

'He said his task would not be difficult, since that king,' Master Luke visibly coloured, 'died a sodomite, a failure as a man, a prince and a warrior. I replied that many saints have led ill lives until their conversion. The imprisoned king might have repented.' The messenger paused.

'And did he say anything else?'

'Alberic kept repeating two phrases, I think they are from scripture. I asked one of the brothers and he said they were.' The messenger screwed up his eyes in concentration. 'The first was, "Put not your trust in princes" and the second, "I said in my excess all men are liars."'

'They are phrases from the psalms,' Athelstan explained. 'Why should Alberic keep quoting them?'

'I don't really know, Brother Athelstan. You see, Alberic said that he would act as Devil's Advocate but he fully expected to concede that Edward II was a great friend of the Dominican Order and that he'd experienced a radical conversion before he died, so he could be a saint. Alberic explained he was only playing a role and that he had serious doubts about the whole process. He asked me, how could you truly judge the mind of a king before he died? He then added that you cannot canonise what is not there.' The messenger took the goblet of white wine Athelstan offered and sipped delicately at the rim. 'And before you ask, Brother Athelstan, Alberic did not explain himself, except on one occasion he murmured, "Berkeley had the truth of it."'

'Berkeley? The castle or its lord?'

'Brother Athelstan, I cannot say. I know very little . . .'

'And yesterday evening, did you come up here?'

The messenger blinked.

'The truth,' Athelstan insisted. He paused at distant shouting and glanced at the coroner, who just pulled a face and shrugged.

'I came up here after Compline. I heard voices speaking, but they were talking in Italian.'

'How many?'

'I don't know. Distant voices, but they were speaking very fast. No English. I heard a name mentioned, Rutrio.'

'Rutrio?'

'Yes, I am sure it was that. I could not catch anything else except the phrase "I dread", but I couldn't continue eavesdropping, as others were moving about.'

'Who?'

'I don't know, but I could hear them on the gallery below, so I left. I thought nothing of it until this morning . . .' His voice trailed off.

Athelstan thanked the messenger then dismissed him. They listened to his footsteps fading on the stairs.

'Brother, what did you make of that?'

'A very handsome young man who caught the eye of our deceased Brother Alberic, who, I suspect – like so many in our order – was drawn to such beauty. However,' Athelstan added briskly, 'that is not our business. Now look, Sir John . . .'
He got to his feet and walked to where Alberic's corpse had been sprawled.

'Athelstan, you dismiss our beautiful young man, but he could be the murderer. I mean, a lover's quarrel, a dagger drawn . . .'

'No, Sir John, God forgive me if I am wrong. I suspect Master Luke is many things besides a messenger, but he is not a killer, not this time. I believe Alberic was showing off to him. I do wonder what those enigmatic phrases really meant. Who was he talking to here? It must have been his Italian comrades. And what does Rutrio mean? It evokes a memory, something I have recently seen or heard, but I cannot recall it. Anyway,' Athelstan began walking up and down, 'Alberic, a visitor here, is brutally murdered in this sealed room with no other possible entrance but the door, yet that was locked and bolted. I can witness to that. Was Alberic beginning to doubt the validity of the entire canonisation process? Did he discover something in his searches which deeply unsettled him? Did the documents stolen from his chancery satchel hold some secret? This brings me back to the one question I keep asking myself. What is it about this long-dead king which provokes such murderous fury? I believe it is responsible for Alberic's death and for two deadly attacks on me in the one day.' Athelstan paused. 'Rutrio,' he whispered, 'Alberic didn't say Rutrio but Butrio.'

'Brother?'

'Butrio,' Athelstan explained, 'that's what Master Luke overheard. Oh, Lord save us!' Athelstan's fingers went to his face. 'I am certain that Pernel owned a medal from Sancto Alberto di Butrio. I wish I had brought it.'

At that moment, Anselm, accompanied by the three Italians, Roger the chronicler and Brothers Hugh and Matthias, came up the stairs, crowding into the gallery.

'Sir John, Brother Athelstan, you must see this.'

'See what?'

'London's aflame! Brother John has summoned us to the main gateway. Come, come, Compline will be delayed.'

Cranston and Athelstan followed Anselm and his group down the stairs, hurrying along narrow stone passageways. The news from the city had swept through the Dominican house, with people hurrying to secure vantage points. The prior led them up on to the stone platform above the cavernous double-gated entrance. Athelstan immediately saw the great fiery glow to the north and an even fiercer one further west along the river, a blazing inferno against the fading blue sky.

'My Lord of Gaunt's palace of Savoy!' Cranston declared. 'It must be.' Even as he spoke there was a further explosion from the inferno at the Savoy, and a great ball of fire shot up into the night sky, followed by jagged flames. 'Good Lord,' Cranston breathed, 'of course the palace cellars house cannon powder.' He paused at another fiery explosion then pointed to a glow to the north of the city. 'The Priory of Clerkenwell!' Cranston declared. 'Its prior, John Hailes, is also Royal Treasurer and, God save him, Hailes is high on the attainder list of the Upright Men. I hope to God he is safe in the Tower. The Earthworms will surely be hunting him. I have

97

sent Tiptoft out, he will bring back further news.'

'Will he be safe?' Athelstan asked, peering through the crenellations.

'Tiptoft is as cunning as a fox and can slink like any cat. He will join us soon enough.'

'But will they?' Athelstan pointed to the crowd gathering before the main gate. Some of the people had come here for sanctuary and were deep in discussion with Gatekeeper John, who had gone down to meet them. Athelstan was more concerned about the number of cloaked, cowled figures standing around in small groups, making no attempt to approach the gatehouse, but watching it closely.

'I see them,' Cranston whispered, drawing close. 'Earthworms or their scouts. They would like to get their hands on some of the people who've fled here, especially Thibault's daughter Isabella, to seize her as hostage.' Cranston plucked at Athelstan's sleeve, pulling him away to the far corner of the parapet walk. 'Brother, Gaunt is in the north watching and waiting like the viper he is. The rebels are seizing London. Sooner or later they will demand to see the King. Wat Tyler will insist on that.'

'And then?'

Cranston gripped Athelstan's arm tightly. 'Whatever happens, Brother, I need to be there. I have made my decision. I cannot control what is happening here or in the Tower or the city, so I must be involved in that meeting.'

'Why?'

'To kill Tyler. Whatever happens, I am committed to that. I will kill Tyler or die trying, that is my God sworn duty. I will not relent on what I intend.'

Athelstan clutched Cranston's gauntleted hand and squeezed. 'Then, my fat friend, good Sir John, I will go with you but, until then—'

'Brother Athelstan, Sir John,' the prior called out, 'we are to adjourn to Compline.'

Cranston gently pushed his companion away.

'Sing for me, Brother. I have an equally important tryst with a certain cook and a venison pie.'

Athelstan attended Compline standing in the darkening stalls, the shadows held back by the darting, dagger-like flames of the candles burning before the different statues and shrines. Smoking thuribles incensed the air as the massed voices of the community recited the verses of the psalms; a rhythmic chant which lulled the soul and quietened the mind. A hallowed occasion where the church itself became a living, breathing thing dedicated to praising and thanking God and, as the darkness thickened, pleading for protection against the night-dwellers, the demons of the air, Satan and his ghastly retinue who prowled that border between the visible and the invisible. Athelstan, despite intoning the lines and shrouding himself with the protection of the church, sensed a very present brooding evil. Blackfriars was supposed to be a House of God and the Gate of Heaven, yet a bloody-minded assassin lurked within its walls, whilst beyond them, fresh dangers threatened and more murderous mysteries swirled. Athelstan's parishioners had been abducted and his world turned upside down by fire and sword. Athelstan was fully distracted

99

now, and he wondered about Cranston's oath to kill Tyler. Would Richard be enticed out to a meeting? So far the King and his council had failed disastrously to curb the growing violence. They sheltered, or rather cowered, in the Tower. Surely it was only a matter of time before the rebel armies laid siege to that fortress?

'Brother Athelstan?'

The friar turned and glanced around. Compline had finished, and the dark, cowled shapes of the community were filing out.

'I am sorry,' Athelstan smiled at Brother John, 'I was distracted.'

He followed the lay brother out across the concourse to the priory council chamber; a high-beamed room, its lime-washed walls decorated with painted cloths depicting scenes from the life of St Dominic, its wooden floorboards polished to a gleam and sprinkled with crushed herbs to provide a pleasant smell. The great iron-bound candelabra had been lowered and the tapers in the rim of the wheel lit to bathe the long council table in a sheen of light. Prior Anselm sat enthroned at the head, the others ranged either side: Procurator Fieschi, Cassian and Isidore along with Brothers Hugh, Matthias and Roger the chronicler, who had bundles of manuscripts before him. He seemed excited and impatient to speak. Prior Anselm began proceedings by intoning the '*Veni Creator Spiritus*', then he welcomed them, explaining that Athelstan was present to take the place of Alberic, who would be buried the following morning. Hugh and Matthias were also here to assist. Matthias would act as the prior's clerk; Hugh would advise on the royal tomb, its possible opening and the care of the King's remains, the usual process when an exhumation took place. In the meantime, the prior smiled, Brother John would serve some food.

The gatekeeper kept coming in and out of the chamber with jugs of wine, goblets and platters heaped with strips of toasted bread covered in a cheese and herb sauce, portions of cold pork with sage and servings of cherry-red pudding. Trenchers, knives and napkins were placed before each person. Prior Anselm swiftly blessed the food and asked his companions to eat whilst Brother Roger explained what he had found.

'It's very interesting.' The chronicler was so impatient he pushed away his trencher, grabbing the goblet of wine to wet his throat. 'The actual death of King Edward II,' he continued, 'does not concern us; strangulation, suffocation, death by natural causes or through a red-hot skillet being pushed up his anus into his bowels, are the different stories of the chroniclers. According to all of them, Edward died on the Feast of St Matthew, the twenty-first of September, 1327.' Brother Roger rubbed his ruby-red face, sheened with glistening sweat. 'However, what happened next is very important. Item,' he held up a stubby thumb, 'the King's corpse should have been brought across country to Westminster; its abbey is the mausoleum of our royal family. The Benedictines of Westminster did send a delegation demanding this, but Queen Isabella and her lover Roger Mortimer declared it would be unsafe to convey the royal corpse across the kingdom lest it stir up agitation amongst the people.'

'Conspiracies are one thing, but popular uprisings in favour of a deposed king?' Athelstan asked sharply. 'Edward still enjoyed such support?'

'He certainly did.' Brother Roger glanced quickly at Prior Anselm, who simply stared down at the table top. 'Father Prior,' Father Roger insisted, 'I know you wish to say something on this matter.'

'Edward II, God rest him,' Anselm lifted his head, 'dead or alive, enjoyed deep support amongst us Dominicans who preach to the people.' He cleared his throat. 'There, it is out in the open, we know that. We accept it as a fact. I have mentioned this before but now I emphasise it with all the authority I can muster. Our order and that of the deposed king have always been intertwined. The Dominican friar Thomas Dunheved was the King's confessor and closest counsellor. When marital relations between Edward and Isabella broke down after she had fled to France and joined the exiled Mortimer, Thomas Dunheved travelled to Pope John XXI to seek an annulment to the King's marriage with Isabella. However, by the time Dunheved returned, Mortimer and Isabella had invaded the kingdom. They swiftly destroyed the Despensers, captured the King, deposed him in favour of his son and despatched him to life imprisonment at Berkeley, a fortified castle close to Mortimer's power on the Welsh March. What happened next accounts for us being here and for what it means to our order.'

Anselm paused, fingers going to his lips, lost in his own world. His words, and above all his tone, seemed to represent the collective memories of the Dominican Order in England about Edward II. Athelstan recalled one old friar telling him that no English king had done so much for the Dominican Order as Edward II. Nevertheless, that king had fallen from power and the Dominicans had not been with him in his hour of need, leaving a legacy of guilt and shame. The prior had certainly summoned up ghosts, memories and stories from the past. Was it simply that Edward II had fallen from power and the Dominicans had been unable to help? Or was it something else, the matter now being touched on here, the actual fate of that deposed king?

Athelstan glanced at his companions. Fieschi's round, cherubic face betrayed his mood. He seemed troubled, glancing swiftly at his two companions, who looked equally uneasy. Roger was nodding in agreement at what the prior had said, though Hugh and Matthias stared in puzzled indifference. Whatever was happening, Athelstan concluded, the past had certainly swept in; the ghost of this long-dead king now stretched across the years with chilling spectral fingers to clutch the living. Something was wrong. Athelstan was convinced, this was now more than just a discussion about a king who had died at Berkeley and lay buried in nearby Gloucester.

'Prior Anselm?' Athelstan tapped the table top. 'What is all this really about?'

'Brother Roger,' Anselm murmured, 'you had best continue.'

'Prior Anselm is correct,' the chronicler declared. 'The Dominican Order in this kingdom had a deep personal loyalty to King Edward II. He always defended our rights and the good brothers responded in kind. When the great earls executed Peter Gaveston, Edward II's beloved favourite, at Blacklow Hill in Warwickshire, the local Dominicans sewed the severed head back on the corpse. They honourably tended the remains, keeping them embalmed above ground until Holy Mother Church ordered their burial in our friary at Oxford.'

'Brother Roger,' Athelstan interjected, 'what are you implying here? We all know the essentials of history here. Edward II was deposed, imprisoned, murdered and buried in Gloucester. What else is there that need concern us?'

'That he escaped,' Roger declared, provoking cries of surprise.

'No . . .'

'Father Prior,' Fieschi intervened, 'I don't know how our learned colleague here has reached such a conclusion so swiftly.'

'I do.' Isidore, his face contorted with fury, half rose until Fieschi pressed him on the arm and he sat down.

'Not for the moment,' Fieschi declared, glaring at the chronicler, who looked rather shame-faced, though he was still clearly eager to reveal what he knew.

'What is not for the moment?' Athelstan demanded. 'What do you mean, Procurator Fieschi? I fully understand our present prince's desire to have a saint in the family, but I have a

104

feeling there is more to this than merely the sanctity of a long-dead king. It is not going to be as straightforward as we thought.'

'Athelstan,' the Prior replied, 'you are on the road to the truth. We all know the accepted story about Edward II's fall and death, but there *is* more to it than that, and Procurator Fieschi wishes to be thorough. He and his comrades arrived at the end of January and have spent the time since travelling extensively round the country.'

'But mainly to Gloucester and Berkeley,' Fieschi intervened, his tongue stumbling over the English place names.

'Yes, and now they are in London,' the Prior continued, 'to meet His Grace the King but also to study the relevant records. They are housed here because they are brothers in our order. We can protect and assist them, particularly you, Athelstan, with your keen mind and sharp wit.' Athelstan smiled bleakly at the flattery, bowed his head and beat his breast as a sign of compliance.

'So, Brother Roger, let us strike at the heart of the problem,' Anselm lifted a hand, 'without interruption.' He let his words hang in the air, the silence broken only by the constant rasp of secretarius Matthias' quill pen racing across the vellum stretched out in front of him.

Brother Roger began again, glaring around to challenge any objection: 'The accepted story of Edward II being buried at Gloucester must be seriously questioned. *Primo*, he allegedly died on the twenty-first of September and was kept above ground until solemn interment at

Gloucester. The corpse was moved from Berkeley to St Peter's Abbey on the twenty-first of October and was buried during a snow storm on the twentieth of December, Isabella and Mortimer being present. We have very little evidence about the funeral. Now,' Roger was thoroughly enjoying himself, 'note how late this burial was, as if there is nothing suspect. Nevertheless, there is.

'So, *secundo*. The corpse was above ground for months but was scarcely viewed. It was exposed for a short while at Berkeley and seen from afar by a number of dignitaries. In addition, at Berkeley the corpse was sheathed in a shroud of pure lead which was then placed in a wooden casket for transport to Gloucester, where it lay in state. Of course the actual body was sealed in and a life-sized effigy of the King placed on top of the coffin casket, the first of its kind, I understand. *Tertio*,' Roger pressed on. 'The corpse was dressed for burial not by a royal physician, leech or apothecary but by a local woman from the Gloucester countryside. She prepared the corpse and removed the heart which, according to the chamber accounts, she placed in a silver casket and took to Queen Isabella.' Roger sniffed noisily. 'When that good lady died at Castle Rising in 1358, in something akin to the odour of sanctity, this silver casket was placed in her coffin before burial at Greyfriars in London.'

He paused, as if gauging the effect his words were having. Athelstan had been listening intently, his mind racing at the possibilities. He was aware of the tension in the chamber, where the daylight

106

was dying and the shadows stretching out from corners and enclaves as if to greet the ghosts now gathering close.

'*Quarto.*' Roger's voice was as harsh as a cracked whip. The chronicler was now a story-teller, a minstrel taking them all back into the bloody, mysterious past. 'During Edward II's imprisonment at Berkeley there were numerous attempts to free him, the most notorious being an assault on the castle during the summer of 1327. The leaders of this enterprise were two Dominican friars, Thomas and Stephen Dunheved. According to a letter written by Lord Berkeley himself, the attackers got into the castle and, in Berkeley's own words, "Took the father of our present king from our guard." In other words, Edward II was freed.'

Athelstan whistled under his breath; the mystery was deepening.

'*Quinto.* Rumours persisted that Edward II had escaped and was hiding in Dorset at Corfe Castle. We know these stories were enhanced and spread by Dominican friars, who even persuaded Edmund, Earl of Kent, Edward II's half-brother, to write a letter to the former king, not dead but in hiding, promising to return him to his throne. Kent boasted that he had the blessing of the Holy Father as well as the support of leading notables in both church and state. People later said all this was just a ploy by Mortimer and Isabella, to trap Kent, a man of straw, a feckless young wastrel. They certainly had their way. In March 1330, Edmund of Kent was condemned as a traitor and arrested at Winchester. He was forced to stand in disgrace at the city gates until a drunken felon cut off his head in return for a pardon.'

Roger sipped from his goblet and reorganised the pieces of parchment before him. Athelstan gazed at a wall painting depicting St Dominic resplendent in a blue-gold chasuble. The great preacher was fending off Satan and his minions, fiends with monkey faces and lizard bodies, tongues of fire erupting from their snarling, fanged mouths. In the dark, troubled sky above them, fresh hosts of demons mustered in black, drifting clouds, ready for battle.

'*Sexto*,' the chronicler continued. 'The royal chamber accounts of 1338 list payments to Edward III, eleven years after the events of 1327 when he was abroad in foreign parts. The money was to pay expenses for going to meet a man called William the Welshman, who claimed to be the King's father. Now, these payments mention the city of Cologne. *Septimo*,' Roger continued, blithely ignoring the exclamations of surprise from Athelstan and the others. 'We have a letter, do we not, from your uncle?' The chronicler pointed dramatically at Fieschi, who, tight-lipped, gazed stonily back. 'Your uncle, Manuel Fieschi, wrote a letter to Edward III in 1342 claiming that the King's father did escape from Berkeley; that he travelled through Europe visiting the shrine of the Three Kings at Cologne before journeying south into Italy and sheltering at the abbey of Sancto Alberto di Butrio.'

Roger paused as the three Italians conversed swiftly in their own tongue. They were deeply agitated, especially Isidore, who kept shaking his

108

head and glaring at the chronicler. Athelstan leaned back in his chair, trying to hide his consternation. Butrio! Pernel had a medal from there, and that was the name Master Luke the messenger had overheard.

Prior Anselm rapped the table. 'Press on, Roger,' he insisted. 'Then we will have the questions.'

'*Octavo*, finally.' The chronicler picked up the sheet of yellowing vellum. 'In 1330 Roger Mortimer fell from power and was arrested by the young Edward III at Nottingham Castle. Mortimer died at Tyburn. Queen Isabella was dispatched into honourable retirement, her beloved son making it very clear that he would accept no criticism of his darling mother and that everything which had occurred over the last four years was Mortimer's fault, not hers. The alleged assassins fled. Ockle was never found. Gurney was arrested in Naples and died on the journey back to England. The two men actually responsible for the royal prisoner, John Maltravers and Thomas Berkeley, fell under deep suspicion. Maltravers fled abroad but was later pardoned. Thomas Berkeley, however, kept his nerve and coolly arrived at Parliament in November 1330, where Mortimer was condemned. Berkeley, too, was summoned to the bar, but he boldly stated, when accused of being involved in Edward II's murder, that he didn't even know the King had died until this present Parliament.'

'What?' Athelstan ignored Prior Anselm's objection to the interruption. 'Sir Thomas, keeper of Berkeley Castle, insisted three years after the old king had died and been buried nearby, that he did not know of it until that Parliament?' Athelstan laughed. 'Of course Berkeley was playing a game.'

'He was presenting the classic defence,' the chronicler agreed. 'How can he, Berkeley, be accused of regicide if the alleged victim is still alive? How can Edward II be murdered when the King had actually escaped?' Roger sipped from his goblet. 'The crown made no response to his plea so that was the end of the matter.'

'Not quite. We have questions.' Isidore, his sallow face suffused with anger rapped the table. 'Prior Anselm, you knew what Friar Roger was going to say tonight?'

'Yes, he told me.'

'What are his sources?'

'We have had records brought here for our use, you know that.'

'And the schedule of documents stolen from Brother Alberic's chancery satchel?' Isidore pointed a finger at Roger. 'All that you say can be found in those documents. Did you steal that schedule? Did you murder poor Alberic?'

'This is nonsense!' All good humour drained from Roger's face. 'Father Prior, please tell them.'

Anselm rose to his feet, his lean, lined face exuding authority as his gaze swept the council chamber. 'You all know, Procurator Fieschi, Brothers Isidore and Cassian, that records have been sent here from both the Tower and Westminster. Brother Alberic, God rest him, had long conversations with Brother Roger. Both historians, they helped each other. Alberic's

110

schedule was not stolen. He loaned it to Roger for his perusal. He did so because Roger himself entertained profound doubts about the accepted story of Edward II's death.'

'Why didn't you tell us that?' Isidore accused.

'Because my father prior told me not to,' Roger retorted, 'well, not until I had read and studied what these documents contain. Alberic loaned them to me; once I have finished my scrutiny, I shall return them. Like you,' the chronicler added sardonically, 'I pursue the truth.'

'What Brother Roger says,' Athelstan intervened tactfully as Anselm retook his seat, 'is both logical and correct. It is more important to answer certain questions on this matter than to argue about who knows what.' He turned in his chair. 'Procurator Fieschi, you were chosen by the Holy Father in this task because you are a Dominican, but you are also the nephew of Manuel Fieschi?'

'Yes.'

'And you must have visited the abbey of Sancto Alberto di Butrio? Did you find any trace of Edward II, either that he stayed there or, more importantly, was buried there?'

'Nothing but rumours, gossip that years ago an English king fleeing for his life and disguised as a hermit visited the abbey. However, there is no real evidence or proof of that.'

'Then let us turn to this corpse at Berkeley. Brother Hugh?' Athelstan asked. 'You are a most skilled infirmarian, leech and herbalist, a man who has prepared many corpses for burial. Now the only time, or so I believe, that Edward II's corpse was publicly displayed was at Berkeley during September and early October. Brother Roger will correct me if I am wrong, but the corpse was viewed by notables, though from afar. My question is this: could another corpse have been substituted for that of Edward II?'

'Certainly.' Hugh's face creased into a smile. 'Remember, those mortal remains in that shroud of lead were prepared by a local woman, probably a village leech who might not even know what the King looked like in life. She would have shorn the hair and beard. I also suggest that the face of the corpse was cupped in a coif, like that of a nun, so only the eyes, nose and mouth could be seen. If anybody did have doubts, you could argue that this was due to the effects of death and the preparations for burial, such as the shaving of the face and embalming work on both mouth and nose.'

'And the leaden sheath?' Athelstan queried.

'The best way to seal a corpse in once and for all. Any attempt to open such a shroud would allow in the humours and elements to decay the remains. Mortimer and Isabella, or so they thought, had sealed the past.'

'Accordingly,' Athelstan held up a hand for silence, 'whether that leaden sheath truly contained the mortal remains of Edward II is a matter of speculation. The case that it did not is based on Edward II being freed and being seen here and there. The only people who know the full truth are those who attacked Berkeley Castle in the summer 1327: the coven led by the two Dominicans, Thomas and Stephen Dunheved. What happened to them?'

'I am searching our records here at Blackfriars.' Matthias the secretarius lifted his head, twirling the quill pen between his fingers. 'Well, I and my learned friend here, chronicler Roger. According to the evidence, the Dunheveds were later caught and flung into Newgate prison.'

'Even though they were clerics?' Athelstan asked sharply.

'Oh, Holy Mother Church protested, as did the Dominican Order. Apparently the Dunheveds came from our house at Oxford, young men who had been scholars there, totally devoted to the memory of Edward II. They led a considerable coven of like-minded priests, yeomen and others.'

'And the Dunheveds' fate?'

'Brother Athelstan,' Roger replied, 'you have visited the Hell pit at Newgate. By the time the church lodged its protests, along with those of the Dominican Order, the Dunheveds were dead of jail fever: their corpses were brought here, viewed, cleansed, blessed and buried out in God's Acre. You will find their tombstones in the Dominican cemetery, their names enrolled in our Book of the Dead.' He paused. 'The prison chaplain at Newgate was Brother Eadred, a member of our order.'

'I know of him,' Anselm intervened. 'A good, saintly priest.'

'I knew him too,' Roger declared. 'I met him once. Eadred ministered to the prisoners and their families. He later became Prior of our house at Oxford and, indeed, Provincial of the Dominican Order in England. Gone to God now,' Roger sighed, 'like so many of our brothers.' Brother

113

Roger's voice trailed away yet, watching him closely, Athelstan wandered what else this skilful chronicler had discovered: he could almost sense Brother Roger's tension, as if the chronicler knew something but was most reluctant to share it.

'What I cannot understand,' Matthias declared, 'is the obvious: if Edward II escaped from Berkeley. If there is a suspicion that an imposter lies buried beneath the flagstones of St Peter's in Gloucester, why did his son build that splendid tomb and send hunters after those accused of being involved in his father's murder, creatures like Gurney?'

'And I could add,' Roger declared, 'if Edward II definitely lies buried at Gloucester, why should his successor, his own son, pay good money to meet someone claiming to be his father?'

'There is the possibility,' Fieschi declared. 'We have the reality and the pretence. Isabella received that heart taken from the corpse at Berkeley to heighten the impression in that it truly was from her husband's body. Secondly, Edward III paid public homage to his father's memory by building that tomb and despatching hunters to capture the likes of Gurney. All this was to sustain the illusion that Edward II did die at Berkeley, lies buried at Gloucester and that his son is determined to punish his murderers as well as honour the dead king. In such a situation the Crown of England would find it easier to manage the illusion and life could move on rather than to have to publicly concede that Edward II is still alive, wandering the byways of England or elsewhere.'

Fieschi took a deep breath. 'If Edward II was

truly murdered at Berkeley and buried in Gloucester, we could proceed with the process of canonisation; those who advocate it could do so from a position of strength. However,' he shook his head, 'if, on the balance of probability, evidence can be produced which demonstrates that Edward II escaped, what can we do? For all we know, the old king might have survived for years after his escape. In which case how did he live? Godly, righteously, or did he indulge in every form of vice? It would be foolish to canonise someone, prince or not, when the greater part of his life, not to mention the details of his death, are hidden from even the most superficial scrutiny.' Fieschi spread his hands on the table and stared around. 'Brethren, that is why we are here and that is the problem which confronts us.'

Wat Tyler, leader of the Upright Men of Kent, felt he had sated his rage that day as a thirsty man would slake his throat. Thursday 13th June had marked a change. Everything Tyler had plotted had broken down. He and John of Gaunt had entered into a secret compact. The self-styled regent would withdraw from London, taking the royal army north to the Scottish march. London and, above all, the Crown would be left unprotected. Tyler would sweep into the city, storm its fortifications and seize the court party. In the violent, bloody mêlée that followed, Richard would die, an unintended casualty. Gaunt would then come hurrying south. He and Tyler would be masters of the city and the realm.

Now all this had been overturned. Gaunt had

marched north but King Richard, advised by the likes of Cranston and his cunning helpmate Athelstan, had checked Gaunt. The regent and his wily henchman Thibault must have realised that Cranston and Athelstan had discovered their murky alliance with Tyler, so the regent and his Master of Secrets had decided to take another path. Any alliance or understanding with the rebel leader was now null and void. Gaunt had marched north but Thibault had disappeared from both the Tower and the city. According to Tyler's spies, Thibault had not panicked and fled but was hiding somewhere in the wild countryside of Essex, feverishly plotting. He was now acting the fervent supporter of the Crown, persuading the great lords of the Soil to whistle up their retinues to unite and march on London. And then what? How long would the Upright Men's peasant levies stand against the mailed might of knights on horseback, of professional mercenaries and phalanx after phalanx of bowmen and hobelars?

Tyler drank deeply from the plundered goblet and stared around the luxurious chamber; a truly opulent room with its exquisitely carved furniture, and thick turkey cloths lying edge to edge on the polished floor to deaden sound. The chair Tyler was sitting on was cushioned with the purest flock pushed into gold-fringed satin cushions. Tapestries of brilliant light-catching hues decorated the pink-washed plaster above shimmering wooden panelling. Once the mansion of Roger Leggett, an assizer, questmonger, professional lawyer and, by public repute, a rogue and enemy to the True Commons, the house stood in its own grounds near St Katherine's Dock. Yesterday it had been Leggett's pride and joy, now it was Tyler's, the new lord of London. Roger Leggett had no need of this splendid mansion. He had gone to his eternal reward.

At first Leggett thought he would escape by fleeing for sanctuary at St Martin's le Grand. Leggett had reached its high altar and wailed for protection. Tyler had stormed the church with drawn sword. He'd threatened the priests and made them step aside. Once he had them kneeling in obedience and begging for their lives, Tyler had marched up the nave with his henchmen and dragged the weeping Leggett out of the church. Tyler had thrown him into a horse trough and crowned him with stinking manure. He then had the unfortunate lawyer stripped to his loin cloth, beaten, pushed along West Chepe and placed in the stocks which stood at the junction of Milk and Bread Street. The mob had then hurled insults and filthy sewage at Tyler's unfortunate prisoner, dancing around and toasting him with the wine and ale they had plundered from nearby taverns. This macabre dance lasted until the Kestrel, Tyler's leading captain amongst the Upright Men, had released Leggett from the stocks and forced him to lie down, fastening his head against a log before hacking it off with a flesher's axe.

Tyler walked out of the solar and along the passageway leading to the gardens. In a chamber above, the Kestrel was now enjoying the plump, glorious charms of Leggett's young mistress, a buxom wench whose cries of protest had been replaced with growing moans of pleasure. The great four-poster bed she was now bouncing on was rattling against the floor. In other parts of the mansion, Tyler's men were hunting for precious items, their leather sacks open, ready to receive goblets, mazers, platters, cups and drinking jugs, as well as Leggett's collection of precious relics, including the lantern Judas allegedly used when he betrayed Christ in the Garden of Gethsemane.

Tyler walked out into the paved garden. Darkness was closing in, but flickering flambeaux and lanternhorns bathed the garden in light, a true pleasance with its herbers, grassy plots, cultivated flower beds and richly stocked vegetable garden, as well as a small orchard. The garden had been transformed into a place of bloody slaughter and gruesome display. Eighteen poles, each bearing the severed head of an enemy of the True Commons, had been thrust into the fresh, black soil. Leggett's head was in the front row; the blood had long since stopped pumping. The scraggy neck, with its bony strip of vertebrae hanging down, looked ghastly set against the velvet glow of an English summer evening. The fruit trees in the small orchard had also been decorated, festooned with dangling corpses, necks tied fast, heads to one side, faces all horrid in death. Tyler called them 'his harvest of rotten fruit come to ripen': lawyers, officials and court flunkies seized in the streets and hanged out of hand.

Tyler clenched his fist. He had certainly wreaked vengeance that day, especially against Gaunt. The rebel leader had turned his full fury at Gaunt's duplicity on the regent's pride and joy, his magnificent palace of the Savoy: a veritable treasure house with its warren of luxurious chambers; the great hammer-beam hall; its jewel of a private chapel surrounded by cloisters, gardens and elegant courtyards. Tyler had plundered the palace from cellar to loft. Everything; furniture, tapestries and a hoard of precious items, beds, tables, chairs and stools, had all been piled on to a soaring bonfire in the great hall. Tyler himself had thrust in the first flaming torch. The fire had spread swiftly as the looters brought barrels of gold and silver, caskets of jewels and coffers full of precious cloth of gold.

Some of the pillagers became drunk and one of them had hurled three tuns of gunpowder on to the bonfire. The immediate explosion had brought timber and masonry tumbling down to block the steps to the palace wine cellars. Thirty of Tyler's followers, feasting on the sweet wines they had found there, were trapped and burnt alive. The rebel leader still had the stench of burning flesh in his nostrils, whilst he was sure he could still hear the shrill cries of the men being scorched to death. Nevertheless, it had all been worth it, and the dance had scarcely begun.

Tyler had decided to throw in his lot with the radical Jack Straw. The kingdom would be purged of princes and prelates, and London burnt to the ground to clear the rat nests of privilege. The destruction of the Savoy was only the beginning. Tyler was determined to teach Gaunt a lesson in ruthlessness. He would make the regent pay for his treachery and double-dealing. And the rest? Tyler raised the jewel-encrusted goblet to his mouth and drank deep of the late Leggett's best Bordeaux before offering a mocking toast to the severed head. 'Farewell,' Tyler whispered. 'I hope Master Thibault's head will soon join yours.' He sipped again, letting the wine wash the dirt from his mouth. Thibault was beyond his reach, but the Master of Secrets' daughter Isabella was sheltering in Blackfriars, along with two others Tyler wished to settle scores with: Cranston and the meddling Athelstan. Tyler had anticipated this. Where else provided safer sanctuary for Thibault's brat or indeed Athelstan, not to mention others, than the sacred precincts of Blackfriars?

Tyler drained the goblet, half listening to the squeals of the dead Leggett's woman. He had his own adherents in those sacred precincts and it was time he paid them a visit. And afterwards, once Cranston and Athelstan were gone? Tyler smiled. He would deal with them all: Gaunt, Thibault and, above all, Richard the King.

Part Three

'True Love Is Away.'
(The Letters of John Ball)

Cranston and Athelstan met in the friar's chamber after the requiem Mass for Alberic and the others ready for burial in God's Acre. Benedicta joined them just as a kitchen scullion served roo broth with chunks of venison, blanche porray, peppered toast, creamed leeks and tankards of what the servant called 'Blackfriars' best ale'. Once he had left, Athelstan described what he had learnt in the friary library about the reign of Edward II. Most of it was already known to Cranston. Benedicta was especially interested in Isabella, Edward's wife.

'They called her the She-Wolf of France,' Cranston declared. 'They say she went mad with grief at Castle Rising. Isabella believed she was haunted by her dead husband's ghost.'

'Whatever that might mean,' Athelstan intervened, 'because on the balance of probability, there is every reason to believe that Edward II escaped from Berkeley.' He rubbed his face in his hands. 'I must admit, I am exercised not so much by this mystery but by the violence it seems to have provoked here at Blackfriars. Benedicta, I have news for you . . .' Athelstan told the widow woman what had happened: Fieschi's mission, Alberic's mysterious murder, the attacks on him and poor Pernel's death. Benedicta heard him out, eyes softening at his description of the Fleming's drowned corpse.

'It may have been a simple accident,' she murmured. 'Pernel was much distracted. I have seen her stagger and stumble along the nave at St Erconwald's.'

'And the attacks on me?'

'You may have it wrong,' Benedicta replied. 'Apart from Pernel's death, could such violence be the work of the Upright Men? I am sure they have their followers here: gardeners, scullions, even the servant who's just served you.'

'But why?'

'Oh, it's obvious, Brother, the disappearance of your parishioners. Sir John is coroner of London, an official marked down for death. Tyler must nourish a personal grudge against you. He must deeply resent your interference, your protection of the young king. I concede the revolt is not what I had hoped for. London is afire, the sky black with smoke. I have been up to the gatehouse. Earthworms now watch all the approaches to Blackfriars. They will also be seething about all the foreigners and lawyers and others who shelter here.' She crossed herself. 'Brother Athelstan, be assured, the likes of Tyler would love to do great violence to you and yours.'

Athelstan agreed. He had wondered about the possibility that the violence in Blackfriars might have nothing to do with the investigation into Edward II, yet he was not fully convinced.

'So we are in great danger?' Cranston demanded. 'Is that what you are saying, Benedicta?'

'Sir John, I think everybody is in danger.'

Athelstan held the widow woman's gaze, noting how beautiful she really was. Those dark, lustrous eyes seemed larger, the skin of her face smoother, as if the soul within responded with all its energies to the dangers pressing close.

'The rebels will turn on each other.' She sighed. 'Did you know they are now hunting Giles of Sempringham, our parish artist?'

'But I thought he was one of the Upright Men?'

'He is also known as the Hangman of Rochester. Some Earthworms maintain he is responsible for the execution of some of their comrades.'

'He is,' Athelstan interjected. 'He had no choice. The men he executed were criminals, tried and judged worthy of death.'

'I agree, Brother, but, as I have said, times have changed. Before this happened we all had to act our part, but now it's harvest time. The reapers are here. Grudges have to be settled, grievances redressed. In your sermons and homilies you said it would come to this. How once the killing began the monsters would creep out of the darkness – well, they certainly have.' She turned to the coroner. 'So, yes, Sir John, you are in danger and you should not leave here.'

'But I have to,' Cranston retorted. 'I must join the King . . .' He paused at a pounding at the door. It swung open and John the gatekeeper almost fell into the room.

'Brother Athelstan, please, it's Friar Roger . . .'

The chronicler's chamber stood just off the

great cloisters, close to the writing desks where Roger could sit to make good use of the light. It was usually a place of serene study, but now agitated members of the community were thronging the enclave leading down to his chamber. Brother John pushed them all aside until they reached the entrance guarded by the burly sacristan, Brother Cuthbert, who let them in. The chronicler's cell was large. The shutters on the lancet window had been thrown back. Athelstan was aware of a bed, chancery desk, chair, wall pegs and, above all, manuscripts stacked on shelves or spilling out of coffers, chests and chancery pouches. Prior Anselm was there along with Fieschi, Cassian and Isidore, Hugh the infirmarian and Brother Matthias. All seemed in shock, staring down at Roger, who lay stretched on the floor, head to one side, his left eye open, locked in an empty stare. The usual jovial face was drawn and discoloured, and even from where he stood, Athelstan could glimpse dirty-white foam coating the chronicler's lips.

'We found him so.' Prior Anselm's harsh face was drawn in sorrow. 'We found poor Roger like this. We had to force his door. He was just sprawled, silent and cold, yet he was so merry, so learned. I have known him for years. He was my brother . . .'

Anselm slumped down on a stool, put his face in his hands and quietly sobbed. Athelstan crouched by the corpse. He too felt a deep pang of sorrow for this fat, rubicund friar who had bustled about Blackfriars, his head full of stories as he studied this manuscript or that, constantly compiling a chronicle of the mother house and all its doings. A friar who loved to regale anyone and everyone with a litany of stories and anecdotes. Roger had been one of Athelstan's teachers, skilled in the use and treatment of manuscripts, a living authority on annals, chronicles and histories. He loved nothing better than to pore over old manuscripts, fingers twitching with excitement. Athelstan murmured a requiem and looked up.

'Nothing has been disturbed?'

'Nothing,' Hugh replied. 'Isidore came to visit Roger and found the door locked and bolted. He returned and, after receiving no answer, alerted Father Prior, who realised that Roger had also not attended Divine Office or this morning's requiem mass. Prior Anselm summoned me and the others. Lay brothers broke down the door and we saw what you now see, only a short while ago. No one has left or entered this chamber except you. And,' he indicated with his head, 'the redoubtable Sir John.'

Athelstan gazed over his shoulder. Cranston framed the broken doorway. Benedicta had not followed them – being a woman, she would not be allowed into the friary enclosure. Athelstan moved to kneel more comfortably.

'I will administer the last rites,' he murmured. He opened his chancery satchel and took out a small leather case containing the phials of sacred oil. He turned the corpse over on its back, trying not to be distracted by the agonised rictus on Roger's dead face. The chronicler had definitely been poisoned: the protuberant eyes, the livid

125

skin, discoloured lips and thickened tongue, as well as the creamy, dirty froth staining the corners of the dead man's mouth, were proof enough. Athelstan anointed the corpse – brow, eyes, mouth, chest and feet – before delivering absolution. The cadaver's skin was cold, the muscles rigid. Friar Roger had been dead for some hours. Athelstan forced open the corpse's mouth but the swollen tongue blocked any real investigation. He pulled back the upper and lower lips and stared pitifully at the yellowing stumps of teeth. He sketched a blessing above the corpse, crossed himself and rose. Prior Anselm had now composed himself.

'Brother Athelstan,' he said dully, 'I want you to investigate all this. Do what you have to.' He joined his hands and raised his eyes, lips murmuring in silent prayer. Once finished, he glanced swiftly at Athelstan. 'Many years ago,' he said, 'we had a novice here, a young man of good family with brothers and sisters, a lovely father and mother. He was one of Brother Roger's scholars, trained to study the past. He decided to write a history of his own father, a man he admired as much as he loved.' The prior narrowed his eyes. 'Now the boy's father had served in the King's array in France. Our young scholar started making enquiries and discovered that his father had been a professional mercenary who had served with the Falcons—'

'I have heard of them,' Cranston intervened, 'Lord have mercy on us.'

'I am sure you have, Sir John.' Anselm smiled thinly. 'They were a free company, notorious for the ruthless savagery they showed the enemy, be it man, woman or child. They burnt and murdered their way across northern France, so vile the Papal Legate excommunicated them. The boy's father not only served with this company but was one of their captains. He amassed a fortune, returned to England and apparently made his peace with God and man: he became a wealthy city merchant with a reputation for helping the poor. Of course, there were many in France who could have told another tale. You see my point, Athelstan?'

The friar nodded. 'Father Prior, I agree, and I have reached the same conclusion myself.'

'The past can be very dangerous. You go back there . . .' The prior blinked and stared down at Brother Roger's corpse. 'You go back there,' he whispered, 'you unlock doors. You open windows. You think what lies within is long dead and forgotten. Wrong! The past is a living thing, full of sweet memories but also monsters. This is what has happened here.' He put his hand on the friar and drew him closer. 'Athelstan, you must go back into the past, find these monsters. Either kill them or put them back in their pits to be sealed forever.'

Athelstan nodded his agreement. He was conscious of other friars gathered near the door, watching him curiously. 'Father Prior,' he replied, 'once we leave here, this chamber must be sealed. Nothing is to be taken from it without my permission. So, what do we have here?' He walked across to the chancery table: its chair had been pulled back, the table top was strewn with manuscripts, some fresh, others yellowing with age. Athelstan glimpsed a goblet of wine and a wooden mazer half full of dried nuts and raisins.

'Roger loved these.' Hugh had followed him across. The infirmarian picked up the goblet, swirled the dregs of white wine, sniffed and, before Athelstan could stop him, drained the cup. He then winked at Athelstan and handed the goblet to him. 'Nothing but the finest wine from the Rhineland, and these,' he picked up the bowl of nuts and raisins, poking them about with his bony fingers, sniffing them carefully, running a few of them across his hand before popping them into his mouth.

'Hugh!' Athelstan gasped.

'Be at peace, Brother,' the infirmarian replied. 'Taste them yourself.' He placed the mazer back on the table. 'I can detect nothing amiss. Examine them yourself. Indeed, if you wish, I can arrange for rats to be caught, caged and fed anything found in this chamber. I assure you, they will only be the better for it.'

Athelstan shook his head and walked around the chamber; there was no more food and drink. In his mind he listed the items Brother Roger might have put to his mouth. He carefully examined the feather-tipped quill pens but could detect nothing amiss. He then studied the room, a large friary cell served by a long lancet window and sealed by a heavy, iron-studded door. Athelstan could tell from the buckled lock, cracked bolts and ripped hinges that the door had been roughly forced. He knelt and scrutinised the dead friar's fingers, bending close to sniff the cold, cracked flesh: yet all he could detect was the faint smell of ink, parchment and sealing wax. Once again, he stared down at the contorted face. He was sure that when the corpse was stripped, tell-tale rashes would be found indicating some powerful poison, probably the garden sort. He glanced up.

'Prior Anselm? Brother Roger has been dead for some hours, probably since late yesterday evening. What happened last night? Where was Brother Roger, what was he doing?'

'Apparently he left our meeting and collected that goblet of wine and mazer from Brother Paschal, our buttery clerk. Roger told Paschal he wanted to study until Matins. The buttery clerk offered to help Roger as our chronicler was never the steadiest on his feet. Roger thanked him and left for his chamber, Brother Paschal following close behind. Apparently,' the prior continued, 'Roger's hands were full of manuscripts, and it was some time before they managed to open the door. Paschal waited until this was done, then took in the wine and mazer. Roger thanked him. Paschal left, and he distinctly remembers Roger locking and bolting the door.'

'And no one else approached this chamber last night?'

'Not that I know of,' Anselm replied. 'Brother John was busy locking coffers and chests in the cloisters, the usual routine when night falls. You know it well, Athelstan. The *Magnum Silentium* descends. All the brothers are to withdraw to their cells, remain alone, study, sleep, pray and make themselves ready for Matins, the beginning of

Divine Office and the Jesus Mass. Brother John has reported nothing untoward, no visitors.'

'In which case,' Athelstan said, 'I have no more questions for the moment. Brother Hugh, would you please take Roger's corpse to the death house. Use the door to this chamber to block the entrance to it. No one is to be allowed in without my permission. I would like this chamber to be guarded by . . .'

'Brother Athelstan!' Cranston had withdrawn for a short while, but now he was bustling back into the chamber. 'Prior Anselm,' he exclaimed. 'I have excellent news. Flaxwith, my chief bailiff, and Samson, the ugliest mastiff in the kingdom, and a *comitatus* of my bailiffs have just been allowed through the watergate. They've been hiding along the mudflats near Westminster. They seized a barge and came here looking for you, Brother, and rejoiced when they also found me. They are all armed and buckled for war.'

'Good,' Athelstan replied. 'And their first task will be to guard this room.' He turned back to the prior. 'They can shelter here? We need every fighting man we can. God knows what the Earthworms are plotting against Blackfriars.'

Anselm agreed to this addition to what he called his 'burgeoning community'. Athelstan and Cranston waited as Roger's corpse was removed. The chamber and enclave beyond gradually emptied as the prior instructed his brethren to return to their duties. Flaxwith and his posse of bailiffs arrived. Greetings and pleasantries were exchanged. Samson, 'God's ugliest creature' as Athelstan called the mastiff, seemed ecstatic at seeing Sir John and greeted him with what was judged to be a howl of pure pleasure. Cranston, who couldn't abide the mastiff, gently tapped it away with the toe of his boot as he fumbled for his miraculous wineskin. At last order was restored. Athelstan carefully checked the chamber. He supervised the repositioning of the door and impressed upon Flaxwith that the room was to be guarded day and night; no one was to be admitted except himself.

'Why, Brother?' Cranston asked. 'Why are you so strict on preserving Roger's chamber?' They had now left and were sitting on a bench in the sun-washed cloisters, watching the scribes retake their seats before their sloping desks to continue their copying and illuminating using an array of brilliantly coloured paints: vermillion, red, blue and gold.

'So peaceful, so beautiful,' Athelstan murmured. 'But to answer your question, Sir John, Prior Anselm and I have an agreement and I am sure you will concur. All these killings are linked to a royal mystery over fifty years old. At the moment I cannot trace any connection. All those involved in that mystery must be long dead. No trace exists of any of the participants surviving and, even if they did, what does it really matter now? And yet,' he turned and looked seriously at the coroner, 'apparently it matters very much. Indeed, a matter of life and death. I suspect Alberic found something and I think Brother Roger did the same. So it stands to reason that there could be something in that chamber which would throw great light on this mystery. No, don't ask me. I cannot even guess, but I do not want the assassin returning to either take or destroy that evidence.'

Athelstan gazed across the cloisters, shielding his eyes against the sunlight. 'This is a place of serenity, of calm, of hallowed prayer and service, or it certainly was until Satan set up festival here. He now presides at a great banquet of blood and this dulls my soul and darkens my spirit. Outside, killing begets killing. Sin prowls the street like a slavering beast to feast on rape, rapine and murder. We are assailed, Sir John, from both within and without, so much so that I am losing sight of who I truly am and what I do.'

'Brother?' Cranston peered at Athelstan; his good friend was almost in tears: his little ferret of a friar who was always so certain, so sure that he lived in the truth.

'Sometimes I wonder, Sir John, I really do. If there is anything beyond the veil, perhaps the veil itself doesn't exist. Perhaps only what we see, hear and feel is real. Nothing else. And yet this reality is not comforting. We are creatures of the dark, Sir John, blood stains both tooth and claw. We hunt and abuse each other. We kill each other in our minds, in our thoughts and, sometimes, if the opportunity presents itself, we actually carry it out.'

'And what about God, Christ?'

'Even if there is a God, even a God made man, let's face it, Sir John, we killed him as well. Christ was murdered, the bloody, well-plotted killing of a totally innocent man.' Athelstan glanced down at his feet. 'This comes of dwelling

132

too long in the halls of darkness. Oh, I think the darkness is real enough, but don't become too alarmed, Sir John. Such miserable thoughts make me fall back on what I truly believe.'

'Which is?'

'Oh, the basic goodness of man and the saving power of Christ. I know in my heart of hearts that, in the end, good will triumph and the resurrection will occur. It's just that sometimes I lose sight of that.' He rose and clapped Cranston on the shoulder. 'Enough sermonising, Sir John. Let's return to the matter in hand. Do you have news from the city?'

'Only what I learn by looking down from the walls of Blackfriars. Tiptoft is a veritable Hermes, a true messenger of God, the best scurrier in the city, but he still hasn't broken through, which means that matters must be going from bad to worse. Thank God I sent the Lady Maude, the two Poppets and all my household into the countryside. Now I must do what I have decided.' Cranston squeezed the friar's arm. 'I know you are busy here, Brother, but I must return to the Tower to rejoin the King and the others.'

'Sir John,' Athelstan murmured, 'we will get you back, so let's think how.' He rose and walked back to the chronicler's chamber. Flaxwith's bailiff helped him move the door, then Athelstan once again entered that shadow-filled room and inspected it carefully. He had left certain items in a particular way and he was pleased to see that nothing had been disturbed. He left and hastened across to the death house. Matthias, Hugh and Brother John were grouped around

Roger's naked cadaver stretched out on one of the mortuary tables. The death house seemed more sombre, a truly ghostly place lit by fluttering lantern flame. Hugh was conducting a service for the dead, a purple and gold stole around his neck. He was blessing the corpse with a stoup of holy water, whilst Matthias incensed it with a smoking thurible which perfumed the air. All three Dominicans had pulled up their capuchons which almost hid their heads and faces as they intoned the *'De Profundis'*, whispering those sombre words: 'If thou, oh Lord, should mark our iniquities, Lord, who would stand before you?'

Athelstan joined them at the table, participating in the responses even as he noticed the mulberry-coloured stains on the corpse's belly and chest. From the little he knew, Athelstan recognised such blotches as clear evidence of a powerful poison. He tried to concentrate on the words of the psalm, closing his mind to the sombre mood of that corpse chamber. Nevertheless, he became distracted by a squeaking in the far corner. A rat had been trapped and its whimpering became more strident. Once the infirmarian had finished the psalm and bestowed the final blessing, Athelstan walked across to where the squealing was becoming more shrill. He stared down at the large, wire mesh cage and the sleek-headed, long-snouted rat, high on its legs, paws scrabbling, nose pushing at the wire, a large, plump rodent, long-tailed and vicious. Athelstan could almost feel its fury at being trapped.

Hugh came across and joined him. 'I cleaned

poor Roger's teeth and gums. I put all the shards of food in that cage and Brother rat has suffered no ill effect. I will leave him there for a while.' Athelstan walked back to the table, and the others crowded around him.

'Roger was poisoned,' Athelstan declared. 'Can you say by what?'

The infirmarian pulled the canvas sheet over the corpse. 'Something natural but noxious,' he murmured, 'a plant or herb which clutched his heart and closed his throat. I suspect death was very swift.'

'And how?'

Athelstan looked despairingly at these three Dominicans, men who had been here long before him. Teachers and practitioners: Brother John had been an entertaining source of stories about everything under the sun. Hugh had instructed Athelstan on so many matters, but especially to observe most critically both cause and effect. Matthias, skilled as any royal chancery clerk, had taught him the secrets of ciphers and the elegant abbreviations so beloved of the professional scribe. And of course Brother Roger had regaled him with stories about London, Blackfriars and the scandals of the royal family. Athelstan smiled to himself, the dead chronicler and Sir John had a great deal in common.

'How,' he whispered, 'did poor Roger die? Who is responsible?' He gazed at his fellow Dominicans. 'What do you think?'

'Gaunt,' Hugh replied. 'John of Gaunt, our self-proclaimed regent. Athelstan, we have discussed this amongst ourselves. Gaunt will be implacably opposed to our young king having a saint included amongst his ancestors.'

'But Gaunt is also a descendant of Edward II.'

'The House of Lancaster was bitterly opposed to Edward II,' Hugh said.

Athelstan stared at a shaft of fading light streaming through a narrow window.

'What Brother Hugh has said is logical enough,' Matthias declared. 'Gaunt and others might fiercely resent the canonisation of Edward II, who proved to be a thorn deep in the side of the House of Lancaster. But what about the Italians, Fieschi and his companions? Are they truly committed to the cause, or do they too have serious reservations? Did they, all or one of them, want this process of beatification to collapse in a welter of confusion, as so many do? After all, the curial offices of the Papacy are crammed with stacks of petitions for the sanctification of this or that person.'

'Brother?' Hugh demanded. 'What do you think?'

Athelstan just smiled at the three friars, sketched a blessing and returned to the chronicler's chamber. He sat at the chancery desk sifting through the different manuscripts and scraps of vellum. Apparently Roger had collected and studied the different records sent to Blackfriars from the royal chancery and the record chambers of both the Tower and Westminster. According to the scrawled notes recorded on a sheet of parchment stretched out under metal weights, Roger had created an index. To a certain extent all the documents dealt with the same issue:

warrants, proclamations and letters concerning the imprisoned Edward II. Most of the letters were directed to the Sheriff of Gloucester, copies being sent to Berkeley and Maltravers. They all carried the same message: conspiracies were being formed, and covens being organised deep in the Forest of Dean to free the imprisoned king. The justices of Oyer and Terminer were being despatched into the shire to hunt down, arrest and indict all such traitors and malefactors. The crown spies were also very busy, royal clerks sent in disguise into the towns and villages close to Berkeley to discover who was involved and where they could be found. Occasionally a memorandum would be published listing the names of these traitors. Each list was always headed by the Dunheved brothers, Thomas and Stephen.

Now and again Athelstan would come across scraps of parchment with the name 'Eadred' by itself, then with a list of titles all written in Brother Roger's hand. Athelstan deduced that Eadred had been a Dominican priest at Blackfriars during the reign of Mortimer and Isabella. He had served as a prison chaplain in Newgate when the Dunheved brothers had been imprisoned and later died there. Eadred had organised the conveyance of their corpses back to Blackfriars for burial. After Mortimer fell from power, Eadred became Prior of the Dominican house at Oxford and Provincial of the entire order in England. Many other names appeared, and Athelstan realised that Roger had been developing a theory that in 1327 virtually the entire

Dominican order in England supported the deposed Edward II.

He was distracted from his close study of the documents by a sound behind him. He turned to see Brother Paschal, the buttery clerk, standing outside with a tray of food and drink. Athelstan beckoned him in. The buttery clerk, mumbling under his breath about Blackfriars being invaded by all kinds of hungry and thirsty people, laid out the pot of ale and the platter of food.

'None of it is poisoned,' Paschal grumbled, 'I tasted it myself.' Athelstan thanked him absent-mindedly then called the buttery clerk back.

'Paschal, last night when you helped poor Roger, did he say anything untoward?'

Paschal glared at Flaxwith's bailiffs, who had stolen some of the cheese from the tray, then he stood and thought awhile. 'Ah, now I remember. Roger said he intended to work until he greeted the Matins bell. He then added, "I know what I have to do. Everyone else is looking in the wrong place."'

'Wrong place?' Athelstan queried. 'What did he mean by that?'

'God only knows, and I mean that. I am just a buttery clerk trying to feed hordes of people.'

Paschal stomped away. Athelstan ate and drank whilst he sifted through different manuscripts: the Book of the Dead at Blackfriars, a chronicle of the mother house, the history of the community, letters to and from a host of individuals. Athelstan could make no sense of the haphazard collection, so he decided to concentrate on his own investigation. He began to list all he knew about the murders of Alberic, Roger and Pernel.

Item: Alberic had been found stabbed in his own chamber, the door locked and bolted; the weapon had been found nearby; the Italian had received his death wound savagely and swiftly. Item: Alberic was a former soldier, fairly young and robust. Surely he would have resisted – so why was there no sign of disturbance, no cry for help, nothing to indicate a struggle? Item: Master Luke the courier had approached Alberic's chamber and overheard a conversation in Italian, with a reference made to Butrio and what was the meaning in English of 'I dread'? Item: Alberic, by his own remarks to Master Luke, fully accepted the story that Edward had escaped from Berkeley. Could that be why he was murdered? Item: in the end, how did Alberic's assassin get in and out of a locked, barred chamber?

Athelstan paused and thought of all those caught up in this matter. Could he imagine Prior Anselm, Brothers Hugh, Matthias and John attacking Alberic so easily? That was a nonsense, surely. All of Athelstan's colleagues were fairly wiry but they were old; they were certainly not like the street fighters Athelstan had encountered in the city. The friar shook his head, picked up his quill pen and continued. Item: Alberic's murder. The how, the why and the who were shrouded in mystery. No member of the Blackfriars community was capable of such an assault. So was it someone else? Was Alberic's killer among his own kind, Fieschi and his companions? After all, according to Master Luke, the conversation in Alberic's chamber was in Italian. Or perhaps the royal courier himself? He was certainly strong and agile enough to perpetrate such an assault, but what would be the motive? For whom did Master Luke really work – the King or Gaunt? Did the regent have a hand in all this mischief, he and his malevolent shadow Thibault?

Athelstan paused and recalled young Isabella's nurse, a fairly young, wiry woman. She or someone else in Blackfriars could be Gaunt's assassin. But why blame Gaunt? Men such as Tyler were ruthless enough. Did the Upright Men, for their own secret reasons, have a hand in this murderous mayhem? Item: why were the attacks launched against him in the tower and the friary church? How was he, a simple parish priest, involved in the mystery of Edward II's death over fifty years ago?

Athelstan paused to look at what he had written and blew his cheeks out. Some of his conjectures didn't make sense. If the assassin was Gaunt or Thibault's creature, surely Athelstan being wounded or even killed would diminish young Isabella's protection? This in turn prompted a fresh question: was the real reason for those murderous assaults on him due to someone bent on inflicting a grievous blow against Thibault through his beloved daughter Isabella? If Athelstan was removed as her protector, the young girl would certainly become more vulnerable. The friar shook his head and decided to move on.

Item: Roger's death. The chronicler had undoubtedly been poisoned. Most noxious potions acted swiftly, yet Roger had returned to his chamber hale and hearty. The chronicler loved to dig up facts and evidence and draw his own conclusions. Apparently on the night he died, Roger was determined to do this, but about what? Why did he say 'they' (whoever they might be) were looking in the wrong place? What did this mean? Item: how was Roger actually poisoned? He had left the meeting and gone to the kitchen for wine and a bowl of nuts. Paschal the buttery clerk had brought them here for him. All the evidence indicated that neither food nor drink were tainted. The only people who had access to it were Roger himself and Paschal, who was innocent in this matter. No other source of poison could be traced in the chamber, so how was it administered? Did Roger receive a visitor? Brother John, working in the cloisters, reported seeing no one. If someone did visit the chronicler and brought poison into the room, again, how was it administered? Surely it must have been quick acting? So how did the assassin leave, locking and bolting the chamber from the inside? Athelstan scratched his chin. He couldn't imagine someone turning up for such a brief visit and offering poisoned food or wine when Roger already had what he needed. Any attempt to taint Roger's goblet and mazer would surely have been noticed by the sharp-eyed chronicler and traces would have been left of this, but there had been nothing.

Item: Pernel, a mad old Fleming who dyed her hair and talked incessantly to herself like some beldame cursed by the moon, a poor soul floating through the life of the parish like mist above the moor. Had this simply been a pretence, a mask against the world? Pernel had certainly been lucid enough to realise the mysterious abduction of her parishioners would be of great concern to her priest, and she had the wit to organise herself sufficiently – the hire of a barge to cross the Blackfriars quayside – but then what? Was Pernel's death a mere accident, stumbling or staggering along that quayside, shoved and pushed by others who would have no time for a witless old woman? Had Pernel been drinking – she certainly loved her pottle of ale – or was it murder? Was her death an act of the deepest malice? Athelstan was tempted to reject such a proposal out of hand if it had not been for what he'd found in Pernel's cottage: a link with the Order of the Poor Clares and those medals from different churches in Flanders and Hainault, and, more significantly, from the abbey of Sancto Alberto di Butrio in Northern Italy, a place caught up in the saga of the mystery surrounding Edward II. Had Pernel been a nun or a novice in the Poor Clares? Was she then known as Agnes? And where was the convent of St Monica?

Athelstan turned back to sifting through the manuscripts collected by Roger, the various proclamations of men long dead, listing the names of the Dunheved coven. He could find no trace of an 'Agnes' or any mention of the Order of Poor Clares, yet all this was part of the spate of murders. Athelstan experienced a feeling of fear and dread. Sin, God's executioner, lurked in the shadows of Blackfriars. He never thought such

142

a place of prayer could become the refuge of demons, and yet it had. Athelstan recalled a travelling minstrel who used to visit his parents' farmstead. The jongleur talked vividly about a veritable camp royal of demons lurking in the woods nearby. The minstrel, in one of his tales, also described murder as a loathsome serpent, a fire dragon, fierce and mottled with fury. Athelstan put down his quill pen. Somewhere, he reflected, here in Blackfriars, that serpent lay coiled, ready to strike again.

Athelstan decided to take some respite and dozed for a while. Benedicta came and woke him to say goodbye. She explained that Father Prior had used her for a certain task, and as a thank you had arranged for the friary bargeman to take her across to Southwark. Once there she would ensure the church and priest's house were safe. Athelstan absent-mindedly heard her out and kissed her on each cheek, muttering at her to keep safe, then she was gone before he realised it. A short while later Prior Anselm greeted Flaxwith's bailiffs and slipped like a shadow into the chamber.

'A fruitful search, Athelstan?'

'No, Father Prior, not yet.'

'Then I have a guest you must meet. No, no, you must come. No one else knows about him.'

Now fully awake and intrigued, Athelstan followed his prior out along the passageways and into the enclosure known as the petty cloisters. A pentile ran around all four sides, protection from the rain and shading against the summer sun which now bathed the cloister garth in brilliant light. At the centre of the garth rose an exquisitely sculptured fountain carved in the shape of a pelican striking its breast. The water gushed out through the pelican's open beak into a huge bowl beneath, brimming to the full, so the lily pads on the surface moved in a constant slow dance. On a bench close to the fountain sat an old man dressed in the brown and cream robes of the Carmelite order. He sat resting his hands on a walking stick, but when he saw Prior Anselm approach, he insisted on clambering to his feet. He exchanged the kiss of peace with Athelstan then sat down on the bench beside him.

'Brother Athelstan,' Prior Anselm declared, his voice scarce above a whisper, 'this is Odo Brecon, a man who might be able to help you. Someone from times past, but his wits are sharp and his memory even keener.' Athelstan gazed at the old man with the rheumy, light-blue eyes of the very old. He had a stubbled, rather inflamed face; his meagre white hair stood up like quills; his dark spotted hands were vein streaked.

'Brother Odo?'

'No, my learned Dominican.' Odo's lips parted in a gummy smile. 'True, I am garbed like a Carmelite but I am a lay person. I have a corrody, a pension at nearby Whitefriars, a gift from the present king's grandfather.' Athelstan nodded understandingly. The crown often rewarded its long-serving faithful retainers with comfortable lodgings for life in some religious house. He recalled at least three old soldiers at Blackfriars, whilst two of his kinsmen lodged in the beautiful abbey of Glastonbury.

144

'I am pleased for you,' Athelstan replied. 'And what was your service to the crown?'

'Let me explain.' Anselm crouched down before both of them. 'Nobody here knows who Odo truly is or why he has kindly agreed to visit Blackfriars. Two Carmelites escorted him here and they will return within the hour. Those watchers outside our gate, the screed of Earthworms, allowed them safe passage through.'

'Ruffians, rifflers, chaff in the wind,' Odo scoffed. 'In my green and supple days . . .' He paused as the prior raised his hand.

'Odo Brecon,' Anselm explained, 'was a captain of hobelars. He once served in the retinue of Hugh Despenser, favourite of Edward II. When that king was deposed and imprisoned at Berkeley, Despenser was barbarously executed at Hereford. Odo, of course, fell from grace. He became a wanted man.'

'I had taken an oath of allegiance to Lord Hugh and the king, God bless them.' The old man's mouth jutted stubbornly.

'Odo,' Anselm continued, 'was swept up in the conspiracy to free the imprisoned king. He was a member of Denheved's coven. He actually fought alongside him . . .'

The prior smiled at Athelstan's surprise.

'I didn't think,' Athelstan declared, 'I mean, that someone would—'

'Brother Athelstan,' Odo tapped his stick noisily on the ground, 'believe me, I have seen the days and I have supped with all the demons.' Athelstan looked at Anselm.

'How did you . . .?'

145

'Poor Roger's work, not mine. He has been immersed in the mystery of Edward II's captivity since the arrival of our Italian brethren. Well, to be truthful, even long before that. In preparation for their arrival the royal chancery despatched the relevant records of 1327 to 1330 to be stored in our library at Blackfriars. Well, you know Roger, he was attracted to such archives as a cat to cream. I don't think there was one he didn't read. Anyway,' Prior Anselm got to his feet, 'when he came across the name Odo Brecon, not only did he recognise it, but he knew where our good friend actually lived.'

'Of course,' Athelstan whispered, smiling at Odo. 'Brother Roger was always on the best of terms with the librarian and chroniclers at Whitefriars. They were constantly exchanging gossip.'

'More than that,' Odo intervened. 'I met Brother Roger. He visited me at Whitefriars to ask about the attack on Berkeley Castle.' The old man squinted up at Anselm. 'But why all the secrecy?'

'Something dreadful is happening here, Odo,' Anselm said. 'It's best for the moment if I don't tell you. What I would like you to do is share everything you know about the fate of Edward II with my good colleague here. Athelstan,' Anselm continued, 'as I said, nobody here knows about Odo Brecon. I asked Benedicta to take a message to Whitefriars. I informed the guardian there that she would greet Odo at the gate at a specific time. I admitted him and brought him directly here. Once the two Carmelites have returned, please escort our friend back to the gate

146

and make your farewells.' Anselm sketched a blessing and left them.

Athelstan stared around the petty cloisters, revelling in the warm, scented air.

'I am ready,' Odo murmured.

'Have you told your tale to anyone else apart from Brother Roger?'

'Oh no.' Odo tapped the side of his fleshy nose. 'Certain secrets are best kept secret. Brother Roger only found out about me when he searched the records. Remember, Athelstan, I am only known as Brother Odo in our community; it is very rare that I give my full birth name. Roger knew mine and recognised it on a warrant issued by the Crown.'

'So tell me your story.'

'I was a henchman of Despenser, a good lord, though, looking back, he was just one slaughter wolf amongst the rest; a glutton for other men's blood as a crow is to carrion, a despoiler of dark design. Despenser dominated the King and eventually alienated Queen Isabella, who fled to France and into the arms of another blood-drinker, Roger Mortimer. In my view, they richly deserved each other. In the autumn of 1326 they invaded England.' Odo shrugged. 'You know the story. Edward was captured and imprisoned, Despenser was taken to Hereford. He was executed on a specially built gallows, fifty foot high. Half hanged, castrated, his entrails plucked out and burnt before his eyes, his body quartered, his severed head paraded through Cheapside before being poled on London Bridge.'

He paused to collect his thoughts. 'I was Despenser's man in peace and war. A liveried retainer. I could expect no mercy. Isabella was a she-wolf leading a slavering pack, a coven of great lords and bishops who detested Despenser and anyone associated with him. I was proclaimed an outlaw and had no choice but to flee into the wet, green mansions of the Forest of Dean, which was the closest and the safest place to where my imprisoned royal master was being held. In time others joined us. We lived in the soaking darkness of the trees. A close, secretive place even during the brightest noon time. Once the sun set you could well believe why the night is the devil's black book, the nurse of cares, the mother of despair and the daughter of Hell.'

'And the Dunheveds?' Athelstan tactfully intervened.

'Oh, they changed it all.'

'What were they like?'

'I knew them from the heady days of court. Thomas, the elder, had been the King's confessor despatched to the Pope to see if the King's marriage to Isabella could be annulled. During his absence Edward was deposed. Thomas was totally devoted to his royal master, fanatical in his loyalty.'

'How old was he then?'

'He had taken his solemn vows at seventeen. An erudite scholar, he was marked down for high office in your order but he attracted the attention of the King. Thomas was the sort of man Edward II liked. Very similar to Peter Gaveston, the long dead but not forgotten royal favourite. Thomas

148

was quick-witted, good-humoured. He could charm the birds from the branches and the rabbits from their warren. He was kind, affectionate, honourable but, when threatened or in danger, totally and utterly ruthless. He was a Dominican in the true sense of the word.' Odo winked at Athelstan. 'A hound of God. He could move in the splendour of Sheen palace but he could also preach a powerful sermon to peasants gathered around their village cross. Thomas must have been in his early twenties when Edward II was deposed. I believe he was also skilled in arms, a sharp-eyed archer and good as the next man when it came to dagger or sword play. Above all, Edward II was his king and master. Thomas passionately believed that once a prince was anointed with holy chrism he was king until he died. Thomas composed a little verse, in which he called himself "Keeper of the royal flame, defender of the King's name."'

'And his brother, Stephen?'

'A little younger than Thomas. In a word, he was his elder brother's shadow. Where Thomas went, Stephen faithfully followed, be it the Dominican Order, the court—'

'And eventually the Forest of Dean?'

'Oh yes. The Dunheved brothers swept in like a summer storm, drawing in all the adherents of the deposed king: former scholars, clerks, priests, soldiers. In turn these attracted royal spies, Mortimer's creatures. Thomas Dunheved dealt harshly with those we unmasked and caught.'

'How?'

'Thomas hanged and disembowelled them

149

and left their steaming remains at crossroads. Of course, Mortimer and his ilk struck back. They sent soldiers and expert huntsmen into the forest . . .' Odo paused as Athelstan raised a hand.

'My friend,' Athelstan leaned closer, 'I must be truthful. The mystery of Edward II's fate does not concern me as much as it might you. Nor am I trying to establish whether Edward II escaped or not.'

'He did,' Odo interrupted. 'To be blunt, the Dunheveds discovered that repair work was being carried out at Berkeley Castle. Thomas suborned a carpenter who opened a postern gate. I was there, though I was not in the group who stormed the keep and reached the royal prisoner. I did see Edward being hurried up some steps by the Dunheved brothers and their closest adherents.'

'And you?'

'Brother, I swear that night marked the end of my adventures with the Dunheveds. The King had been freed. I heard the three horn blasts, the sound wailing through the darkness, the agreed sign for us to withdraw. I fled through the postern gate and into the forest. I was a seasoned soldier. I realised what was going to happen and sure enough it did. The following morning, Mortimer despatched a veritable army to search about. We had stirred up a tempest and the storm swept through all our hiding places. I was a fortunate one. I never stopped. I didn't hide. I didn't think to lie low like some fox. I stole a horse and rode like the wind until I reached London. I became lost in the gloomy dungeons of the city's under-world, the haunt of blood-red blades, dark souls and cruel hearts. I hid where the demons muster and the prowlers lurk.'

'And what happened to Dunheved and the King?'

'Oh, I met various people who told me stories about how the Dunheveds had spirited the deposed king out of the realm. These were rumours. Members of the Dunheveds' coven crept into the city like I did. They brought their stories, the gossip of their coven. One I remember, a young clerk, I forget his name, he claimed that Edward II was sheltering in a hermitage in Lombardy, an abbey—'

'Sancto Alberto di Butrio?'

'Yes, that's the one, I am sure of it! I recall the story. How the old king was supposed to have fled there. How some of Dunheved's closest followers had also journeyed to stay with their former king . . .'

'But not you?'

'Oh no, Brother Athelstan. When Mortimer fell from power I sued for a royal pardon. Through the good offices of the Despenser family, I not only received this but a good position in the garrison of the Tower. I settled down. I ignored the past and it ignored me. I married Yvette. Lovely lass,' he added dreamily. 'But she died in childbirth, the baby with her. I married again but the sweating sickness swept through the city and took her away. After that my heart could tolerate no more pain. I lived a soldier's life. I served here, I served there. Nobody from the past ever bothered me. Well, not until today. Eventually I became too weak and the crown provided a corrody amongst the good brothers at Whitefriars. It's a peaceful, gentle life.'

Athelstan nodded in agreement and gazed across the sun-filled garden. 'The Dunheveds,' he asked, 'were they alike in looks? How would you describe them?'

'No,' Odo screwed up his face, 'they didn't look alike, even though they were brothers. Remember, Athelstan, the Dunheveds were young, very resourceful, especially Thomas. He had a wise old head on very young shoulders.'

'And their appearance?' Athelstan insisted.

'They were soft-featured, at least then. They both grew moustache and beard; you Dominicans are usually clean-shaven.'

Athelstan nodded in agreement.

'The Dunheveds were different, they deliberately copied the King with his well-clipped beard and moustache. On this they were insistent. When they were at court their hair was flipped and dressed. During our days in the forest, like all of us, they became extremely bedraggled.'

'Any distinguishing marks?'

'Not that I saw. You see, Athelstan, I was not truly of their coven, I was not one of their comrades. I was just one of the many dispossessed after the Despensers fell from power. The Dunheveds were different, devoted to their king, and around them grouped a small coterie of equally fervent supporters.'

'And the women? Did you know someone called Agnes, a possible novice with the Poor

Clare Order?' Odo snorted with laughter but then paused, his head going abruptly back.

'Lord save me, Athelstan,' he breathed. 'The Poor Clares, yes! They had a convent. I forget the name, somewhere between Stroud and Gloucester, I am sure the good nuns gave sustenance and support to the Dunheveds.'

'Such as?'

'Brother, I cannot say. Just a rumour. You must remember we had places to hide, especially the Dunheveds. Now and again, if we were fortunate, good food would appear on our forest table and people would ask where it came from; that's when I heard the rumour about the Poor Clares.'

'And what happened to the Dunheved brothers?'

'I fled. I wanted nothing more to do with them, it was becoming too dangerous. Whispered gossip said they slipped in and out of the country until they were caught in London and confined to Newgate. Of course, the Dominicans protested, but before anything could be done both brothers died of jail fever. I believe they are buried here, or so Roger said.'

'Did Roger ever talk about having enemies here?'

'No, he told me very little. He believed the Dominicans had done a great deal to hide their involvement in royal matters during the dark days of 1327.'

'Were other Dominicans involved in the Dunheved conspiracy?'

'Oh, yes. You see, the Dunheveds were from the friary in Oxfordshire, the very same friary who looked after and cared for the mortal remains of Edward's great favourite, Peter Gaveston.'

'They collected the favourite's corpse, didn't they, but he was killed in 1312,' Athelstan said, then added, 'the Dunheveds would have been too young to have been involved in that crisis, wouldn't they?'

'Ah yes, but the Dunheveds were educated in that house. The cult of the King and his favourite was part of their training. Think of the Dunheved coven as a beehive. At the heart of this was a group totally dedicated to King Edward.'

'Yes, you have said that. Why do you repeat it?'

The old man crossed himself. 'The Dunheveds were ruthless. I heard rumours, chitter-chatter, that anyone who threatened them disappeared. Some say murdered. I truly wonder what is the truth behind all of this, but more than that, I cannot say. Come, we will talk as we make our journey back.'

Athelstan helped the old man up. He heard a sound from the pentile directly across the cloister garth. The pelican fountain blocked a complete view. Athelstan stared as he and Odo moved out of the shadow of the fountain. Narrowing his eyes, Athelstan glimpsed the window in the wall shaded by the pentile: its shutters now hung open. He saw swift movement, a shape in the darkness; there was a sharp click followed by the whirr of a crossbow bolt which shattered against the fountain.

'Sweet Lord save us!' Athelstan shouted even as he tried to push the startled Odo back behind the protection of the fountain. Again, that ominous whirring; Athelstan felt Odo plucked from his grasp. The old man stumbled back, face twisted in agony at the crossbow bolt buried deep in his chest. He tried to stagger towards Athelstan, arms going out, when a third bolt shattered his skull as it would soft fruit. The old man collapsed in a welter of blood, crumpling on to the grass. Athelstan, tears in his eyes, crouched behind the fountain and continued his cries for help.

Doors opened, followed by the patter of sandalled feet. Prior Anselm and other brothers appeared and stopped in shock at the ghastly scene. Hugh, Matthias and John the gatekeeper hastened to help, along with others. Cranston, bellowing at the top of his voice, sword and dagger drawn, forced his way through. He resheathed his weapons and, one arm around Athelstan's shoulder, guided the friar out of the petty cloisters and back to his chamber in the guesthouse. Once there, Cranston forced Athelstan to take generous mouthfuls from the miraculous wineskin. Athelstan thanked him, lay down on the bed and dozed for a while, half muttering prayers to calm his body and quieten his soul. When he awoke Cranston had been joined by Prior Anselm, who sat on a stool staring sadly at him.

'*Pax et bonum*,' Athelstan whispered. 'God save us, it was the suddenness, the speed, the blood spattering in such a serene place. That old man, so venerable, so full of life. A soldier who had survived so much. Then,' Athelstan snapped his fingers, 'his life gutted out as swiftly as a snuffler does candle flame.' He swung his legs

155

off the bed and sat head in hands, then he glanced up. Cranston, for all his bluster, looked shocked, even a little cowed. Athelstan drew a deep breath. 'Father Prior, who knew Odo Brecon was in Blackfriars to meet me?'

'You, me and no one else.' The prior swallowed as if trying to catch his breath. 'I told you. Benedicta took a message to Whitefriars. Two of the brothers there escorted Odo here. That was safe enough; after all, it is not far and the rebels have no cause against them. I was waiting to receive him. No one else knew or was informed. I brought Odo into the petty cloisters and fetched you. From what I know, Athelstan, the assassin entered the grain store which overlooks the petty cloisters. There is a window which opens up over the garth.'

'Yes, I saw it. Odo and I sat behind the fountain which served as a defence. Once we moved, the assassin struck. Did he intend to kill me, Odo or both of us?' Athelstan beat his fist against his leg. 'God knows what is happening.' He got to his feet. 'Father Prior, I must see Fieschi and his companions now.'

'Why?' Anselm, clearly alarmed, also rose. 'Athelstan, you are not going to accuse him of involvement in this attack? Remember, they are accredited envoys . . .'

'No, Father Prior, I am going to accuse them of lying.'

Fieschi, along with Cassian and Isidore, sat on one side of the council table; Athelstan, flanked by Cranston and Anselm, on the other. All three

156

Italians had expressed their concern and shock at what had happened. They asked who the victim was and had the assassin escaped? Had the poor man's death anything to do with their visit? Athelstan simply sat staring at them whilst the prior made non-committal replies and Cranston muttered beneath his breath. Fieschi seemed highly nervous; his round, smooth face had lost its perpetual jovial smile, whilst his two young companions seemed to be harder-faced, rather solemn, as if they were bracing themselves against the coming storm.

'Brother Athelstan,' Fieschi forced a smile, 'you are silent, yet I understand you asked for this meeting. Why?'

'To see if you are lying.'

Fieschi pushed himself away from the table as if making to rise and leave, his two companions likewise. Anselm brought them to order, slamming both hands down on to the table.

'Brothers in Christ,' Anselm grated, 'you are guests here. You have been sent to complete a certain task. Outside the walls of our friary, violence prowls like some famished scavenger desperate to break in. Yet, in a sense, a worse predator has broken through. Murder has been committed in the hallowed precincts of a Dominican friary. Horrid deaths which, somehow, seem linked to your arrival here. I know,' Anselm pulled a face, 'one of your brethren has been a victim of the abomination lurking here. We mourn for him. We grieve for you. We deeply regret it. Nevertheless, the only way this can be resolved is through the truth. Pilate asked, "What is truth?"

And, according to scripture, didn't wait for an answer. We shall certainly wait to establish the truth. Brother Athelstan, do continue.'

Fieschi and his companions, still bridling at Anselm's bluntness, made themselves comfortable on their chairs.

Athelstan leaned forward. 'Brother Fieschi, I say this to you. I have only recently been brought in to investigate Edward II's fate at Berkeley. Nevertheless, it is obvious to me that the King must have escaped. You and your companions are more skilled and learned in this matter than myself. Nevertheless, I ask myself, why all this investigation when the outcome is so obvious? Let us be frank. Your comrade Alberic believed this to be the case: he hid behind quotations from the psalms and enigmatic references to Lord Berkeley's statement at the parliament of 1330, but Alberic accepted that Edward escaped from Berkeley, I am certain of it!' Athelstan cleared his throat. 'His Grace the King has petitioned the Holy Father in Rome for his support in the beatification of his ancestor. We know there is a rival Pope in Avignon. To a cynical observer,' Athelstan paused for effect, 'it might appear that our Holy Father is using this matter to gain the support of the English Crown.'

'In what sense?' Fieschi demanded. 'Brother Athelstan, be warned you should be most prudent in your reply.'

'Oh, I shall be more than prudent, learned Father. I shall be truthful and blunt. If you rule that Edward II did escape, the process of

158

canonisation is brought to an end. However, if you state that, despite all the evidence available, Edward died at Berkeley, then the possible beatification is a matter to be considered. Should you decide on the latter course, despite the weight of evidence, the Papacy, and of course yourselves, will be the recipient of our king's generosity and support. Pope Urban VIII would certainly treasure that, as would you.'

'But why all this work, this public manifestation of what our king intends?' Anselm asked.

'Because Brother Fieschi and his companions here, and correct me if I am wrong, are being closely watched by Clement, the rival Pope in Avignon. He is supported by the king in France, is he not?'

Fieschi just smiled and shrugged.

'Ah,' Anselm sighed, 'I see what road you are taking.'

'England and France are at war,' Athelstan stated. 'Pope Clement wishes to ridicule Pope Urban's authority, whilst the French certainly do not want the English royal family to acquire a new saint. If Edward II is beatified, the Pope in Avignon, not to mention the French crown, will fiercely object. They will conduct their own investigation and do their utmost to bring this process into disrepute. Consequently, Brother Fieschi, you and your companions must prove that you have been thorough and rigorous. Nevertheless,' Athelstan concluded, 'the vexed question of Edward II possibly escaping is one the French and Pope Clement will seize on. They could use that to heap ridicule upon this new saint and all those who supported his canonisation.'

'I agree with Athelstan,' Anselm intervened. 'What he says is both logical and obvious.'

'Father Prior, Brother Athelstan, you are most correct.'

Athelstan flinched at the smug smile on Fieschi's face, realising the Italian had a ready answer.

'First, I am the accredited envoy of the Holy Father to the English court. I do not care what that public sinner, that arch-heretic in Avignon, that false pope says or does. Nor do I care what the French king believes in. So, to answer your own question, undoubtedly Berkeley Castle was stormed and a prisoner was released, but that does not mean it was Edward II.'

'A look-alike?' Athelstan queried.

'Very much so. My own uncle, who purportedly heard the confession of a man claiming to be Edward II, later had doubts and left a memorandum expressing such reservations.' Fieschi spread his hands. 'I can understand that. Remember, Athelstan, Edward II's half-brother, Edmund, Earl of Kent, truly believed the King had escaped and was alive in Corfe Castle. The use of look-alikes in the mystery surrounding Edward II could have prompted one story after another, such as that mysterious figure, William the Welshman, whom Edward III met when he visited the Shrine of the Three Kings at Cologne.'

'But those who stormed the castle and reached the prison, the Dunheveds and their coven, would be more knowledgeable,' Athelstan insisted, recalling what Odo had told him.

'Really?' Cassian scoffed. 'A man bearded and long-haired, well tutored in the speech and manners of the deposed king, a prisoner seized from a dark dungeon in the dead of night. Heaven knows, it might have been days, weeks before the Dunheveds realised they had been tricked. Nevertheless, Mortimer and Isabella realised the dangers, there would be no second attempt, so the real Edward II was murdered. How, we cannot say.'

'And the look-alike, surely the Dunheveds would have killed him?'

'Why, Brother Athelstan, surely it would be much better to let such an individual wander Europe creating confusion and sowing doubts?' Isidore retorted. 'So the legend took root, used by men such as Berkeley in their defence. How can anyone be accused of regicide if the royal victim had allegedly escaped? That was a story Edward III, now free of his mother and Roger Mortimer, did not want to be publicly debated. The new king believed, as we do now, that his father had been murdered.'

Athelstan stared at Fieschi and his companions. Their answer was too glib, yet a brilliant move across the chessboard. All the evidence pointing to Edward II escaping could be summarily rejected on the grounds that a mummer, a look-alike, had been freed, while the true king, enduring the pain and anguish of royal martyrdom, went nobly to his cruel death. In truth, these Dominicans didn't really care about what had happened to Edward II. They were more determined to use the issue to persuade King Richard and his council to move closer to Pope Urban in Rome rather than the anti-pope Clement in Avignon. Accordingly Fieschi and his colleagues would deliberately mislead Athelstan, taking him up and down alleyways, throwing sops at him to quieten any criticism. Nevertheless, they had made one dire mistake and Athelstan was determined to use this to shatter their smug complacency.

'Well, brother?'

'I tell you this, my friend,' Athelstan warned, 'and you have already learnt to your cost that your investigations are not dusty theorising such as debating a problem of logic in the schools. You hope to prove, at least to those in power, that Edward II died a martyr's death in Berkeley and so beatification is a possibility. However, we all now know to our cost that there are others, nameless at the moment, who, in my opinion, are resolutely opposed to your presence here and to what you are doing. Or it could be one person. Somebody who believes in that phrase from scripture, "Leave the dead to bury their dead." He, or them, is warning you that the fate of Edward II and his burial are not be interfered with under pain of death.'

Isidore would have replied but Fieschi put a restraining hand on his arm. He gazed sadly at Athelstan, lips parted, dark eyes sorrowful, almost as if he was on the brink of tears.

'Brother Athelstan,' his voice was just above a whisper, 'I accept your warning. We are all in great danger, but what can be done?'

'Unmask the assassin,' Cassian declared, glaring

at Athelstan. 'Father Prior has given you that task.'

'And I am doing my best to complete it.'

'Who could it be?' Isidore demanded.

'Anyone,' Athelstan retorted. 'It might even be one of you.'

'Preposterous!'

'No, Brother Isidore,' Athelstan insisted. 'Someone in this friary is resolutely against this investigation into Edward II's death. It could be anyone. Therefore, logically, it would be most prudent if you bear this in mind in dealing with each other. Now, if there's . . .'

He paused at a knock on the door and Brother John entered. 'Athelstan,' he gasped, 'you'd best come to the gatehouse. There is someone very strange demanding to speak to you.' His lined, craggy face broke into a smile. 'I think it best if you saw for yourself.'

Athelstan and Cranston made their excuses and hastened from the chamber. They followed the scurrying gatekeeper across cobbled yards, pushing their way through a press of people congregating on the great paved bailey which stretched from the cloisters down to the main gate of the friary. Dusk was falling. The air had grown a little colder but the breeze was rich with different smells, the sweet odours from the great kitchens, now busy all the time to feed the growing crowd of those seeking sanctuary. The cooking smells mingled with wisps of incense, candle smoke, horse dung and the gritty tang from the charcoal braziers which had been fired against the cold night air.

Athelstan noticed that the few men-at-arms employed at Blackfriars were deployed near the main gate. They were fully armed and dressed in sallets, mailed harness, with weapons at the ready. Athelstan glimpsed a crossbow resting against the mailed leg of one of the soldiers. Once again he recalled that murderous attack on Odo Brecon. Was that old man the intended victim, or was it himself? He murmured a prayer and followed Brother John up on to the parapet walk above the stout double doors of the main gatehouse.

Athelstan stared over the fortified wall. Daylight was fading, yet he glimpsed Earthworms camped about their fires and smelt the stench from the horse, some lord's destrier, which they had slaughtered and were now hacking up to be grilled over the dancing flames.

'The wasteland of Hell,' Athelstan murmured.

'And who are these?' Cranston pointed at two figures who'd stumbled out of the murk. The taller one carried a sconce torch, which he lifted to illuminate a macabre scene. Athelstan stared in disbelief at the two grotesques: both men had their heads cleanly shaved, the skin glistening from the lard or oil they had rubbed in. The taller one had a blindfold across his eyes and grasped the hand of his shorter, much fatter companion whilst moving the spluttering torch backwards and forwards.

'Athelstan?' the torchbearer bellowed. 'Brother Athelstan, we bring you clear warning.'

'I recognise that voice,' Athelstan murmured. 'But for the life of me . . .'

'Why do you talk of one devil?' the torchbearer bellowed. 'I tell you this, Friar, something I have learnt on my travels. There is not a room in any man's house but it is pestered and close packed with a host of demons. No place on earth, be it no bigger than a pock-hole on a man's face, but it is closely thronged with demons. Indeed, infinite millions of them can hang swarming about a worm-eaten nose . . .'

'Giles of Sempringham,' Athelstan exclaimed, 'one of my beloved parishioners, and I am sure,' he narrowed his eyes, 'that is Master Bladdersmith or, as he sometimes styles himself, Bladdersniff, our parish beadle. Well, well, well. Brother John, allow them in.'

Athelstan and Cranston went down to wait in the bailey. The two grotesques almost threw themselves through the half-open postern door which the gatekeeper slammed hastily behind them. Bladdersmith immediately went down on his knees, hands joined in prayer, whilst Giles of Sempringham, also known as the Hangman of Rochester, lifted the blind from his eyes and threw the spluttering torch on to the ground.

'Follow me,' Athelstan called and, turning on his heel, led both men through the cloisters, across the yards and into the guesthouse refectory. Both the Hangman and Bladdersmith washed at the *lavarium*, sat down at the table and swiftly devoured the hot pottage, bread, cheese and dried meats brought from the nearby kitchen. For a while Cranston and Athelstan watched them eat. Both men reeked of the sewer, their clothes nothing more than motley rags. The Hangman

165

was his usual enigmatic self; his straw-coloured hair had been completely shaven off, which made his skull-like face look even harsher. Bladdersmith couldn't stop sobbing with relief until Cranston fed him generous mouthfuls from his miraculous wineskin.

'Well, my beauties!' the coroner declared as both finished eating, licking their horn spoons clean.

'Oh, lord save us,' Bladdersmith wailed.

'Tell us what happened.' Athelstan leaned across and gently touched the Hangman's wrist.

'The day the rest were taken, I mean Watkin and the rest,' the Hangman raised his eyes heavenwards, 'and by all the angels, Father, I have no idea who took them, why or where they have gone. I swear to that. Anyway, I was down at the gallows near the bridge. I had to hang two felons arrested by the sheriff for breaking into a house. One of them struggled and tried to break free, that took some time. It always does.' He added sorrowfully. 'I don't see why they don't just let me get on with it.' He stretched out his hands as if examining his almost feminine fingers which could so expertly tie the knot of a noose around a convicted criminal's throat for swift despatch as well as grasp a paintbrush to depict the most startling scenes on the walls of their parish church. Athelstan touched him on the shoulder.

'What happened?' he asked.

'Oh, yes.' The Hangman recollected himself. 'By the time I returned to St Erconwald's, the men had been taken; their womenfolk and

166

children, deeply distressed, milled about not knowing what to do. You have been back there Father?'

'Yes I have. Strangely deserted though I understand that. Doors and shutters firmly closed against anyone and everyone even,' Athelstan added sadly, 'their priest.'

'Many of them have fled,' Bladdersmith blurted out. 'Frightened they are, gone into the countryside. Scattered,' he sniffed noisily, 'like sheep without a shepherd.'

'Their shepherd,' Athelstan retorted tartly, 'was busy elsewhere. What happened to you?'

'He was drinking,' the Hangman declared. 'Weren't you?' He nudged Bladdersmith. 'Fell asleep, he did, in the Poor Man's Plot in God's Acre, so no one saw him in the long grass. He awoke just as I arrived.' The Hangman drew a deep breath. 'And so it began.' He paused and looked under his eyebrows at Athelstan. 'You were correct, Father, the Great Community of the Realm and Upright Men began this revolt, but others have usurped it. The Earthworms swarmed all over St Erconwald's searching for Watkin and the rest. I made a mistake. I always thought I was safe. I attended the conventicles and councils of the Upright Men. I regarded myself as one of them. However, whilst sheltering at the Piebald, Bladdersmith and I learnt that the Earthworms were searching for any official, be it of the court, the crown or the city . . .' the Hangman gestured at Bladdersmith, '. . . which included him. As for me, I heard they held me responsible for executing some of their companions. Father, Sir

167

John,' the Hangman of Rochester spread his hands, 'I had no choice over whom I hanged, when, where and why. All I can say with clear conscience is that I never knowingly executed anyone who was innocent.'

'True, true,' Athelstan replied absent-mindedly. He glanced at Sir John: the coroner was strangely quiet, apparently distracted by his own problems. 'And then what happened?' Athelstan asked.

'We realised we were hunted men,' the Hangman declared. 'The Earthworms wanted us seized, they would have hanged us out of hand, so we changed our appearance. We shaved our heads and faces,' he tugged at his ragged jerkin, 'we made ourselves appear as if we were moon-touched like mummers in a play, the blind prophet and his guide. The Earthworms were convinced, and I can see why. Believe me, Father, all kinds of strange creatures are crawling out of the darkness. We were just two more who were insistent on delivering a message to a Dominican friar.' He paused. 'Anyway, Father, Sir John, do you know where the rest are – Watkin, Pike and the others? Who abducted them?'

'I don't know, nor does Sir John. I have been back to Southwark. Our parish is deserted, or at least it was when I was there.' Athelstan paused. 'I must tell you: old Pernel, the Fleming woman, is dead. Oh yes,' he answered their exclamations, 'apparently she came across to Blackfriars looking for me. Heaven knows what happened to the poor thing. She must have stumbled or missed her footing. She was found floating near the water-gate. I wish—'

'She not only came looking for you, Father,' Bladdersmith blurted out.

'What do you mean?'

'Well, Father, do you remember a few days before the prior summoned you across here? You told us you had to go. You announced it after the Jesus mass. How you were to visit Blackfriars where there were special guests, Italians, Lombards, led by someone called Fi . . .'

'Fieschi,' Athelstan replied, all intrigued.

'Yes, that's it. After mass, Pernel chatted to me and Godbless. We met in God's Acre to share a jug of ale. It was a glorious morning and the jug was a big one . . .'

'Fieschi?' Athelstan warned.

'Oh yes, Pernel said she must go to Blackfriars. How she knew an Italian called Fieschi, a name from her distant past. She asked me to accompany her but I refused.'

'Poor thing,' Athelstan intervened. 'She must have intended to go when the others were seized, that must have decided her. Anyway, did Pernel say how she knew Fieschi?'

'No, Father, but that was Pernel. Sometimes she would act all moonstruck, fey in her wits. At other times, she could be as clear as a summer's day.'

'Did she ever talk about her past?'

'Sometimes. Once I teased her about dyeing her hair. I said it was ugly, dirty. I didn't mean to hurt her, but she replied swiftly that in her youth it had been beautiful, as golden as summer corn, but she had shaved it off to become a nun.'

'Where?'

'I can't recall, some place in the west country.'

'And?'

'Pernel said she had fled her vows, that she had travelled abroad where her heart had been broken by a man. Father, I don't know if it's the truth. Pernel would say such things and, when I tried to question her, she would retreat into herself, start clawing at her hair as she crooned some lullaby, like some mad woman grieving over a lost baby.'

'You mean she had a child?'

'God knows, Father, but that's all I can tell you about Pernel.'

Athelstan urged both men to eat, gesturing at Cranston to join him near the refectory lectern where the reader would declaim during mealtimes.

'So Pernel did know someone here,' Athelstan whispered. 'Can that be a coincidence? Sir John, I am sure her death was no accident.'

'Father?' the Hangman called, and Athelstan and Cranston returned to the table. 'I must tell you this. I don't know if they were bluffing, but the Earthworms who let us by said it didn't matter who entered Blackfriars.'

'Did they say why?' Cranston raised the miraculous wineskin to his lips.

'Because, Sir John, one of them muttered that once darkness fell they would enter Blackfriars themselves . . .'

Cranston took the warning seriously. He told the Hangman and Bladdersmith to prepare themselves, then he almost dragged Athelstan from

170

the refectory to repeat the warning to Prior Anselm.

The prior was not surprised by the news. 'Our guards on the parapet walk also believe the Earthworms are massing just out of sight. Moreover, we continue to receive warnings from the rebels about sheltering enemies of the "True Commons and the King". They insist that the Upright Men have the right to search our precincts for any undesirables, but that is nonsense! Blackfriars is church land. These precincts are consecrated ground. I am certainly not opening the gates to a horde of ruffians.' The prior smiled thinly. 'We now become the church militant. We have every right to defend ourselves. I am certainly not going to be the prior who allowed this great mother house to be sacked by a coven of outlaws.'

'Father Prior,' Cranston clapped him on the shoulder, 'I couldn't ask for better. So let's prepare a meal to serve up to these rifflers who, I think, are going to get the shock of their lives.'

The friary readied itself. Darkness fell. The watchmen on the walls reported that all fire and torchlight had died in the Earthworms' camp, though the noise of grinding cart wheels could be clearly heard.

'They are preparing a ram,' the infirmarian offered as he, Matthias and Brother John gathered close around Cranston and Athelstan in the great cobbled bailey stretching down to the gatehouse.

'You have been a soldier, Brother Hugh?' Cranston teased.

171

'*Deo Gratias*, no, Sir John but I have been up on the walls and noticed the carts arriving late this afternoon. They are certainly not bringing in supplies.'

'Brother Hugh, where did you serve, I mean, before you came to our London house?' Athelstan asked.

'At Yarm in Yorkshire, then Coventry, King's Langley and Oxford. King Edward II used to visit those places. I remember meeting him. He was bluff and hearty. He loved nothing more than jesters and acrobats; he also loved our order. From what I gather he would stay with us rather than at a royal palace.' Hugh shook his head. 'It's true what they say, he never forgot us Dominicans.'

'And the Dunheved brothers, did you ever meet them?'

'Outlaws.' Matthias laughed throatily. 'Oh, we heard about their exploits. For a while they were regarded as legendary, heroes like Robin Hood, Will Scarlet and their merry men.' Matthias made a face. 'You know how it is, Athelstan, all things pass, all things change. A new king emerged, a different regime, a fresh beginning, and our order returned to its usual business.'

'And the Dunheveds are buried here?'

'Oh yes,' Matthias replied. 'I have the Book of the Dead showing where their graves lie in God's Acre. Tomorrow, after this nonsense is over, I will show you their tombs. Now, Sir John,' Matthias picked up an arbalest lying on the ground beside him, 'if you would be so good as to show us . . .'

Cranston did so, demonstrating to all three friars

how to wind back the cord and insert the barbed bolt in the groove. How to take aim and loose. Much merriment was caused with all three friars getting it wrong. Fieschi, Cassian and Isidore joined them. Athelstan noticed that the Italians had donned coats of mail and seemed most skilled in the use of a crossbow. When questioned, all three declared that in their youth they had served in the militia of various city states. Athelstan was recalling his own days as a soldier when he felt his sleeve plucked, and turned to see Luke the royal messenger standing there. He too was garbed in a hauberk, a helmet over his coifed head, a drawn sword in his hand. He gestured at the friar to come away. Athelstan followed him into the darkness.

'What is it, Luke?'

'The lady Isabella, Master Thibault's daughter, where is she? Is she safe?'

Athelstan stepped closer. 'What is she to you, sir?'

Luke sheathed his sword, opened the small pouch on his warbelt and produced a red, glazed seal which Athelstan recognised as Thibault's.

'That could be forged.'

'It isn't, Brother, and you know it. Now, the lady Isabella?'

'In the guesthouse with her nurse.'

'Oh, the Medusa!' Luke scoffed. 'When the Earthworms try to wriggle in here, I will be guarding her.'

'Do you think they want her?'

'Of course.'

'Where is Master Thibault, Luke? He and his

173

shadow Albinus appear to have vanished from the face of the earth.'

'My master believes he should bend before the storm as well as prepare for what comes after it.'

'You are not really a royal courier, are you?' Athelstan glanced over at a burst of laughter from the Dominicans clustered around Cranston. He turned back. 'You have been given a false name, a false background and a task which is only a pretence.'

'Very true.'

Athelstan could see the courier was grinning through the darkness at him. 'Master Thibault arranged for me to be here, and you know how influential he is, so our Italian guests could use me as an envoy to take messages back and forth between Procurator Fieschi and the King. Master Thibault wants to know what is going on; he has a finger in every pot. He arranged it that way. Of course, the revolt and the unrest in the city have interfered with the best-laid plans of those in power.'

'But your real task now is to keep a close eye on young Isabella?'

'In the main, yes. But listen.' The courier's voice fell to a whisper. 'My true name, Brother Athelstan, is John Ferrour. I am Thibault's man in Southwark. I had nothing to do with you or your parish, but I kept an eye on other parts of that vineyard. I am here in Blackfriars for various reasons, some of which you know. However, now we have something in common. We are both trapped here, Brother Athelstan. Sir John Cranston is growing restless; sooner or later, he will try to leave for the Tower. I know he must. He wants to be with the King. I must go with you, promise me that . . .'

Athelstan gazed back at Cranston still trying to persuade the three English Dominicans that the crossbow would not harm them. He heard his own name shouted. The Hangman and Bladdersmith, now garbed in Dominican robes, were hurrying towards him. Both men had been given weapons from the barbican. The Hangman was resolute enough, though Bladdersmith was shaking and fearful. Athelstan gestured at them to keep away.

'Brother Athelstan,' the courier hissed, 'do you promise—'

'Luke, John Ferrour, whoever you are,' Athelstan gestured around, 'if all goes well here—'

'Harrow! Harrow!' one of the sentries on the parapet walk cried out. Athelstan glanced up. Fiery streaks flamed against the night sky.

'Fire arrows!' Cranston shouted. 'Have tubs of water at the ready . . .'

Ferrour grabbed Athelstan's arm and pulled him away even as arrow shafts shattered on the cobbles. A bell began to toll the tocsin. Men-at-arms appeared, edging out into the darkness, taking shelter where they could. At first there was confusion. Sentries shouted that they could see no one though the fire shafts continued to pepper the night sky. Cranston joined Athelstan in the shelter of an outhouse overlooking the cobbled bailey. He shouted orders, telling the men-at-arms to fall back and wait. Silence descended, then was shattered by screams of

'Harrow!', *'A l'aide! A l'aide!'* from both left and right.

'They are testing our defences,' Cranston muttered, 'as well as trying to confuse us.' He pointed to the main gate. 'That's what they want. They will force it if they can.'

Athelstan glanced to his right and glimpsed shapes emerging from the darkness. A horn blew and friary men-at-arms, shields locked, charged a group of Earthworms who were clustered with their spears jabbing. Athelstan grasped the mace Cranston pushed into his hand and followed the coroner out across the cobbles. The ominous silence before a battle had been riven by shouts, screams and cries of war. The great cobbled bailey swiftly became a battlefield. Apparently Earthworms had scaled the friary walls on both sides. They planned to outflank the defences, secure control of the fortified gate and so open a postern door for those waiting outside. Prior Anselm had prepared for this, holding back a cohort of men-at-arms to bring the Earthworms to battle and kill them.

The struggle in front of the main gate was now the heart of the battle. Spear, sword, axe, club and mace rose and fell. Athelstan tripped over a corpse and stared down at the mashed face of an Earthworm, the cobbles around turning greasy with blood. The friary men-at-arms along with others were trying to push the Earthworms back against the walls. Athelstan glimpsed Matthias, Hugh and John, each armed with an arbalest, standing grouped together; a hapless huddle searching for a target. Ferrour and the Hangman were fighting comrades; standing together each had found a kite-shaped shield, locking them close. Bladdersmith, looking rather ridiculous with a cooking pot on his head, protected their backs.

Athelstan closed with a spear-wielding Earthworm even as he heard the pounding of a ram against the main gate. The Earthworm dodged and feinted. Athelstan waited for his opportunity. The Earthworm jabbed his spear. Athelstan swiftly stepped aside, bringing the mace cracking down against his opponent's hair-matted skull. The Earthworm collapsed. Athelstan was grabbed by a sword-wielding Cranston who roared at those around him to stay close. The coroner had come into his own; as swift as any dancer, he turned and twisted, sword jabbing out like a viper's tongue.

The crashing against the main gate now thundered above the cries and yells of the mass of fighting men who surged backwards and forwards. The cloisters bell began to toll, followed by a roar of voices, '*A l'aide*, St Dominic – St Dominic, come to our help.' Prior Anselm, a coat of mail over his robes, led a group of friars along with Flaxwith and his bailiffs out of the darkness, a throng of fighting men whirling both sword and club. Their arrival proved too much for the Earthworms, who began to slip away, racing back into the blackness of the night, desperate to reach the siege ladders which they had left propped against the walls. Some of them became lost, unsure of the way, and they had no choice but to turn and defend themselves against bloodthirsty knots of defenders led by Cranston and Flaxwith. For a while Athelstan followed, but the struggle was now becoming a massacre as individual Earthworms were trapped and cut down.

Athelstan retreated into a shadow-filled enclave. He crouched against the cold wall, eyes growing heavy, a feeling of utter weariness creeping through him. The strident noise of men killing each other subsided. Figures emerged out of the darkness, their blood-smeared weapons glistening in the flame of the torches they carried. Athelstan wearily rose and joined the rest gathering on the cobbled yard of the great bailey. Men-at-arms patrolling the walls reported that a great silence had descended on the blackness beneath them. No sound or sight of any enemy.

The dead of both sides were laid out. Wounded defenders were helped off to the infirmary and hospital. Little mercy was shown to Earthworms who had been wounded or captured. Cranston, the battle fury still throbbing through him, displayed his seals of office, declaring he was the King's own officer with the power of axe, tumbril, sword and noose. Prior Anselm, who had suffered a slight hand wound, seemed too exhausted to protest. Fieschi and his two companions, who had not been in that bloody, frenetic struggle, now appeared, quietly watchful, as if what was happening was not really their concern.

Cranston had the eight Earthworm prisoners brought before him; stripped of their armour and weapons, they were pushed forward and made to kneel. Flaxwith and his bailiffs, cudgels in one hand, a fiery torch in the other, created a pool of light around the ghastly scene. Some of the Earthworms were wounded, two of them grievously, but their moans, groans and pleas were ignored. Cranston, holding his drawn sword by the blade as if it was a cross, intoned the solemn words of justice dealing with traitors caught in arms against their king.

'By law and due process,' he thundered, 'you should be condemned to be drawn, hanged, disembowelled, your heads struck off and your bodies quartered. Justice, however, will be swifter. You will be hanged. Sentence to be carried out immediately. You,' Cranston pointed at one of the friars, 'will shrive them if they want that. Let it be swift.' Cranston supervised the hapless prisoners being dragged to their feet and pushed up the steps to the parapet. In the fitful light from the juddering sconce torches, Athelstan watched as the Hangman of Rochester placed a noose over each prisoner's head, the other end of the rope being lashed around one of the crenellations. The faded words of absolution spoken by a breathless friar carried on the breeze. Figures moved in the murk. Athelstan walked away as Flaxwith's bailiffs began to toss each of the prisoners over the wall to jerk and shudder in that last ghastly gallows dance.

Athelstan felt sick, sweat-soaked. Tiredness numbed his body whilst his frantic mind seemed dominated by macabre images. He murmured a prayer for the executed prisoners. There was nothing he could have done for them. They were guilty of rebellion, attacking church property and the slaughter of innocents. He reached his chamber in the guesthouse and sat on the edge of the bed. Undoubtedly the Earthworms intended to seize all of those sheltering at Blackfriars, especially Thibault's daughter Isabella. However, he wondered if the attack was also connected to Fieschi's mission here. Had they been encouraged in their assault, enticed to attack what they thought was an undefended friary, not realising that the presence of Flaxwith and others would mean fierce resistance? Athelstan tried to list what he had seen and heard, but his eyelids were growing heavy. Wrapping a blanket around him, he lay down on the bed and fell asleep.

He woke long before dawn. He washed, shaved and laid out fresh robes. Once ready, he went down to the refectory where a sleepy servant provided a cup of watered ale. Others were also busy; Hugh, Matthias and John the gatekeeper had come from the infirmary, where Hugh cheerily declared that the dead were laid out, absolved, anointed and destined for God, whilst the wounded had been made comfortable and sent into the land of dreams with a powerful opiate. Despite their mask of good humour, all three Dominicans looked tired and drawn, but they agreed that after mass, they would take Athelstan out to God's Acre and the burial plots of the Dunheved brothers.

By the time they had finished celebrating mass and divested, dawn had broken, though the rising sun was still not strong enough to burn off the thick river mist which curled around the ancient yew trees, sturdy shrubs and the lines of battered crosses and crumbling tombstones of the dead. An eerie, ghostly place, God's Acre stretched out like some blighted wasteland. Here and there, pinpricks of glowing torchlight and the muffled thud of mattock, hoe and spade showed where the ground was being prepared for the burial of those slaughtered or executed the night before. Crows and ravens cawed noisily, then lapsed into silence. Brother Hugh, carrying the Book of the Dead, led his two constant companions and Athelstan along the pebble-dashed path to a far corner of the graveyard and two heavy crosses, each carved with the names 'Dunheved Thomas, Brother' and 'Dunheved Stephen, Brother'. Both the crosses and tumuli looked neglected, worn down by wind, rain and freezing winter. Athelstan knelt on the prayer stone between the graves and murmured the requiem, then rose to his feet.

'So little,' he declared, pointing down at the graves. 'Here lie two men who shook throne, crown and church. What secrets died with them, eh?' He glanced at his three companions, cowls pulled up against the drifting mist. 'Does Blackfriars hold any records on these two brothers?'

'I don't know,' Matthias the secretarius answered. 'Poor Roger was the authority on such matters. As you can see, Athelstan, these are two lonely tombs, and what the Dunheveds said or knew is now known only to God. Well, are you finished?'

Athelstan stared around the mist-hung cemetery. A seed of an idea was taking root. A suspicion was beginning to surface that the dead, despite the apparent paradox, were very much active amongst the living. Odo Brecon was a relic of the past and he had been brutally killed. Pernel the Fleming woman had, in her own fey-witted way, wandered into a dark place ruled by the past and she had forfeited her life. Brother Roger, busy probing the past, had been cruelly struck down. Athelstan threaded a set of Ave beads through his fingers. Odo Brecon and Pernel were gone, murdered for what they knew, Brother Roger for what he had discovered – or threatened to. Athelstan was walking the same path as the dead chronicler. Roger had stumbled on something, so it was vital that his chamber remained sealed and guarded until the truth was discovered.

Lost in his own thoughts, Athelstan thanked his companions, then walked out of God's Acre and across to the guesthouse. A grim-faced, unshaven Cranston was already there, his clothes still splattered with blood. He was deep in conversation with John Ferrour whilst they broke their fast on crispy pork slices under a caraway sauce, with brimming tankards of ale beside them. Cranston, however, seemed more interested in what Ferrour was saying than satisfying his hunger. The coroner turned as Athelstan sat down on a stool beside him.

'So, Friar, you know who this young man truly is?'

'I certainly know what he claims to be: John

Ferrour of Thibault's household masquerading as a royal messenger.'

'And a veritable source of information. Apparently the King and his council are hiding in the Tower. The rebel armies are massing to the north-east of the city. Rumours run riot, but it would seem that the King and his council are prepared to concede to the rebels' demands . . .' Cranston paused as Athelstan rapped the table and pointed at Ferrour.

'How do you know all of this?'

'We hanged the Earthworms.' Ferrour's face creased into a grin. 'I helped the Hangman of Rochester despatch those devils into the dark.'

'And he has a special knot,' Athelstan intervened, 'which,' he snapped his fingers, 'causes a swift death. You would offer this as a bribe to the Earthworms,' Athelstan crossed himself, 'and the Earthworms talked.'

'They certainly did, like sparrows on the branch,' Cranston declared. 'That's how we know, and it is serious. The rebel armies now occupy London and are preparing to lay siege to the Tower. I truly believe they intend to force entry.'

'And seize the King?'

'Or worse, Brother, kill him as, I suspect, a few of the rebel leaders always intended.'

Cranston leaned against the table. His face had lost its colour, becoming thinner and, Athelstan thought, strangely younger. He felt he was glimpsing Cranston as the coroner must have been years ago, a ruthless swordsman, a warrior about to enter the lists, to joust in the

183

tourney. However, this was no mock tournament but, as the heralds would declare, a fight to the death.

'Athelstan?' Cranston grasped the friar's hand. 'I must go to the Tower. The city is no longer under royal control. Master Ferrour here wants to accompany us. A good swordsman would never be refused, and you, Athelstan, must come with me. There is someone in the Tower I would like you to meet.' He let go of Athelstan's hand. 'So all three of us are going, but how? To go along the riverbank would be dangerous; the quaysides and the main thoroughfares will be under the control of the Earthworms. We will have to go by boat, barge or wherry, even if I have to row it myself—'

Cranston broke off as Fieschi, flanked by Cassian and Isidore, entered the refectory. The Italians raised their hands in salutation as they sat at the far end of the common table. Ferrour got to his feet, saying he would find a boat or barge and then return. Athelstan followed him to the door, then turned to look at the Italians clustered together talking quietly in their own tongue. Fieschi glanced up, caught Athelstan's gaze and smiled. Athelstan stared back and, without warning, a deep coldness seized him, a feeling of creeping, crawling danger. He stood gasping for breath, wondering if his wits were wandering, yet the logic of what was happening at Blackfriars made it brutally obvious. Anyone involved in this investigation into the mysterious death of Edward II was vulnerable to vicious attack. He had been targeted, as had Pernel, Brecon and the two

Dominicans, Roger and Alberic. Athelstan stared at the Italians. One or more of them could be the assassin and, if he was correct, could turn swift as a viper and lunge at another victim.

'Brother?' Cranston, grim-faced, was standing close behind him. 'We should go.'

Part Four

'Truth Has Been Imprisoned Under A Lock.'

(The Letters of John Ball)

They left Blackfriars a short while later in a skiff rowed by Brother John and three men-at-arms from the friary. They deliberately hugged the riverbank, slipping past Castle Baynard, the Wardrobe and other riverside mansions. Cranston was correct: the city was in the hands of the mob. Clouds of grey smoke drifted up against the sky. The glow of fiercely raging fires was commonplace. The riverside gallows were heavy with corpses, whilst here and there rose clusters of poles driven into the ground, each bearing a bloodied severed head. The occasional horseman raced along the quayside. Strident cries and clamour drifted across whilst the stench of burning mingled with the usual fishy smells of the riverbank. Further along flaming plumes of smoke shot up from warehouses put to the torch. Foreigners and those marked down for vengeance had been summarily hanged just above the water line.

Athelstan glimpsed two corpses bobbing in the swollen river, and one of the rowers claimed he'd seen three more, all chained together. A man-at-arms murmured that the Earthworms had allegedly impaled some prisoners on sand banks further down the river. Certainly fear seemed to hang over the usually busy Thames: wherries, barges, fishing boats, cogs and bumboats had all disappeared. Ships from foreign parts had slipped their moorings, moving downriver towards the safety and security of the gull-swept waters of the estuary.

Cranston gestured towards the city. 'They will all be there,' he muttered bitterly. 'They'll have swarmed out of their dungeons of eternal night, their filthy mumpers' castles, cellars and sewers which never see the daylight, Madcap and Mudfog, Cut-throat and Back-stabber, Daniel the daggerman and Richard the riffler, garbed in shit-strewn rags but armed with the sharpest blades. Harvest time has arrived with easy plunder and pretty pickings . . .'

'And how do you think this will end?'

'Someone, Athelstan, will have to strike, and strike swiftly, at the very heart of this chaos. Now, brace yourself.'

The small wherry began to rise and fall on the growing swell which hurtled them towards the arches of London Bridge, its pillars and columns protected by sturdy starlings. The noise of the river grew to a constant thundering, drowning even the clacking of the mills and filling their nostrils with a salty tang which almost concealed the rank smell from the nearby tanneries. Athelstan glanced up at the bridge: even that had not escaped the fury of the mob. He glimpsed darting flames and a moving pall of black smoke.

'May the guardian angel of the bridge protect us!' one of the men-at-arms shouted, the usual prayer of those who were brave or rash enough to shoot the turbulent, thrashing waters between the arches. Athelstan closed his eyes, murmuring, '*Jesu Miserere*' and then they were through, aiming like an arrow towards the Tower quayside. Athelstan immediately sensed something was wrong. All the gates, windows and towers over-looking the river quayside were firmly shuttered, and he glimpsed men-at-arms behind the crenellations on the soaring walls. Smoke spiralled from braziers lit in preparation for any assault.

On the quayside a mob was gathering, streaming down from Smithfield and Tower Hill, a surging mass of men and women, yet 'the rabble', as Cranston called them, seemed highly organised, being quickly marshalled under the floating black and scarlet banners of the Upright Men. Most of the rebels were well armed, many carrying warbows and quivers crammed with feathered shafts swinging over their backs. Tower archers and royal men-at-arms patrolled the different entrances uneasily, and their officers sheltered in the shade of the yawning Lion Gate, now firmly closed and barred, admission being only through narrow postern doors. The officers kept looking over the shoulders as if to make sure that, if they had to, they could swiftly retreat through one of these openings. For the moment the mood of the rebels was watchful rather than aggressive. The peasants who'd flooded in from the shires were completely overawed by the baleful majesty of the Tower, its soaring walls and menacing fortifications. Moreover, the clamour and noise, the growls and roars of lions and other savage beasts in the royal menagerie kept the peasants distracted and surprised.

'For the moment we are safe,' Cranston murmured. 'The Upright Men who have brought them here are curious, not hostile. But I doubt that will last for long, so come.' The coroner, cloak tightly drawn about him, his beaver hat pulled down over his eyes, shouldered his way through the crowd, Ferrour and Athelstan close behind. Cranston approached an old acquaintance, John Nettles, captain of the Cheshire archers, the King's own bodyguard, Richard's personal insignia of the White Hart emblazoned on his leather jerkin. Cranston whispered to him. Nettles nodded, turned and rapped the hilt of his dagger on the fortified, iron-studded Lion Gate. A postern door opened wide enough to allow Nettles, Cranston and his two companions in before slamming shut behind them.

Athelstan stared around. The Tower was a narrow, strait place of winding gulleys, steep cobbled lanes, needle-thin as any coffin path: these wound up past the brooding bulwarks, soaring towers and fortifications so powerful in appearance that many thought the Tower had been built by giants. Every approach and twisted passageway was under the careful watch of bowmen whose arrows could turn such runnels into a place of bloody slaughter. Nettles led them deeper into the Tower precincts, strangely silent except for the pigs penned in their sties, from which they would be dragged out to have their throats slit. At last the maze of pathways debouched on to the cobbled bailey around the soaring white-painted keep.

Athelstan stared up at the great four-square tower built in grey Kentish ragstone and painted white to shimmer in the sunlight. Across from this stood the gloomy Tower chapel of St Peter in Chains and the black and white timbered houses of the officials who lived and worked in the Tower. A number of people – soldiers, servants and scullions – milled about. Somewhere children played, their screams carrying on the breeze to mingle with those of the hogs being slaughtered in the killing pens. Dogs barked, animals in the menagerie answered. Majestic, sombre ravens, the so-called 'Guardians of the Tower', floated serenely around, glossy black wings flapping, eyes and beaks sharp for any morsel.

A captain of hobelars in a chainmail hauberk came clattering down the outside steps of the White Tower. Nettles introduced Cranston and his two companions. The bewhiskered soldier gestured around.

'Don't you find it strange?'

'Yes, I do,' Athelstan answered quickly. 'The Tower seems well garrisoned, but apart from the guards outside, people seem to be drifting aimlessly as if they know something is wrong but are not too certain.'

'The King has left,' Nettles declared. 'He and some of his councillors have ridden to Mile End to meet the rebels. He has insisted that they gather there in ranks under their banners.'

'So who is here?' Ferrour demanded.

The captain of hobelars stared at Ferrour. 'Who are you? Do I know you? I am sure I do.'

'John Ferrour.'

'Who is here?' Cranston repeated the question.

'Archbishop Sudbury,' the captain of hobelars replied, 'tax assessor Legge and Hailes, Prior of the Hospitallers and Treasurer.'

Athelstan closed his eyes and repressed a shiver. The three men just named were responsible for the hated poll tax levied on every individual in the kingdom. All three were condemned and, in the words of the Upright Men, 'adjudged traitors to the True Commons and so worthy of death'.

'You cannot go up,' the captain of hobelars added wearily, gesturing at the outside steps to the White Tower. 'Archbishop Sudbury is conducting what he calls, "the vespers of death". He firmly believes, and the others with him, that they are going to die this day. He has issued strict instructions that no one else is to be admitted to the Chapel of St John. The archbishop will wait there for whatever God decides.'

'Could the White Tower be defended?' Cranston demanded.

The captain of hobelars just shook his head. 'Archbishop Sudbury has ordered us not to resist; there must be no bloodshed, particularly in the chapel.'

'All we can do is wait,' Ferrour explained. 'Wait and wonder, and that is what I shall do.' He bowed and walked off towards the chapel of St Peter ad Vincula. Nettles and the captain of hobelars drew away. Cranston plucked at Athelstan's sleeve.

'I promised you we could meet someone who was once involved in the business you are investigating at Blackfriars. There is time enough. Come, Brother.'

Intrigued, Athelstan followed the coroner across the great bailey. Cranston stopped by the women busy at the washtubs. He bent down and talked to them while Athelstan gazed around. The Tower was an eerie place, a fortress and a prison yet home to many royal officials. A haunt of ghosts crammed with memories of the past, a place which had figured prominently in the vicious power struggles which had raged in both London and Westminster. 'As it does now,' Athelstan whispered to himself. Cranston returned and led Athelstan across to the white-plastered guest hall with chambers on all three galleries above it. They climbed the stairs to the first and Cranston knocked on a door displaying a red heart pierced with a sword.

'Come in.' The woman's voice was strong and carrying. Cranston lifted the latch and they entered a spacious, comfortable chamber. The whitewashed walls were covered with heraldic, gaily coloured cloths as well as a Greek icon displaying the face of the crucified Christ. Soft cord matting covered the scrubbed floorboards, the furniture elegantly carved and polished to shimmering in the light pouring through the mullion glass window overlooking the square of garden beneath. An old woman, garbed in blue and white like a nun, sat in a comfortable cushioned chair next to a narrow four poster bed, its murrey-coloured, gold-tasselled drapes pulled close.

'Mistress Marissa Langen?' Cranston asked.

The old woman's lined face was redeemed by eyes bright and sharp as a spring sparrow. She nodded, pointing a bony finger at the coroner. 'You are Jack Cranston.' She smiled, and her thin face, framed by a starched, white wimple, seemed to grow younger. 'I remember dancing with you!' She cackled. 'Thirty years ago. The May Day celebrations, a lovely summer's evening, eh? I never forget a face or certain parts of a man's anatomy.'

Despite the circumstances, Athelstan grinned while Cranston noticeably coloured, coughing and stamping his booted feet in embarrassment.

'Oh yes, Jack Cranston. I have heard of your achievements in both the battlefield and bedchamber. And this must be your secretarius, Brother Athelstan?' She poked the air with her fingers. 'I also know what is going on at Blackfriars. Oh yes, the clerks who moved the manuscripts there chatter and gossip, like the noddle-pates they are. No one asks me.' She sniffed primly. 'But I can talk, eh Jack?'

'And that, mistress, is why we've come. Now . . .' Cranston pulled up a stool, indicating that Athelstan should do the same, so they sat like errant schoolboys before this sharp-eyed, keen-witted old woman.

'What is it you—' She broke off at a swelling roar which carried across the grounds of the Tower. 'The wolves gather,' she murmured. 'They

194

will do no harm to an old woman, former hand-maid to a queen, living out her days here as a pensioner.'

'They will not hurt you,' Athelstan soothed.

'No, they won't,' she retorted. 'The wolves hunt other prey: those three unfortunates Sudbury, Legge and Hailes. I have heard the chatter. They brought in the poll tax and they will now pay for it with their heads.' She crossed herself swiftly. 'I have seen all three on their knees in the Chapel of St John; only God can save them. So,' her fingers fluttered, 'Jack Cranston and his keen-eyed little companion. Why are you here? Queen Isabella?'

'Queen Isabella,' Cranston agreed. The old lady rocked backwards and forwards in her chair.

'Now you must remember I was not with her during the hurling days. I have no knowledge of the power of Mortimer, though I think he was a constant memory for my mistress the Queen Mother.' She sat back in her chair, gesturing at Athelstan to pass the pewter cup from a side table. He did so and she sipped, then studied both of them over the rim of the goblet. 'I entered Queen Isabella's service in the spring of 1353, the twenty-sixth year of her son's reign. Isabella, Her Grace,' she added briskly, 'had been closely protected by her son after Mortimer's fall and there,' she smiled faintly, 'is the root and the rub of this matter. Brother, Mortimer was hanged naked on the elms at Tyburn, his corpse left dangling for two days and nights. Rumour had it that Isabella was pregnant at the time with Mortimer's child.'

'I heard something similar,' Cranston grunted.

'Anyway, true or not, they say Isabella's wits were turned, her mind became unstable. So, for the first two years after Mortimer's death she was confined to Windsor Castle.' Marissa blew her cheeks out. 'She recovered and moved into the eastern shires, staying at Hertford for a while, but, for most of the time, at Castle Rising in Norfolk. You know it, Jack, I'm sure. A great towering donjon surrounded by half-timbered dwellings and protected by rough-hewn, powerful walls pierced by only one entrance.' She repressed a shiver. 'A gloomy, murky place, especially when the sea fogs roll in to cloud the eye and muffle all sound. A pagan place with its morasses and marshes. At night strange sounds can be heard drifting in from the wasteland. It was—'

'Can you tell me about her husband's heart?' Cranston interrupted, growing more and more distracted by the growing clamour from outside.

'Oh, that. She carried it as a priest would a pyx containing the sacred host. A small, silver-bejewelled vase covered with a pure silk cloth sewn with gold. Where she went, her chaplain and physician, Master Laurence, followed carrying the heart.' Marissa looked pityingly at Athelstan. 'And so it was until about five months before her death in August 1358. She was poisoned.' Marissa paused. 'I am sure she was poisoned, and her mind began to drift again.'

'But surely that was old age?'

'No, no, listen, Brother. In the late winter of 1358, after the Feast of the Annunciation, my mistress Isabella was visited at Castle Rising by a mysterious group of men; cloaked, cowled, hooded and visored. The constable of the castle said they rode like wraiths out of the mist demanding an immediate audience with the Queen Mother. The constable challenged them, asking their names.' Marissa held up a spotty, vein-streaked hand. 'I remember this most clearly; their leader replied, "Sancto Alberto di Butrio". That's what the constable told us later, that's all that was said.'

'You are certain?' Athelstan insisted.

'I remember that evening very distinctly. Isabella was sitting in her chair before the hearth in the royal solar. I was with her when the constable reported what had happened.'

'And what did the Queen Mother do?'

'Brother Athelstan, I assure you, I have never seen her so startled, so frightened. She screamed at us to go, we were to leave immediately. Everyone, ladies in waiting, servants, guards. We hastened out and the four strangers were admitted.'

'You saw no faces?'

'Nothing at all. Just four black shapes like ghosts from the gloaming coming up those steps, boots scraping the stone, the clink of weapons beneath their cloaks. There was something frightening about them. One of them spoke; his riding boots were wet and he slipped on a step. He cursed and I am sure the tongue was Italian, a few words of abuse. But then we were ushered down and they swept in.'

'How long did they stay?'

'All night, apparently, closeted in that solar. The constable became so concerned he went back to the solar but the door was locked and bolted on the inside. He knocked. Isabella came to the grille in the door and pulled it open. The constable said her face was like that of a ghost, waxen-white and drawn, eyes much enlarged. She whispered hoarsely that under pain of death she must not be disturbed any further.' Marissa sucked from the goblet, silently toasting Cranston as he took generous mouthfuls from the miraculous wineskin before passing it to Athelstan to do likewise.

'The mysterious visitors,' Marissa continued, 'left just before dawn. They came out of the castle bailey. Naturally, the grooms and ostlers had inspected the horses and harnesses but these could yield nothing about the identity of their riders. They left immediately, riding into the mist and disappearing into the desolate wasteland around Castle Rising. After they had gone Isabella became deeply disturbed, even fey-witted. She never uttered a further word about her midnight visitors, nor would she allow us even to refer to it.'

'Did Isabella understand Italian?'

'A little,' Marissa shrugged, 'but, there again, they would probably speak the language of the court, Norman French.'

'Could one of those visitors have been her husband,' Athelstan asked, 'allegedly slain at Berkeley, though some say he escaped?'

'True.' Marissa nodded in agreement. 'I heard the rumours. Anyone close to the Queen Mother did, but none dared voice it. The "Days of Mortimer", as they were called, were forbidden

198

fruit. We knew they were there but not for discussion.' She sipped from the goblet. 'Afterwards, the Queen Mother's mood slipped deeper into darkness. Within two months of those visitors leaving she began to feel unwell.' She tapped the arm of her chair. 'I remember there was wine in the solar. Isabella liked that. Most of it was drunk that night. I sometimes suspect her midnight guests secretly distilled some noxious potion which began a growing rot within her; she sickened and died in the August of that year.'

'And those midnight visitors, was anything ever discovered?'

'Brother, I assure you nothing—'

She paused as the door was flung open and Nettles burst into the chamber.

'Sir John, Brother Athelstan,' he gasped, 'you are needed now in the Chapel of St John.'

Cranston and Athelstan hastily made their excuses to the old lady and hurried out into the bright sunlight. Despite the warmth, Athelstan felt a chill as a roar of angry voices echoed across the bailey. They hastened up the steps and into the chapel of St John the Evangelist, built so its apse projected out of the south-east corner of the White Tower. The chapel was oval in shape. Along either side of it ranged six drum-like pillars ornamented at top and bottom with acanthus leaves. Each pillar, representing one of the apostles, was lavishly painted with scenes from that particular saint's life. Behind each set of pillars was a narrow gallery separating them from the outside wall, which was pierced with windows through which the sunlight poured. The chapel was dominated by a finely decorated rood screen depicting a crucified Christ flanked either side by life-size statues of the Virgin and St John painted in the glorious, eye-catching colours of England's royal house, the Plantagenets: gold, red, blue and silver.

On that particular day the hallowed beauty of the royal chapel had been shattered by those taking refuge there. A gaggle of frightened women, cloaks wrapped around them, surrounded Joan the Queen Mother who, her lovely face ravaged by both time and excess, sat in the throne-like sanctuary chair. Others lurked deeper in the dappled shadows. Athelstan saw Sudbury, Archbishop of Canterbury, waxen-faced, white-haired and sharp-featured, garbed in a stained sulpice. John Legge, the chief tax assessor, knelt before Sudbury, hands clasped. Beside him crouched Robert Hailes, Prior of the Hospitallers and Treasurer of England. All three men were deep in prayer, and, from the still burning candles and the sacred vessels strewn across the altar, Athelstan realised mass must have just finished. Sudbury and his companions were now quietly reciting the litany of the saints.

Others too sheltered behind the altar. Henry of Derby, Gaunt's elder son, who, at Cranston's insistence, had been left in London with others of the self-proclaimed regent's household. Henry of Derby, with his close-cropped black hair and solemn face, looked the only one ready to confront the boiling rage of the gathering rebels. The Queen Mother, lost in her own hysterics, glimpsed Cranston and stretched out her hands in supplication, her sobs almost drowning Sudbury and the others now chanting the '*Placebo*' and '*Dirige*' psalms, the conventional prayers for those about to die.

Athelstan and Cranston both sensed a deep spiritual gloom pervading that small jewel of a chapel. There was a growing disorder which could easily tip into chaos. The coroner drew his sword and beat the blade against a pillar. All noise ceased, everyone's eyes on the coroner.

'We must flee this place,' Cranston declared. 'Now, it's only a matter of time . . .' He paused as Ferrour, cloak thrown back, clattered into the chapel. 'You, sir,' Cranston pointed at the new arrival, 'will help us. Now,' the coroner bowed towards the Queen Mother, 'Madam, this clatter and chatter must cease. Master Nettles, collect as many Tower archers as you can and accompany us.' Cranston beat his sword against the pillar. 'Now, now, now!' he shouted. Immediately the people in the chapel hurried to obey, dividing into two groups. The Queen Mother and her ladies-in-waiting assembled under Cranston's direct protection and that of his archers. Athelstan summoned the rest to gather around him.

'The water-gate,' Cranston ordered, 'swiftly, now. You must only carry what you need.' He gestured at the sobbing Queen Mother and her distressed ladies in waiting. 'I beg you to be calm. Brother, we must go.'

Athelstan grasped Sudbury's cold, vein-streaked hand and gently tugged. 'My Lord Archbishop, please?' He turned to the others, Legge, Hailes and a Franciscan friar, who were all beside themselves with fear, their eyes bloodshot, faces unshaven, robes and tunics grubby with food and wine stains. Athelstan tried to ignore the stench of sweat, urine and vomit. The chapel now reeked like the taproom of some shabby alehouse, the tightening grip of fear dulling the wits of these hunted men.

At last everyone was ready. They left the chapel and hurried down the steps along Red Gulley to the cavernous water-gate where a group of Tower archers had prepared two great war barges. The river water in the moat was swollen, heavy and sluggish, while the stench was offensive. Black shiny shapes scurried across the pillars either side of the gates, river rats disturbed in their plunder of the refuse the river swept in. The other side of the moat was deserted. Athelstan wondered if the stench had driven the mob away. The roar of the rebel army now gathering before the Lion Gate and other entrances rolled like thunder on a summer's day. Athelstan sensed something was wrong. Why was the other side of the moat facing the water-gate unguarded? True, the moat reeked like a sewer, but something else must have drawn watchers and spies away.

A fresh rolling growl of angry voices echoed ominously. Athelstan glanced over his shoulder. Perhaps Ferrour could discover what was happening elsewhere, but that enigmatic intruder had apparently disappeared. The throng around the water-gate grew even more unruly, the prospect of imminent escape deepening their hysteria. Cranston supervised the embarkation of the Queen Mother, her ladies-in-waiting and other individuals on to one barge. He then turned, clasped Athelstan by the shoulder and drew him close.

'Little monk.'

'Friar, Sir John!'

'My little friar, my greatest friend, follow swiftly. The barges will take us down to the Great Wardrobe at Castle Baynard, close to Blackfriars. Be there.' Cranston tightened his grip then let Athelstan go, brushing the tears brimming in his eyes as he urged the royal party to settle comfortably and sit quietly. Accompanied by Flaxwith and his bailiffs, Cranston clambered in. The barge had taken all who could be safely berthed. Cranston shouted an order and the barge pulled away, its oars lowered, and the barge swiftly cut through the water of the moat, heading for the river.

The second craft prepared itself. Athelstan grasped Sudbury's arm, gesturing at him to get ready, when a shout went up. The friar glanced across the moat and his heart sank. An old woman had appeared, her walking cane jabbing the air like a spear, her strident voice echoing across the murky water. Immediately others appeared even as an archer came running down Red Gulley screaming that the Tower had fallen and the rebels were within its walls.

Chaos descended. Across the moat bowmen appeared; they knelt, bows strung, and feathered yard shafts whistled through the air, shattering against the grim walls behind them. The war barge was still empty, except for its crew of Tower archers, who were now desperate to get beyond the reach of the rebel bowmen. One of them shouted, shaking his head, and the barge swiftly pulled away. Athelstan glanced around; some of those who had been with him had already fled.

'We should seek sanctuary,' he murmured. He led his little group back along Red Gulley to the White Tower and the relative safety of the Chapel of St John. Sudbury, Legge, Hailes and a few others including Henry of Derby clustered for sanctuary around the altar framed by the gorgeously carved rood screen. Verses from the psalms rang out: 'The snares of death overtook me, the cords of Hell tightened around me,' and 'From my enemy, save me, Lord. Rescue me lest he tear me to pieces like a lion and drag me off with no one to save me.' These and other chilling verses echoed ominously through St John's as Athelstan heard the pounding on the stairs outside.

The doors to the chapel were flung open, the archers on guard pushed aside as the rebels burst in. A sweat-soaked, filthy rabble, they poked the archers' bellies and pulled their beards though they offered no further violence. Athelstan realised what must have happened. Gates and postern doors had been forced or likely opened through treachery. The Tower had fallen, there was nothing to be done. The rifflers who surged into St John's Chapel now glimpsed Sudbury and the others through the rood screen, and they howled with delight, mittened hands brandishing knobbly cudgels and rusting blades. Athelstan took a deep breath, murmured a prayer and stepped across to block entrance to the rood screen. The insurgents thrust themselves forward led by a dwarf of a man garbed in a black, dusty robe, a coarse robe girdle around his waist, and stout marching sandals on his feet. This rebel leader was heavily bearded, though his head was completely shaven and shiny with sweat, his deep-set dark eyes bright with a blazing anger.

'You are Athelstan?' the dwarf asked. 'I have seen you, though of course you did not see me. But the time for such hiding and concealment is over. London will be bathed in the light and fire of God's justice. I am John Ball, priest of Kent, chaplain to God's army.'

'In which case you will respect God's house,' Athelstan retorted, staring at this self-proclaimed Vicar of the People, a hedge priest with a virulent hatred for Sudbury, who had imprisoned Ball on numerous occasions at Maidstone and Lambeth.

'Stand aside, Brother.' Ball lifted his crozier carved more like a war club than a pastoral staff.

'Leave him!'

A voice echoed from the chapel doorway. Despite the moans and chants from those huddled around the altar, everyone turned as Ferrour shouldered his way through the mob still bristling with weapons. Ferrour carried a seal in his left hand, a large green blob of wax with an insignia carved in red, the All Seeing Eye of the Great Community of the Realm. Everyone, even Ball, had to defer to this. Ferrour suddenly grabbed Athelstan by the shoulder and pushed him aside. The friar made to resist. Ferrour snapped his fingers and two of Ball's henchmen grasped Athelstan by the arms and pulled him back between two of the pillars.

'Stand away and stay away, Friar,' Ferrour hissed. Athelstan stared at this man who seemed to change from one form to another. He abruptly recalled Ferrour disappearing just after they had entered the Tower.

'You let them in?' Athelstan gasped. 'You disappeared; you opened some postern door. You told them about the water-gate; you—'

'Enough!' Ball shouted. 'Seize our prisoners!' Athelstan could only stare in heart-wrenching pity as Sudbury, Hailes, Legge and Gaunt's personal physician Appleton were dragged from the altar and pulled through the rood screen to be greeted with raucous abuse. Henry of Derby was also pinioned but again Ferrour intervened. He plucked Gaunt's fifteen-year-old son from his captors, whispered in his ear and shoved the lad through the crowd and out through the chapel door. Meanwhile the rebels had turned on their prisoners, stripping them of their clothes, throwing them to the floor to be kicked and punched. Sudbury tried to intone the litany of the saints whilst his comrades replied, through bloodied lips, the heartfelt pleas of *Orate Pro Nobis* – pray for us.' Ball ordered all four to be dragged out of the chapel and into the fierce glare of sunlight. Athelstan was also seized. John Ball, lips curled like a snarling mastiff, assured the friar he was safe in life and limb but he would have to act as the condemned men's chaplain.

'Condemned by whom?' Athelstan tried to argue, but his words were drowned by the cries of the rebels waiting outside. The hedge priest held up his hands in salutation. Athelstan stared down at the rabble swirling across the great bailey. Here and there stood Tower soldiers, archers, servants and scullions, who were left unscathed on the unspoken agreement that they did not interfere. The rest of the mob which congregated there included peasants in their drab colours of brown, black or green. Others, the denizens of the notorious dungeons, mumpers' castles and hell-holes of Whitefriars, Southwark and the Fleet, were dressed in garish garb, some of it undoubtedly plundered from the shops and stalls of Cheapside. They were all armed, many carrying warbows and quivers along with weapons stolen from both the Tower barbican and elsewhere.

The appearance of Sudbury and the others provoked roars of approval followed by a litany of curses and abuse. The mob surged forward, weapon blades pointed at the prisoners. Nevertheless there was some order and discipline among the rebel ranks. Earthworms, gathered beneath the great, floating scarlet and black banners, moved through the mob which parted to allow Ball and the prisoners to be brought down the steps of the keep. An execution party emerged, and men led forward four hog-maned horses, undoubtedly taken from the Tower stables. Each horse dragged a simple, crude sledge, and the prisoners were forced to lie down and be lashed to one of these.

The macabre procession then moved off. John Ball, chanting a psalm, was followed by the four horses and their sledges ringed by fearsome Earthworms, their faces hidden by the mask of

207

a dog, weasel or some other creature. The mob, when it could, threw dirt and other refuse at the condemned men. Athelstan walked behind the last sledge and kept his eyes down as he tried to intone the vespers of the dead. Shouts and yells dinned about him, drowning the agonised cries of the condemned men, their naked backs cruelly shredded on the sharp cobbles and rutted track-ways of the Tower.

They left the fortress through the Lion Gate. An even greater horde was waiting to escort them up Tower Hill to the soaring, stark execution platform rising black against the summer sky. A clod of earth hit Athelstan. He staggered. A horn blew and a group of Earthworms immediately surrounded him, a shield against the ordure and filth now being pelted at the condemned men. Despite the obvious horror, the procession had assumed the air of some bloody carnival. Anarchy reigned under a council of monsters. Had Hell emptied, Athelstan wondered; were all the fiends of the pit streaming up to congregate alongside him to watch the grisly spectacle on the summit of Tower Hill?

They reached the execution platform. The prisoners were roughly released from their hurdles and pushed up the ladder to the waiting executioners, whose faces were masked, unsteady on their feet after all the ale they had downed. Athelstan had no choice but to follow. He climbed on to the platform, now slippery with the blood from other unfortunates who had been brutally despatched, their blood-soaked, decapitated cadavers lying in a pile of sawdust, their heads stacked in a wicker basket nearby. Sudbury was the first to be hustled to the block. The frenzied crowd shouted their delight, though Athelstan heard other voices, more pitying, intoning the psalms and various songs of mourning. The friar sensed the horrors were gathering. He was sweat-soaked, sick to his stomach, yet he administered a general absolution to all four prisoners even though the words, 'I absolve you from all your sins,' seemed to stick in his dry mouth.

Sudbury's head was forced down even before Athelstan could finish the prayer. The archbishop knelt but then his fettered feet were brutally pulled back so his head crashed against the rough-hewn execution block. A blast of heat from a spluttering brazier carried across along with trailing plumes of black smoke to irritate the nose and mouth. The drunken flesher kicked Sudbury to be still and brought his cleaver down. Unsteady on his feet, the flesher missed the prisoner's neck, slicing the archbishop's half-turned head. Athelstan watched in horror. Sudbury was trying to get up, one hand raised in blessing, lips mouthing a prayer. Again the flesher struck blow after blow in a thickening spray of blood which splattered Athelstan's face. More smoke billowed across. The crowd were baying like a host of fiends. The flesher was now using a knife to saw off Sudbury's head. Legge and the others were crying piteously. Athelstan tried to walk forward but he couldn't. The execution platform was moving, turning. Athelstan tried to stand still to free himself from the clammy terror which seemed to grasp his soul. He stared up at the sky and then collapsed in a dead faint.

Athelstan opened his eyes. Benedicta was leaning over him. She forced a goblet between his lips, making him drink the mulled herb wine. Athelstan took a generous mouthful, sat up and stared around the dappled, shadowed orchard.

'I have been here before.' He grinned weakly. 'It is not the garden of Eden, though you might be my Eve.' Athelstan paused as others came out of the green darkness behind Benedicta. He gently pushed away the goblet and stared around the widow woman at those coming to greet him.

'Well, I never!' he breathed. Crim the altar boy, Imelda, Mathilda and other women of the parish gathered, all sorrowful-faced, to stare down at him. 'Look,' Athelstan pushed himself up against a tree, 'don't be so mournful. I am alive. I simply became weak. So much violence, the blood-splattering, the screaming and the yelling. Anyway, never mind that.' He shook his head. 'More importantly, what are you doing here?'

Athelstan took the goblet and sipped. He felt better, cooler and calmer. Memories of the grue-some executions flooded back but he responded to these with a silent prayer. He looked about him. He was in a small tree-ringed glade. In the centre of this stood a broken fountain.

'The Round Hoop tavern,' he whispered as Benedicta and the others crowded around him. 'Of course,' Athelstan smiled, 'I've had dealings with this place before.' He blinked. 'Almost a lifetime ago when all this trouble was still bubbling to the top of the pot. Now tell me, why are you here?'

'We came looking for you, Father,' Imelda, Pike the ditcher's severe-faced wife, declared. 'When they took our men, we fled, we hid. Now we have returned to hear dreadful stories.'

Benedicta took up the story. 'Now that the village menfolk have swarmed into London, the shire lords are raiding villages and hamlets out in the countryside.'

'Raiding?'

'They and their retainers. They take liveried men along with their chancery clerks who are taking careful note of who is missing and asking where they could be.' Benedicta patted Crim, who crouched all smudge-faced next to her. 'Not even children are safe. So,' she gestured around, 'we thought we could come and see if you, and Sir John especially, could help us. We crossed to Blackfriars. Brother Hugh the infirmarian informed us that you and Sir John had gone to the Tower.' She sighed. 'By the time we arrived the fortress had fallen and the rebels were swarming within. We watched the execution procession leave. I could see what had happened, that you were as much a prisoner as poor Sudbury. We had to stay to see what happened. On the platform you staggered and fainted. No one really cared.'

She pointed at Imelda. 'Father, she is a true iron-hard, warrior woman.' Imelda blushed. 'Oh yes, you were,' Benedicta continued. 'Imelda fought her way to the steps, screaming that the friar was our priest, an innocent in all this

211

business.' Athelstan smiled his thanks at Imelda and sketched a blessing in her direction.

'We all climbed up the steps and carried you down. No one objected.' Benedicta wiped a sheen of sweat from her face. 'We brought you here and—'

'What about the others?' Athelstan asked. 'The prisoners?'

'Poor Sudbury's head was hacked off; the others followed him to the block. The executioners were drunk, they were booed as butter-fingered fumblers. In the end they nailed Sudbury's mitre to his head, then poled it and the others on staves.' She looked away. 'Paraded like rotten apples, necks all ragged, mouths stuffed with shit-strewn straw. They were exhibited up and down Cheapside before being spiked on London Bridge.'

'What has caused all this?' Judith the mummer's voice quavered as it did when she delivered her lines in some miracle play. 'Why the violence, the hunting down of certain individuals, their barbaric execution?'

'Rumour,' Benedicta replied. 'Rumour claims that when King Richard met the rebels at Mile End, he offered them pardon charters for all crimes and treasons committed. Richard allegedly gave them royal licence to hunt down whomever his True Commons deemed to be a traitor.'

'Which would explain the attack on the Tower and the capture and execution of Sudbury and the others,' Athelstan remarked as he struggled to his feet. 'I must go and find our Lord High Coroner.'

'I suspect Sir John and the others have gone

to La Royale, the great Wardrobe at Castle Baynard. Brother, we could take you there. Oh, by the way, I have told them,' Benedicta continued in a rush, 'about poor Pernel.'

'Did any of you . . .' Athelstan stood up. He felt better; his strength was returning and he was determined to join Sir John as quickly as possible.

'Did any of us what?' Judith the mummer asked.

'Did Pernel ever talk to you about her past?'

Imelda spoke up: 'Once. Pernel had been sharing a pot of ale with Godbless. Deep in her cups, she was. Anyway, she talked about Ghent, Dordrecht and the towns of Hainault, Zeeland and Flanders. She babbled like a child about being in a nunnery, of falling in love, of being rejected, but it was all prattle and nonsense. I suspected she was telling bits about other people's lives. She could become so confused, though.' Imelda paused. 'On two occasions she lapsed into a foreign tongue, I am not too sure what it was. Ah well, she is gone now.' Imelda sighed. 'And so has her house.'

'What!' Athelstan exclaimed.

'Burnt to the ground,' Imelda sniffed, 'consumed by a roaring fire, red flames and black smoke. Definitely arson. We could smell the oil they used. Rioters, plunderers,' she continued, 'nothing is safe.'

Athelstan nodded in agreement. He felt a strange sadness about Pernel. The poor woman had been murdered, then someone had crossed the Thames to burn her house, destroy her possessions and make sure there was no link to the past.

213

Athelstan turned and walked into the cool green darkness. A thrush warbled its song to mingle with that of the constant cooing of the wood pigeons. The air was sweet, heavy with the scent of ripening apples and the fragrance of crushed grass.

'Was Eden like this?' Athelstan whispered to himself. 'And beyond the walls, did the demons throng as they do now, their throats full of threats, mouths crying murder and mayhem?'

'Brother?' Athelstan looked around. Benedicta, holding Crim's hand and surrounded by the other women, beckoned him urgently.

'We must go Brother,' she called.

'Yes, we must,' Athelstan agreed.

They hurried out of the orchard, across the stable yard of the Round Hoop and out into the runnels leading down to the Tower quayside. The rebel horde had moved on but the streets still stank from the violent bloodshed. Tattered red and black banners floated from open windows. The corpses of two Flemings caught out in the street dangled from a tavern sign. A herald, garbed in the garish livery of the Upright Men, stood on a pile of rotting refuse and proclaimed sentence of death against the King's uncle, Gaunt. The herald was sottish with drink but his voice was still clear as he proclaimed the regent, 'An instigator of treachery, a cesspool of avarice, the charioteer of treason, the receptacle of malice, the disseminator of hatred, the fabricator of lies, an artful backbiter, notorious for deception . . .'

Athelstan and his party hurried on. The tanning yards around the Tower had closed, but the stench from the workshops polluted the summer air, and the ground underfoot was still greasy with slops from the tanning vats. Athelstan walked carefully, lost in his own thoughts. He sensed that the blood-letting on Tower Hill had drained most of the hatred which had welled up along these needle-thin lanes around the fortress. Shops however remained shuttered, stalls removed, tinker tubs rolled away. The Tower wharf was empty though still a place of gruesome horror, the slime on the riverside mingling with the blood of other foreigners caught, summarily beheaded and gibbeted on the soaring scaffolds.

Some of the women began to sob quietly, huddling together for comfort. A barge master, touting for business, approached them, realising that a Dominican friar and a group of women would pose no threat. Athelstan handed over some of his precious coins and they clambered into the barge, the friar insisting the women sit in the canopied stern whilst he squatted with the oarsmen.

The journey was mercifully short, the barge hugging the riverbank. They could see houses were burning and columns of grey smoke billowed against the sky. Here and there shooting flames created flashes of violent scarlet. Dowgate, the Wine Wharf, Queenhithe and the rest were relatively free of ships. The only people on the quayside were those bent on mischief. Athelstan wondered what was happening deep in the city, places like St Sepulchre outside Newgate, one of the most infamous hunting runs for the wolf-sheads of the city. The bargeman tapped him on the shoulder and pointed to the approaching quayside dominated by the soaring, gloomy mass of Castle Baynard.

'I will be swift, Brother. I will land you, then take the ladies across to Southwark. The safest place for them will be the Priory of St Overy . . .'

A short while later Athelstan climbed the steep steps to the postern door in Castle Baynard's water-gate. He turned to bless the parish women grouped in the stern of the barge staring mournfully at him. He then continued on until he was challenged by Nettles, the captain of the Cheshire archers. Athelstan pulled back his cowl, and the rough-faced soldier grinned and beckoned him through.

'The King is here,' he whispered. 'Poor, frightened boy. His councillors are divided.'

'And Sir John?'

'Good Sir John is in the castle chapel. He is in a strange mood, Brother. He has drawn both sword and dagger and placed them close to the Lady altar. He is kneeling there like a Knight of the Grail.'

Athelstan pulled a face and hurried into the bailey. Castle Baynard was a grim, dark-stoned fortress, its towers and walls rising sheer all around him. A gloomy place, built for war as well as for protecting the great Wardrobe which housed royal supplies, be it cloth of gold for the court, or weapons, which were stored in the great squat, drum-like barbican. The bailey was busy with archers, hobelars, men-at-arms and knights of the royal household in their resplendent livery. Cheshire archers, master bowmen, weapons at the ready, guarded all entrances. Athelstan walked across the bailey then paused and glanced around. He noticed a group of the King's own council, some of whom he recognised: Nicholas Brembre, a leading alderman; William Walworth, Mayor of London; and Sir Robert Knollys, a seasoned veteran. Athelstan was pleased to see these experienced soldiers, courageous and of the same mind and temperament as Sir John.

Athelstan drew up his cowl and continued on, deftly avoiding the grooms and ostlers exercising the great destriers stabled there. He slipped up some stairs and into the chapel royal. The nave was narrow and vaulted. The only light came from narrow lancet windows as well as the stacks of candles burning before this statue or that sacred painting. The altar and sanctuary were cloaked in gloom, the only glow being provided by the tapers flickering in the lady chapel to the left of the high altar.

Cranston was kneeling at a prie-dieu; on the tiled floor between him and the statue of the Virgin lay his sword and dagger. Athelstan tapped the coroner gently on the shoulder. In the candlelight Cranston's face looked paler, younger, leaner, the merry eyes now ice-blue hard, the usual full lips a bloodless line.

'Jack!' Athelstan teased. 'Sir Jack?' He pointed down at the coroner's weapons. 'What is this? You keep a knight's vigil before combat?'

'Yes, that is what I am doing.' Cranston kept staring at the statue of the Virgin. 'I heard what happened at the Tower earlier today. Poor Sudbury and the others.' He squeezed Athelstan's arm and let it go. 'I am so pleased to see you, little friar. I prayed for you. So, what happened?'

Athelstan told him. Cranston, kneeling back on his heels, listened intently, shaking his head in disbelief. Now and again he would grip the friar's wrist tightly, keeping his eyes on the statue before him. Once Athelstan was finished, Cranston rose and led the friar across to one of the wall benches.

'I keep vigil here,' he whispered. 'I wish to be God's true knight and that of His Grace the King. Listen, Brother, when Richard met the rebels at Mile End today he made a hideous mistake. He offered them pardons.'

'I heard of this,' Athelstan replied. 'He also told them to hunt down traitors.'

'But there is more.' Cranston's voice was a hoarse whisper. 'Tomorrow, the young king has agreed to meet Wat Tyler and the rebel army at Smithfield. We know, you and I, Athelstan, about Tyler's sinister designs against the King. I believe tomorrow's meeting will lead to murderous mischief, and he has the support of other leaders.' Cranston fished in his belt wallet and took out a scroll of parchment. 'We intercepted this, a copy of a letter the hedge priest John Ball has sent to other malignants in his coven. Read it, Brother.'

Athelstan unrolled the manuscript. The message was in English but then translated by a royal clerk. Athelstan read it carefully, mouthing the words. First the original in the common tongue.

Johon schep some time seynte marie priest of Yorke. and now

of Colchestre. Greteth well Johan Nameless
  and Johan the
Miller and Johon Carter
he biddeth them that they be wary
of guile in the borough and standeth (together)
  in God's name.
He biddeth Piers Plowman. go to his work. and
  chastise
well Hobbe the Robber.
Taketh with you Johan Trewman
and all his fellows and no more.
Remember Johan the miller hath ground small
  small small.
The kinge's son of heune shall paye for al.
Be ware or ye be woe
Knoweth your friend or foe.

Beneath was the translation: 'John the shepherd, formerly priest of St Mary's in York and
now of Colchester, warmly greets John Nameless,
John Miller and John Carter and bids them to
be wary of deception in the borough and they
must stand together in God's name. They must
instruct Piers Ploughman to get on with his work
and ruthlessly chastise Hobbe the Robber. They
have to take with them John Trewman and his
companions and no others. Remember, John the
Miller has ground exceedingly small and the
King, the Son of Heaven, shall pay for all. Be
wary lest you be sorry. Know your friend from
your foe.'

'What does this all mean?' Athelstan asked,
handing the parchment back.

'Like all such letters, little friar, they are written

219

in cipher. God knows who John the Nameless is, or John the Miller. I am sure the borough refers to London. Hobbe the Robber might be Gaunt or indeed the entire royal family or council. What I find chilling is the reference to John the Miller grinding small. I believe John the Miller stands for the Mills of God. Everything and everyone will be reduced to the same. God knows,' Cranston murmured, 'in a perfect world we would have no need for what we have to do now. But I am the Lord High Coroner of London, and that, Brother is the life that I have, the life that I lead. I must act in the situation I find myself. I did not compose the music I dance to any more than you do, Athelstan. However, we have been brought to the ring and dance we must.' He handed the document back to Athelstan. 'Look, the royal clerk has translated the line of that doggerel poem as "the King of heaven's son shall ransom them all . . ."'

Athelstan unrolled the scroll and read the transcript, then studied the original in coarse English: 'The Kinges sone of heune shall paye for al.'

'Yes, I see what you mean,' he exclaimed. 'A first reading might make you think it is a reference to Christ the King, but he has already died for our sins. Here, the king of heaven's son is going to do this sometime in the future.'

'In a way,' Cranston declared, 'the business at Blackfriars is relevant here. Richard wants a saint in his dynasty because he truly believes that he rules by heaven's mandate. This is a reference to Richard, not Jesus. Tomorrow our boy king, Heaven's Son to so many, will pay for all the grievances the rebels can muster, and believe me, if they fail, they will keep trying until they achieve their end. Richard is the lamb dressed for sacrifice.'

'And what will you do, Sir John?'

'I shall, with God's grace, be there tomorrow and, again with God's grace, I shall do all in my power to stop them.' Cranston's face became even more stubborn. 'Not only will I stop them, I swear I will do all I can to remove the threat forever. I fully intend to kill Tyler.'

'In which case, Sir John, I shall be with you.' Cranston made to object. 'No, Jack, my friend. I will be with you, I must be.' Athelstan let his words hang in the air. The chapel lay quiet and dark around them. Candle smoke, like the souls of the departed, floated in great wisps and swirled through the air. Athelstan was surprised at his own vehemence. He had spoken before he had even reflected, yet he was committed, his decision sprang from the very marrow of his being.

'Will you now, my little friar?' Cranston whispered. 'Will you, my closest friend? It will be very dangerous . . .'

'Not for the first time,' Athelstan replied tartly, 'and, I am sure, not for the last.'

'In which case,' Cranston gave a deep sigh. He went down on his knees and, before Athelstan could stop him, made the sign of the cross. In the close silence of that chapel, Sir John intoned the words of a penitent in confession, 'Bless me, Father, for I have sinned . . .'

Athelstan could only sit, head bowed, as Cranston spoke from the heart, not so much about

221

any sin he had committed but the good he had failed to do. At the end he sat back on his heels and pointed to his weapons still lying before the Lady Altar. 'Tomorrow, little friar, I openly confess, I am going to try and kill a man, albeit a criminal whose mind is set, I am certain, on striking down our king, our liege lord, Christ's anointed.'

'Do you want to?'

'No.' Cranston half smiled. 'To quote your good self, I think no man ill. I say no man ill. I do no man ill but I feel I have to. I have no choice in the matter.'

'Sir John,' Athelstan replied, 'you are the King's own officer: the Lord High Coroner of London, a knight of the body who has taken an oath of fealty to our king. Jack, you must follow your conscience and do your duty. Now, is that all?'

Cranston nodded. Athelstan lifted his hand and gave absolution. When he had finished, Cranston eased himself back on the bench. 'And my penance?' the coroner asked.

Athelstan narrowed his eyes. 'Bearing in mind what might happen tomorrow, I would say at least three cups of the best Bordeaux and the juiciest meat pie this castle's cook can muster.' Crowing with delight, Cranston almost dragged Athelstan out of the church and across to the small refectory where others had gathered. The coroner took Athelstan over to a table in the far corner. He managed to collect two stools and, having slipped a coin to a scullion, ordered the best Bordeaux and a pie with the freshest, spiciest venison mince both for himself and his 'black monk friend'.

'Friar,' Athelstan insisted as Cranston slid on to the stool opposite him.

'Who cares?' The coroner grinned. He licked his lips and rubbed his hands together. 'Sometimes, Brother, a goblet of wine and hot, diced mince can become the centre of your life. Now,' he leaned across the table, 'this business of Blackfriars. I see you have left your chancery satchel behind?'

Athelstan tapped the side of his head. 'I have it all up here, everything I have seen, heard and felt is being milled and ground.' He smiled. 'John the Miller is not the only one intent on grinding small.' He paused as a servant brought a tray of goblets, platters, a wine jug and a dish of venison to share, as well as napkins. Athelstan placed his napkin over his arm and insisted on serving Sir John, what he called the 'royal portion' of both the meat and the wine. He then sat and waited until the coroner, now cheery-faced and bright-eyed, had satisfied the pangs of hunger.

'First,' Athelstan began, 'the death of Edward II. Undoubtedly there are two strands, that he was murdered at Berkeley and lies buried at Gloucester, or that he escaped and some mammet or look-alike was buried in his stead, which is a strong possibility.'

'And secondly?'

'Secondly, my dear coroner, there is this investigation into the death of Edward II being carried out by Fieschi and his companions. The Holy Father wishes to please our king. He is prepared

223

to consider the possible canonisation of Edward II and entrust this matter to Matteo Fieschi, whose ancestor claims to have heard the escaped king's confession. Moreover, the Fieschi family are prominent, or so I gather, in the area around the abbey of Sancto Alberto di Butrio. So, the papal delegation eventually arrive in this country. They travel here, they travel there before taking up residence at Blackfriars, a logical choice. Blackfriars is the mother house of the Dominican order in this kingdom, and it holds its own archives, a wealth of documents.' Athelstan rubbed the stubble on his chin. 'I must remember that,' he whispered. 'Brother Roger's chamber desk is littered with our archives. Of course,' he continued, 'the English crown is eager to assist Fieschi and the canonisation process. Documents from the Exchequer, Chancery and King's Bench are sent to Blackfriars for examination. Fieschi's party as well as Brother Roger scrutinised these.'

'Now let's stop there,' Cranston intervened. 'You describe the way things are, but what is the real truth of the matter?'

'Undoubtedly the Holy Father wants to please our king. He chose Fieschi as his envoy because of that family's association with stories that Edward II had escaped. In a word, Sir John, I believe Fieschi is under strict instruction to quash such rumours, to declare that Edward II was martyred at Berkeley and so the process of canonisation can blithely proceed.'

'So what happened? What went wrong?'

'Two things. First, the evidence for Edward II

escaping is probably greater than anyone imagined. This has surprised the papal delegation.'

'And secondly?'

'Ah, Sir John,' Athelstan replied wearily, 'what I call the dark heart of this affair. Someone, for their own sinister reasons, is trying to impede the investigation, and will do anything, including murder, to block its progress. But why? What does it really matter now if Edward II escaped or not?'

'If it was proved he did, the process of canonisation would falter, even collapse.'

'True, Sir John, so I ask myself, is that the reason for all this murderous mayhem? Alberic stabbed so mysteriously in his chamber, Roger poisoned in his, poor Pernel drowned, her house burnt down. Odo Brecon killed so barbarously. Then there is the murderous assaults on myself.' Athelstan tapped the table. 'We must not forget the one common factor in all of this, be it the year 1327 or that of the present year of grace, 1381.'

'The common factor?'

'Dominicans,' Athelstan replied. 'Dominican friars were deeply involved in the fate of Edward II, and some fifty-four years later Dominican friars are immersed in that king's fate and possible sanctity.' Athelstan paused, fingers to his lips. 'That's it, Sir John, that's the way forward. I will leave the fate of kings to others whilst I construct two paths. The first will be the role of the Dominicans in 1327 and afterwards. The second will be the doings of certain Dominicans over the last few days at Blackfriars. However, that will have to wait for a while.' Athelstan pushed the platter away and wiped his fingers on the napkin. 'Sir John, I have asked this before and I ask you again, do you have any news of my parishioners?'

'None.' Cranston shook his head. 'I do wonder about their disappearance, and that of Master Thibault and his constant shadow Albinus. I have heard rumours about what is happening in the shires, as you have. The Lords of the Soil are gathering whilst the rebel horde streams through London. They are hanging rebels they find isolated or vulnerable. One rumour describes how, when a dead man's relatives removed the corpse from the public gibbet, these lords compelled them to re-hang the remains using the same worn chains, even though they were covered in putrefaction. Now that,' Cranston added grimly, 'is what Thibault could be involved in. So we have the Lords of the Soil busy in the shires, but nothing, except for me and a few others in London, to afford our king protection. Tomorrow, God willing, such protection will make itself felt . . .'

Athelstan rose late the following morning. He celebrated mass at a small side altar in the castle chapel and waited on events. Cranston arrived all freshly barbered, beneath his murrey jerkin a coat of the finest Milanese steel, his war-belt strapped tightly about him, a dagger concealed up the sleeve of his cloak. At about noon King Richard appeared in the castle bailey. He walked up to mount his destrier, finely caparisoned in scarlet, blue and gold. Cranston knelt and helped the King into his stirrups and then up on to the high horn saddle. Richard looked like some angel come down from heaven. He was dressed in royal cloth of gold; his blonde hair, oiled and combed, framed his smooth, delicate face set in a mask of cold serenity, those strange, light blue eyes staring, almost unseeingly, in front of him. Now and again Richard's bejewelled, leather-gauntleted hand would touch the precious chaplet around his head as if to ensure that it was still there.

Others of the royal entourage gathered, men sworn to serve the King both body and soul. Cranston, principal amongst these, rode on the King's right with Mayor William Walworth on Richard's left. At Cranston's instruction, Athelstan gingerly mounted a small sumpter pony close behind the coroner. The noise and clamour of the great bailey rose as others saddled and prepared to leave. Heralds unfurled the royal war banners of England, the red cross of St George, the golden lions of England and the silver Fleur de Lys of France against a dark-blue background. Trumpets brayed and horns blew. Men checked their war-belts, the hilts of sword and dagger, to ensure all was well.

Everyone in the royal party knew this could slip into a day of wrath, a time of slaughter. Royal advisors like Cranston and Walworth were committed. They truly believed the rebel army should be militarily confronted and summarily defeated. It was only a matter of time before the rebel leaders realised they needed to seize the great offices of state, the Chancery and the Treasury at Westminster. Once they had control of these they could begin to dictate orders to sheriffs, bailiffs and harbour masters; all those royal officials in the far-flung shires would see the council seal and act accordingly. Sitting on his gentle palfrey, Athelstan again wondered about his parishioners. He closed his eyes and said a swift prayer. Trumpets brayed again, horse hooves skittered on the cobbles. Cranston turned his mount, standing high in the stirrups.

'Gentlemen!' he bellowed. 'We march out to confront the rebel leaders. This meeting could end in sword and dagger play. Blood will be shed, but whose blood is a matter for God to decide.'

Athelstan's heart skipped a beat at the coroner's next words.

'I cannot speak for you, but I give you good advice on what I will do for myself. I do not intend to be taken prisoner. I will not be mocked, reviled and dragged through Cheapside to be taunted by the very rogues I would cheerfully hang. However,' Cranston paused for effect, 'this day will be ours. Before that sun sets His Grace the King will have won his city back. God be with us all. St George! St George!'

'St George! St George!' the royal party echoed back. A last shrill of trumpets. The King, who had sat immobile throughout, lifted a hand and the royal party clattered across the lowered drawbridge, the sharpened hooves of the destriers echoing sombrely like the roll of a drum on the day of battle. They were planning to go to Smithfield, but Richard wanted to visit the

Plantagenet mausoleum at Westminster. He needed to pray to the saintly King Edward and draw strength from the spirits of his ancestors. Cranston had agreed, though he had insisted that they ride with all speed and not delay.

They crossed the stinking Fleet river choked with animal corpses and all the filth of the city. Beneath the bridge the Fleet swirled a black, oozing mass. A place of horror and foul odours where carrion birds, feathery wings touching, almost covered the slime-coated mess, their beaks constantly stabbing for morsels. The summer sun and the breakdown of order in the city meant the midden heaps had been allowed to fester and poison the air more thoroughly. The King and his escort, covering mouth and nose, rode on, following the river road past the grim signs of pillaging and arson. The Temple buildings, ransacked and battered, were covered by a heavy pall of smoke fed by fires still smouldering within. Other houses and inns had been wrecked beyond repair. Walls torn down, gates and fences shredded, their inhabitants smoked out to face degradation, torture and summary execution at different places along the way. They passed scaffolds, gibbets and gallows festooned with corpses or decorated with bloody body parts and severed heads. Mounds of documents had been seized, cut up and cast to the breeze, so the scraps whirled in the air like dirty snowflakes.

An eerie, brooding silence hung over this usually busy ward of the city, the meeting place for lawyers, clerks and all the royal officials who worked at Westminster. Here and there small bands of rebels, armoured and buckled for war, gathered at the mouths of alleyways. Occasionally Earthworms in their grotesque garb would also appear, but they prudently kept their distance from this well-armed royal party. They continued on into the deserted, stricken village of Charing, where they were met by a party of priests from the Collegiate Church of St Stephen, gorgeous coats and mantles about them, shaven heads bowed in prayer, bare feet slipping on the muddy trackway, softly chanting a psalm and incensing the air with thuribles. The priests accompanied the royal party until they were under the gorgeous mass of Westminster Abbey, now desecrated by the murders which had taken place there recently.

The royal party dismounted and entered the abbey. Athelstan followed Cranston into the cold, sweet-smelling darkness. In public protest at the outrage perpetrated by the rebels, no candle or taper lit the gloom. No incense bowl glowed, no brazier crackled. The King, now escorted by the abbot, prior and other leading black monks, made his way up the abbey nave and into the royal sanctuary, where the tombs of former kings and queens ringed the splendid shrine of Edward the Confessor. King Richard, on his knees, mounted the steps smoothed by the visit of countless pilgrims over the centuries. The King crossed himself and pressed his face against the cool marble tomb of the Confessor.

Afterwards he declared he wanted to meet the abbey anchorite whose cell stood in a nearby garden. The royal party then broke up, some going to pay their respects to the shrine, others drifting into the darkness for whispered heated discussion. Cranston was led away by the rubicund, burly-faced mayor, William Walworth. Both men stood, heads close together, arguing fiercely, now and again their fingers dropping to brush the hilt of sword and dagger as they rehearsed for the final time what they intended to do at Smithfield.

Athelstan, feeling tired, sat down beside one of the pillars, resting his sweaty back against the cool, grey stone and letting his mind return to the murderous mystery shrouding Blackfriars. The true fate of Edward II had to be ignored, he reflected. He must now construct those two paths, two lines of strict enquiry: the attacks and murders recently carried out in and around the mother house; and the close link between the events of 1327 and 1381, namely the Dominican order. He felt a slight nudge and glanced up. Cranston was standing over him.

'Brother, it is time, we must go.'

They left the abbey. Cranston helped the King back into the saddle and the royal party, bristling with weapons, made their way out and down to the city. A company of White Hart archers joined them at Ludgate and served as a screen around the royal party, hemming them in, so Athelstan could see little of the city they passed through. Nevertheless, it was a heart-chilling experience. The air reeked of fetid smells, smoke and the salty, iron tang of blood spilt like wine pouring from a cracked vat. The usual noise and clamour of London had died to a murmur of voices, an occasional strident yell or a piercing scream.

Flames still licked the sky and, when the escort of horsemen parted slightly, Athelstan glimpsed corpses hanging from shop and tavern signs. He wondered how safe the King truly was from any malignant master bowman possibly lurking in an upper chamber of one of the houses they passed. He and Cranston had once feared that Gaunt might arrange his nephew's sudden, brutal death in such a way, but that threat had now receded. Treasons had a life of their own, and those who plotted them had to change and adapt to the politics of the hour. The revolt had, at least in the city, been grimly successful. Consequently, all the former conspiracies, intrigues, alliances and secret confederacies would have to respond accordingly. The revolt had now turned into a mêlée where anyone could seize power and win victory.

Cranston urged the royal party to move swiftly. He and Mayor Walworth now rode very close either side of the King. Athelstan felt a cold tension seize him. He could not see Cranston's face, yet he was certain the coroner was now lost in his own world: he had decided on what to do and nothing under the sun, not even the threat of death, would deter him. To distract himself, Athelstan tried to concentrate on the murderous mayhem at Blackfriars. Alberic, vigorous and strong, a former soldier stabbed in his chamber, the door closed, sealed and locked, no sign of any resistance. Pernel was as mad as a March hare yet canny enough. Just what had happened to her? Or to Brother Roger, poisoned so mysteriously? Odo Brecon, murdered in a place where no one knew he was, except for Prior Anselm and Athelstan himself . . .

'Be prepared!' Cranston shouted. Athelstan glanced up. They were approaching Smithfield, breaking free of the city and entering that ancient site, the great open-air trading ground for cattle, horses and other livestock. Smithfield, or Smoothfield as it had once been called, provided the stage for tournaments, markets, festivals and races, the haunt of magicians' booths who offered all kinds of potions and remedies. Smithfield was also the execution ground for East London, good use being made of the long-branched elms clustered to the north beyond the horse pool. Here traitors were dragged on sledges to be strangled, castrated and gutted, their bowels burnt before them, their bodies hacked into steaming quarters, to be boiled and tarred like their severed heads before being displayed on London Bridge or above the city gates. A sombre place where numerous Upright Men and Earthworms had been executed. The rebel leaders had chosen well.

The royal party skirted the soaring towers and gables of the Augustinian priory of St Bartholomew and abruptly paused at what lay before them. They broke up, spreading out into a line. Athelstan's heart skipped a beat. The rebel army, deployed for battle, was waiting for them only two bowshots away. Long columns of men massed into serried ranks under their floating red and black banners. Many of the rebels were armed with warbows at the ready, stakes thrust into the ground before them to deter any sudden attack by horsemen. Organised, menacing in their

233

silence, the rebel army was a formidable battle array: disciplined under their serjeants the Earthworms, who stood ready to give the order to advance. Many of the royal party were dumbfounded. A few turned their horses to ride away. Cranston and Walworth, however, seemed unimpressed.

Determined not to be cowed, they gestured at the King to stay as they spurred towards the rebel lines. Athelstan had no choice but to follow, his sumpter pony delicately picking its way over the grassy soil cut by countless horses' hooves. Closer and closer they drew to the rebel lines. Some of the archers began stringing their bows. Cranston and Walworth reined in. The coroner, standing high in the stirrups, bellowed for Wat Tyler to approach His Grace the King and present his petitions. Athelstan held his breath. Cranston was playing a deadly game of hazard, placing everything on one throw of the dice. Again Cranston made his demand.

The rebel ranks rippled and broke; a lone horseman emerged, gently urging his small palfrey across the grass towards Cranston. He rode coolly, calmly, leisurely and in open mockery of the hasty royal summons. The rider continued such mummery. He paused to adjust the reins, turning slightly in the saddle, one mittened hand raised to acknowledge the salutations of his followers clustered under their banners. The rider came on. He was dressed simply in jacket, leather leggings and shabby boots, his head and face almost hidden by a deep capuchon. He pushed this back as he approached to reveal a hard-lined, unshaven face, deep-set eyes under beetling brows, his hairlip even more pronounced by the self-satisfied smirk.

'You are?' Cranston bellowed.

'You know me well, Coroner. Wat Tyler of the True Commons,' the rebel leader yelled back and his followers roared their approval.

Athelstan threaded the reins of his sumpter pony through his hands and scrutinised Tyler. This Kentish captain was truly a dangerous man. Trusted by the Great Community of the Realm, the Earthworms and the Upright Men, and, both Cranston and Athelstan suspected, in secret alliance with Thibault – or at least he had been. The storm which now swept London and the eastern shires had led to many changes. Was Tyler considering seizing power for himself, and was this charade a part of it? Tyler was certainly acting. He was dressed simply, posing as the Everyman of village plays, Simple Simon or Piers Ploughman, a true Son of the Soil, a representative of the ground-hacking world of the manor peasant, the honest, upright, rustic litigant seeking justice. Athelstan knew it to be a lie. Tyler was as greedy for the trappings of power as any avaricious clerk at Westminster.

'You, sir, may approach His Grace,' Cranston roared.

Tyler arrogantly reined in, swaying slightly in the saddle. Athelstan wondered if the rebel leader had drunk too deeply of London ale. One hand on the hilt of his dagger, Tyler cocked his right leg over and slid arrogantly from the saddle. He carefully brushed himself down then sauntered towards the King, half curtseyed, then lunged forward, grabbing Richard's arm.

'Brother?' Tyler rasped. 'Be of good comfort and stay joyful, for you shall have, in the fortnight yet to come, forty thousand more commons than you have now and we shall all be good companions.'

'Why do you not go back to your shires?' Richard's voice betrayed his desperation.

'Neither I nor my companions will return to our shires until we have our charters.' Tyler scowled, head cocked to one side, like a master reproving his apprentice. He drew close to the King's horse and began to lecture Richard on the True Commons' demand: a lengthy but blunt description of the rebel grievances. Richard replied that he would grant everything as long as the rights of the Crown were both protected and respected. After that, silence.

During Tyler's harangue, Cranston and Walworth had moved their horses slightly in front of the King's. Tyler swayed on his feet. 'I am thirsty,' he rasped, 'I need a drink.' Someone in the King's entourage hastily fetched a pannikin of water. Tyler took a generous mouthful, swirled it around and spat it out contemptuously in front of the King. A growl of disapproval rose from the royal party. Cranston's hand had slipped beneath his cloak. Tyler now demanded a jug of ale, this too was brought. Again the rebel leader washed his mouth out and spat it on to the ground, making Richard's horse whinny and start. Tyler gave a loud sigh. He insultingly turned his back on the King and remounted his

236

own horse. Cranston moved forward, hand still beneath his cloak.

'You, sir,' Cranston bellowed at Tyler, 'are nothing better than a low-born varlet, a wolfshead worthy of hanging, a criminal from Kent who should decorate the stocks and gibbet. How dare you insult your king!'

Tyler drew his dagger, pushing his horse forward.

'Treason!' Cranston shouted. 'It is treason to draw your blade in the royal presence.'

'Arrest him!' Walworth cried, spurring forward, sword drawn.

Tyler thrust at the mayor but the blade buckled on the chainmail shirt beneath Walworth's jerkin. Cranston, dagger drawn, now hemmed the rebel in from the other side, pushing him away from the King. Tyler turned to lunge at the coroner. Cranston parried the blow, thrust his own dagger deep into Tyler's neck, drew it out and struck again, smashing the blade into the rebel's skull. Tyler jerked wildly, blood splattering everywhere. Others from the royal party now surrounded the rebel leader. Cranston struck again. Tyler, slumped across his horse, managed to turn his mount, spurring it back towards the rebel ranks. The small horse, however, frightened and skittish, stumbled and swerved, pitching Tyler from the saddle. Walworth, joined by others, turned away.

The rebel ranks, watching in stunned silence, abruptly broke into shouts and yells. Archers, under the direction of the Earthworms, hurried forward. Bows were strung. One line knelt down; a second line stood behind them. Arrows were plucked from quivers, feathered shafts were fitted. The deadly arc-shaped bows swung up, twine pulled back between leather-coated fingers.

'Now, Sire!' Cranston yelled. He pushed his horse alongside the King's, whispering heatedly. Richard nodded, spurred his mount forward and, followed by Cranston and a bemused Athelstan, galloped towards the rebel ranks even as arrow shafts ripped through the air.

'Will you loose at your king?' Cranston bellowed. He reined in, gesturing at Richard to do likewise.

'I am your liege lord,' Richard, high in the stirrups, proudly proclaimed. 'I am Christ's Anointed, your king. I command you as my True Commons to desist and follow me.'

'Follow His Grace,' Cranston shouted, 'out of here to Clerkenwell fields.'

Athelstan stared in utter disbelief. Richard's courageous action, Cranston's authority, their leader lying prostrate on the ground and the sight of the royal party, swords now drawn, moving as a force behind their king, froze the rebels' wits and blunted their hostility. Despite the screamed orders of the Earthworms, bows were lowered, arrows removed and the rebel ranks broke up, becoming more of a milling crowd than an army. Other members of the royal party now took up position. A phalanx of knights and mounted archers surrounded the King, swords drawn, shields at the ready. Messages were hastily despatched to the Tower, Castle Baynard and Westminster with the startling news that the rebel army was breaking up, and both King and rebels were moving towards Clerkenwell.

Cranston, however, refused to leave. Clutching the reins of his horse, he stared down at the little friar mounted beside him. Athelstan had never seen the coroner in such a mood. The fat, jovial-faced, wine-swigging law officer was now all hard-eyed, lips half-open, chin aggressively tilted. He continued to peer down at Athelstan as if the friar was a complete stranger. Athelstan glanced around. Smithfield was emptying fast. Like sheep who had found their shepherd, the peasants were now flocking around the King as if he would personally lead them to the New Jerusalem.

'You struck hard,' Athelstan murmured.

'Yes, I did, and I am not finished.' Cranston pointed to where a group of Earthworms were now taking the fallen Tyler on a makeshift stretcher through the gates of St Bartholomew's. Apart from those few loyal followers, the fallen rebel leader seemed to be both forsaken and forgotten.

'In France,' Cranston muttered, as if talking to himself, 'we always struck at the leader. Walworth and I decided on the same strategy. Now we have to finish it. Ah, at last . . .'

Athelstan turned to follow Cranston's direction. Flaxwith and his bailiffs were striding across the open field, swords and cudgels at the ready. 'Good,' Cranston breathed. 'Let's complete what we've begun.'

The coroner led the bailiffs across through the yawning gateway of St Bartholomew's priory and hospital. Athelstan followed like a dream walker. Deep in his heart the friar accepted what Cranston had done was legal, moral and very necessary. The coroner had defended his king against both abuse and murder. Cranston had kept faith and now he would deal with the consequences of that. Athelstan felt his shoulder shaken. He stared up into the coroner's icy-blue eyes.

'You must stay with me, little friar. I am no assassin but the King's own officer, Lord High Coroner of London.' Cranston pointed towards the main door of the hospital. 'Tyler is a rebel who mocked our king and drew his weapon in the royal presence. We must make an example of him.' They entered the cool darkness of St Bartholomew's, Flaxwith and his bailiffs trailing behind. The hospital was in uproar with white-aproned servants hurrying around tending to those brought in from the turbulence in the city. Brother Phillippe, the chief physician, appeared highly agitated. He and Athelstan exchanged the kiss of peace. The master of the hospital immediately began to defend what his brothers had done. According to their charter and their oath, they did not distinguish between rebels and those loyal to the crown.

'Never mind that.' Cranston grasped the physician by the shoulder. 'I have come to claim one man only. You know who it is. A rebel and a traitor worthy of death.' Brother Phillippe, his furrowed face all anxious, his popping blue eyes full of fear, nodded and sank to his knees, hands clasped.

'Tyler is in the common dormitory,' he

240

whispered. 'There is little more we can do for him. He is beyond all practical help.'

'But not beyond mine,' Cranston retorted. 'Master Tyler is headed for a meeting with God and it is time I hurried him on his way.' The coroner strode deeper into the hospital, sword and dagger drawn, the good brothers scattering before him. He went up the stairs following the trail of fresh blood which led into the dormitory. Athelstan hurried to keep up with him, fingering the rosary beads he had in his wallet. Tyler lay on a truckle bed just to the side of the door, the wounds to his face, chest and head swilled with blood. The Earthworms had left him there and fled by a different route. Cranston strode over to the rebel leader. He stared down at him for a few heartbeats before gesturing at Flaxwith. 'Not here,' he rasped, 'out in the open.'

Tyler was lost in his own delirium. The bailiffs dragged him to his feet and pushed him down the stairs. Brother Phillippe was waiting for them in the hallway.

'He is not in sanctuary,' Cranston declared. 'He is nothing but a wolfshead. Stand aside, Brother.' Phillippe did so. Cranston led Flaxwith and the prisoner out of St Bartholomew's and across to the execution platform in the centre of Smithfield. No one objected. No one resisted as Flaxwith and his bailiffs shoved a gibbering Tyler up the steps on to the scaffold, pushing him down, pressing his head against the execution block. Athelstan approached and whispered words of absolution. Cranston, cloak thrown back, lifted his great two-edged sword. He stood above the

241

kneeling prisoner, now soaked in blood and sobbing at the pain from his wounds.

'For taking arms against the King,' Cranston intoned, 'drawing his weapon in the presence of His Grace the King. For this and other manifest crimes and horrible treasons.' He stepped back slightly, swung his sword and in one clean, scything cut, severed Tyler's head to send it bouncing like a ball across the planks. Cranston lowered his sword, digging the tip of the blade into the wood as he watched the severed corpse pump out its life blood.

'Judgement carried out,' the coroner breathed. 'Justice is done.' He pointed at the severed head. 'Flaxwith, put that on the end of a pole and take it to His Grace the King at Clerkenwell.'

Part Five

'Falseness And Guile Have Reigned Too Long.'

   (The Letters of John Ball)

Athelstan sat on a stone garden bench over-looking the deep carp pond of Blackfriars. A lovely warm summer's afternoon. The flower beds, herb plots and shrubberies were bright with butterfly colour and pleasantly noisy with echoing birdsong. Athelstan watched a heron float majes-tically backwards and forwards across the pond, its keen eyes and beak ready to seize one of the fat, golden carp moving sinuously beneath the water lilies. Brother Hugh had noticed Athelstan strolling in the garden and given the friar a stick with a plea that he'd guard the carp pond until the heron grew weary of its siege. Athelstan absent-mindedly shook the cane at the marauding bird.

Five days had passed since Tyler's hoodless, severed head had been publicly poled, first at Clerkenwell Fields and then at London Bridge. The death of their leader had led to the sudden and unexpected collapse of all resistance by the rebels to the Crown. The peasantry broke apart. They streamed out of London into the shires, only to encounter troops under manor lords and great seigneurs such as Hugh Despenser, the warlike and aggressive Bishop of Norwich. In the city, loyal aldermen such as Brembre and Walworth had whistled up their rifflers and their roaring boys whilst the guildsmen were also organising their levies. Law and order were being ruthlessly enforced; the gallows, scaffolds and gibbets hung heavy with the corpses of malefactors. Cranston had never been busier in his judgement chamber at the Guildhall.

Athelstan, left to his own devices, had spent his time reflecting on what had happened at both Blackfriars and the Tower. He had been through most of Brother Roger's manuscripts, stumbling on to the fact that the chronicler, just before his death, had been busy drawing up memoranda on the Dunheved brothers. He had concentrated on their opposition to Queen Isabella and Mortimer, their seizure and imprisonment in Newgate and the work and intervention of Brother Eadred. The latter was proving most interesting. A former member of Blackfriars, Eadred had served as chaplain in Newgate before being appointed as prior to the Dominican house in Oxford and eventually provincial of the entire order in England. Apparently Eadred had ministered to the Dunheveds when they were in prison: after they had died there, probably of jail fever, he organised the removal of their corpses for proper burial in God's Acre at Blackfriars.

Athelstan had also tried to talk to Fieschi and his two henchmen, Cassian and Isidore, but the Italians were more intent on drawing up their conclusions and drafting a letter to both the King and the Abbot of Gloucester about opening Edward's tomb in Gloucester Abbey. Athelstan was still deeply suspicious about what Fieschi intended. Would they, Athelstan wondered, at the behest of their master the Pope, draw up two reports? The first would suggest that Edward II was martyred at Berkeley Castle in September 1327 and so worthy of sainthood. The second report, however, could argue that, according to the evidence, Edward II had probably escaped from Berkeley. Consequently, his last years and death were shrouded in mystery and so the process of canonisation would have to be adjourned. Would the papacy use these two possibilities to wring recognition and support from the English crown? Certainly it would be a persuasive ploy by the powers-that-be. From what he knew about the papacy in Rome, Athelstan thought such blackmail might well be intended. After all, Richard II would be horrified that his great-grandfather did not lie buried in Gloucester, and the magnificent tomb which he and others had patronised was no more than a sham.

'Athelstan, in the name of God . . .'

The friar started as Brother John the gatekeeper swept into the garden, almost stumbling over a flower bed. Behind him his two companions Hugh and Matthias seemed equally agitated.

'Brother Athelstan, you had best come, you have visitors . . .'

Athelstan, when he arrived in the bailey, could only stare in absolute amazement at the high prison cart with its narrow bars, pulled in by two great dray horses, the reins held by soldiers, their

245

heads and faces hidden behind gleaming basci-
nets. Men similarly armed served as the cart's
escort and the great cobbled bailey of Blackfriars
echoed to the clatter of their horses' hooves, the
morning air reeking of sweat, leather and horse
dung. One of the leading riders swung himself
down from his high saddle. Two others followed
suit, their cloaks billowing out. Helmets were
removed and Athelstan gazed into the light blue,
innocent eyes of Master Thibault, John of Gaunt's
Master of Secrets, a man Athelstan secretly
considered to be the devil incarnate.

'Well, well, well.' Thibault, hands extended, a
lazy smile on his cherubic face, turned so all
could see him. Then, laughing to himself, the
Master of Secrets tossed his helmet to Albinus,
his perpetual shadow and most willing accom-
plice in all the mischief his master hatched and
plotted. Athelstan nodded at Albinus, raising a
hand in greeting. He noticed that Albinus' snow-
white hair was closely cropped, his pallid face
twisted in a grin, those eerie, pink-rimmed eyes
studying Athelstan closely. The other visitor was
John Ferrour, who looked as if he was about to
attend a royal tournament, his blonde hair all
crimped and coiffed, his smooth face gleaming
with sweet-smelling nard.

'St Michael and all his angels!' Athelstan
exclaimed. 'The warriors of England have
returned. And these?' He gestured at the heavily
armoured men sitting in their saddles like the
heralds of Hell.

'My Genoese boys,' Thibault lisped. 'Lovely
lads. They have been very busy on my behalf.

246

But come, Brother Athelstan, we are so pleased to see you. I know you must have missed us. I can tell that,' he added sardonically, 'by your eyes. You must have wondered where I was?' Thibault pointed at Ferrour. 'I was never very far, either in the flesh and certainly not in spirit. So greetings, Brother.'

Athelstan had no choice but to exchange the kiss of peace with all three men. Prior Anselm and the other friars who had been watching proceedings walked forward, curious about the cart. Thibault smiled and raised a hand, and the huge tailgate was unbolted, crashing down against the cobbles. 'Bring them out.' Thibault smiled at Albinus. Two of the horsemen dismounted, climbed into the back of the cart and helped the prisoners within to clamber down into the bailey. The men, eyes blinking, hands raised, stumbled out of the prison cage, staring around in surprise and amazement.

'Impossible!' Athelstan breathed. 'God's angel in heaven!' The friar, aware of Thibault's mocking laughter, could only stare in amazement as the men of his parish staggered around, rubbing their faces. They were all there: Watkin, Pike, Ranulf, Hig, Crispin, Joycelyn, Moleskin, Merrylegs and the rest, what Athelstan called 'the motley crew'. They looked unshaven and unwashed, but in good spirits. Athelstan could see no harm or wound had been inflicted upon any of them. The bailey was now transformed into a noisy, bustling throng. Young Isabella appeared with her severe-faced nurse and ran to greet her father, throwing herself into his arms.

Athelstan's parishioners, once they realised where they were, crowded around their parish priest asking a spate of questions as they half answered his. At last Prior Anselm imposed some order. The parishioners, along with their escort, were herded off to the main refectory and the ministrations of the priory kitchen. Athelstan led Thibault, who had now gently eased Isabella back into the arms of her nurse, across into the church, Ferrour and Albinus strolling behind. They went up through the hallowed silence of the nave into the Lady Chapel. Athelstan gestured at Thibault to sit on the wall bench whilst he took a stool to face this 'master of intrigue' and 'lord of misrule'. Thibault seemed totally unabashed, his soft, choirboy face wreathed in a simpering smile which never quite reached his eyes. The Master of Secrets undid his cloak and let it slip down. Athelstan glimpsed the Milanese steel hauberk beneath the costly padded jerkin, and the war-belt which Thibault now loosened around his waist.

'You have looked after yourself well, Master Thibault?'

'As I have you and yours, Brother Athelstan,' Thibault simpered. 'I am, and I always will be, eternally grateful for your protection of dearest Isabella during these days of bloody storm. She was safer with you than ever with me. So.' Thibault peeled off his gauntlets. 'My Lord of Gaunt has taken his army north to the Scottish march. I was instructed by him to leave the Tower and London. I had no choice . . .'

'Of course, you never do.'

'Quite. I set up house in Castle Hedingham in

Essex, a formidable fortress with an impregnable keep. I have secretly, with my Lord of Gaunt's permission, signed confidential indentures with Alessandro Brescia and his Genoese companions.' Thibault's smile widened. 'The lovely boys came ashore at Orwell on the Essex coast along with their horses and impedimenta.'

'Ah,' Athelstan interrupted, 'so you have brought mercenaries in and fortified Hedingham?'

'Oh, we did more than that. I recalled my great debt to you, Athelstan. So one of my tasks before I left London was to arrest every one of your parishioners. My Genoese boys did that. I left no hint of my involvement but, once we had them, they went for a short stay in the dungeons of Hedingham. Now that sounds much worse than it is.' Thibault slapped his gauntlets from one hand to the other. 'Ask them yourself, they were well treated. They had good food, some fine ale and even a cask of my favourite wine. And so, Brother,' Thibault's smile faded, 'when the vengeance comes, and believe me it will, all your parishioners, Upright Men or Earthworms, I don't care, cannot be indicted for rebellion or depicted as traitors to the King. They are innocent because they are not guilty of anything. During the revolt they were detained at the Crown's pleasure pending certain enquiries. These have now been completed so they are released without charge both to their priest and their families.'

Athelstan stared at this cunning contriver. Thibault had undoubtedly plotted with that chief of serpents Gaunt about what they would do and now it was evident. During these last few hurling days both Gaunt and Thibault had withdrawn from any active plotting, adopting instead the safest strategy: to withdraw, watch and wait, though, where possible, they would give matters a helping hand.

'Very, very clever,' Athelstan whispered. 'My parishioners can't be indicted and neither can you or my Lord of Gaunt. Oh, you didn't do anything wrong but, apart from helping my parishioners, you really didn't do anything right, did you? You just watched and then jumped. And Master Ferrour was one of your helpmates, I assume?'

Thibault just smiled.

'You used him,' Athelstan continued, 'on matters at Blackfriars and, above all, at the Tower, especially amongst those poor unfortunates who were murdered there.'

Thibault's face tensed.

'I do wonder,' Athelstan murmured, 'yes, I do. I have reflected on what happened. Sir John, Ferrour and myself journeyed there. The coroner managed to escape; I did not, at least not immediately. Now while I was in the Tower somebody, Master Thibault, opened a postern door and let the rebels into the fortress. I suspect it was some forgotten, narrow entrance but wide enough for a group of determined Earthworms. The main gates and doors were eventually forced, the rebels streamed in and mayhem ensued. A number of royal councillors – Archbishop Sudbury, Treasurer Hailes and the tax assessor Legge – were brutally executed. No one could save them, though Ferrour was there to protect Gaunt's son, Henry of Derby. In the end the rebels did not make a clean sweep.

To achieve that, they would need to take your head, Master Thibault, and that of your royal master.'

Thibault was now as watchful as a hunting cat. 'You will publicly mourn Sudbury, Hailes and Legge,' Athelstan continued, 'but at the same time they were not of your party, your persuasion; all three would often oppose you and my Lord of Gaunt. But they will not do that any more, will they? They have gone to God whilst you, Master Thibault, and my Lord of Gaunt can sweep back into London as the saviours of both King and kingdom, ready to dominate the royal council. Nevertheless, Master Thibault, I warn you, in this sacred place: King Richard will not forget what actually happened during these last few weeks. Who was where, when and who did what. Richard now recognises how close he became to being toppled and how only he, together with my good friend Sir Jack Cranston, Lord High Coroner of this city, saved the day. Remember that, Master Thibault, for if you forget it, you do so at your own peril.'

Thibault sat on the bench, head down, staring at the floor. When he glanced up all his bonhomie had faded. He simply stared at Athelstan, then nodded, lips moving as if speaking to himself. He called for his henchmen and swept out of the church. Athelstan lit a taper before the statue of the Virgin, murmured an 'Ave' and followed suit.

He crossed to the refectory where his parishioners were regaling Brother Paschal about what had happened at Hedingham. They had eaten well on strips of goose and fresh lamb, soft white

251

bread and fruit from the priory orchard. They'd drunk even better, downing jugs of Paschal's rich brown ale, so they greeted their parish priest with raucous shouts of welcome. At first all was confusion as Pike explained that they had first thought their kidnapping had been the work of Athelstan and Cranston, but they had soon realised the plot had been hatched by Thibault. They were all relieved and happy to be free. Athelstan sensed they knew what was happening in Southwark and elsewhere. All was breaking down. The Great Community of the Realm, the authority of the Upright Men and the power of the Earthworms had been shattered.

There was a mixture of heady relief amongst Athelstan's parishioners at their escape and a dawning realisation that, as their parish priest had always prophesised, in the end the Lords of the Soil would have their way. No New Jerusalem would arise along the banks of the Thames. The doggerel chants about the brotherhood of men and their equality before God would be brutally swept away and trodden underfoot. The Day of the Great Slaughter had come and gone. They were under no illusion about what was happening. War cogs had appeared on the Thames. Lines of horsemen, dust rising above them, thundered into the city and behind them marched column after column of archers and men-at-arms. Despite their bravura, the men of St Erconwald's were secretly cowed. Tales of the bloodletting in the city and the eastern shires were sweeping the friary. Any desire amongst Athelstan's parishioners to be further involved in the unrest had been destroyed.

These were family men who, like the thousands streaming back into Kent and Essex, simply wished to be away from it all, at home with their kith and kin.

Athelstan made sure his parishioners remained well and safe. They were fed, their clothes laundered. Athelstan even managed to secure a small amount from the alms box to help them on their return. Moleskin offered to secure a barge to get them all across to the Southwark side. Athelstan assured them that when they returned home they would find all was well, except for poor Pernel. He described her death, though he gave no hint that she may have been involved in something much more sinister. The men crossed themselves and, when their parish priest questioned them about the old Fleming, they added very little to what he already knew: her foolish chatter and her fondness for a pottle of ale. Athelstan then excused himself, explaining that business at Blackfriars would detain him for some time. He warned them that, once back safely in their homes, they should all lie low, avoid any confrontation, even avoid assembling together in the Piebald Tavern or elsewhere. The friar explained it would be best if the church remained locked and sealed until he returned. He also pleaded with his flock, before he gave them his most solemn blessing, to look out for the great one-eyed tomcat, Bonaventure. Privately the friar cheerfully conceded to himself that Bonaventure, his constant dining companion, possessed more wit and sense than all his parishioners put together.

Athelstan returned to Brother Roger's chamber and began to itemise everything the chronicler had collected. Brother John came to report that all the parishioners had left, adding that he had forgotten to hand over Pernel's clothing and the few tawdry items found on her. Athelstan nodded absent-mindedly and placed the sack on a stool near the door. For a while the friar just sat looking at it. Now and again he would murmur a requiem for the woman's soul as he idly wondered what would happen to Pernel on her journey into eternity. So many souls in London had taken that long road over the last few days, and the terrors had still not ceased.

Cranston was busy enough in the city. Both he and Athelstan were amazed by how swiftly the rebellion had collapsed. Its leaders, men such as John Ball and Simon Grindcobbe, were now fleeing for their lives. No mercy, compassion or pardon were being shown. The lords were hiring mercenaries. In the city the likes of Walworth and Brembre were combing the streets looking for former rebels. Grievances and grudges were being settled. Some of the city's merchant princes wanted a bloodbath, eye for eye and tooth for tooth, pushing for a campaign of revenge and retribution. Brembre had broken into a poorly guarded Newgate. He had dragged out thirty rebel prisoners and, at the dead of night, marched them to Foul Oak in Kent where he'd beheaded them all as a warning to the rest. Villages were being sacked and burnt. Crown spies and royal approvers were pointing fingers. Rewards were being posted and all the Judas men were ready to betray their closest for the usual thirty pieces of silver or, in this case, much less.

Rousing himself from his chilling, deadening torpor at the way the world had turned, Athelstan got to his feet. He stretched, murmured a prayer and crossed himself, then took the sack containing Pernel's meagre possessions and emptied them out on to the cotbed. He sifted amongst the now-dry clothes, though the river water had both coarsened and hardened the fabric of the dead woman's gown, kirtle, stockings and undergarments. Athelstan felt a lump in the shabby, muddy cloak. He put his hand in and drew out a St Dominic Blessing, the remains of the hardened biscuit slightly green after being soaked in the Thames. The friar stared in astonishment at the token. He recalled what he had been told about Pernel, then sat trying to make sense of it, to impose order on his tumbling thoughts.

He had always accepted that Pernel was somehow involved in the mystery of Edward II but now he could sharpen his suspicions about Pernel's killer. He placed both the crumbling pieces of the blessing in a small dish and sat staring at it as the day began to die. Dusk appeared at door and window. The first bells for night prayer echoed across the priory. Candles and lanterns were lit. Voices of the brothers chanting the evening psalms carried their own dire message about the devils who prowled the darkness and the demons who lurked in corners and crevices. Athelstan continued to reflect. He did not wish to disturb his own teeming thoughts by grasping pen and parchment, at least not now.

He simply wanted, in his own mind, to rework those two converging lines of argument: the actions and fate of the Dunheveds some fifty years ago and the murderous activity which had erupted in and around Blackfriars over the last few weeks.

Cranston arrived, full of news from the city. The King and his council were now in full control. The Guildhall had exerted its authority. Cohorts of archers and men-at-arms patrolled the streets. Chains had been pulled across the entrances to the main thoroughfares. Mounted men-at-arms and knights gathered at every crossroads. The King's peace, enforced with the strictest curfew, had been imposed throughout London; the moveable gallows, scaffolds and gibbets manned by Thibault's mercenaries also enforced it with a rigorous cruelty. Athelstan only half listened. Cranston snorted with laughter. He recognised that this 'little ferret of a friar' was now deep in the burrows of an investigation, pursuing some murderer with all the passion of his sharp mind and stubborn will.

'I will be ready to talk when you are.' Cranston patted Athelstan on the shoulder. 'Vespers is over. So I will join the good brothers in feeding the inner man. You will join us?'

Athelstan murmured he would think about it and returned to smoothing out the piece of parchment before him. He was perplexed. He now entertained the deepest suspicions but he could not guess where they would lead him. He dozed for a while, and when he awoke, he realised how hungry he was. He was about to leave for the refectory when the main bell of the priory sounded the tocsin, its ominous clanging proclaiming that some great danger threatened. The tolling pounded like a drum, drawing all the brothers and guests out of the refectory, church and chambers.

At first all was confusion with bobbing sconce torches illuminating the night. Doors and windows were flung open. People shouted questions. Cranston appeared. He had returned to his usual mood of the roaring boy; sword drawn, he shouted out a spate of questions. Prior Anselm and the almoner Brother Paschal emerged out of the darkness to whisper to Cranston, encouraging the coroner to impose silence and order. This was swiftly achieved. Paschal, his face white as snow, eyes agitated, beckoned with fumbling fingers for the prior and others to follow him down the stone-paved passageways. Anselm led the way. Cresset torches blazed from their sconces on either side of the iron-bound door leading into the guesthouse. Athelstan felt a cold, wrenching dread. Paschal's face told him everything. Some horror lurked within. The murderous spirit which had taken up residence in Blackfriars had struck again.

'This business,' Athelstan whispered to himself, 'will never be over until you are trapped and slaughtered like the wild beast you are . . .'

'Brother Athelstan, what did you say?'

'It is not relevant now, Father Prior. I simply dread what awaits us.'

They entered the guesthouse. Paschal opened a door to what Athelstan knew to be Fieschi's chamber and beckoned them in. Athelstan went first and stared around. Candles burnt fiercely, their flames dancing in the pools of blood creeping across the stone-paved floor. All three Italians lay sprawled in death: Procurator Fieschi on his back, Cassian on his left side and, a short distance away, Isidore, slightly propped up, his head resting against the wall. All three had their eyes open in the glassy stare of death. The sheer horror of the room lay in its hideous contrast: a monastic cell, its walls adorned with crucifixes and painted cloths, a set of Ave beads hanging from a hook above the bed. Coffers and chests stood around, their lids half-open. Candles provided a glowing light whilst perfuming the air with their smoke, yet this was also the devil's banqueting hall. Three Dominican priests had been struck down, each one hit in the chest by a stout, feathered crossbow bolt.

'To the heart of each,' Athelstan murmured as, carrying a candlestick, he moved from corpse to corpse. He murmured prayers, trying to ignore the sightless, dead stare of the victims, faces shocked that their lives had been snatched brutally away in a matter of heartbeats.

Prior Anselm said he would anoint all three corpses once they had been removed. He begged Athelstan to continue his examination and the friar nodded in agreement. Hugh, Matthias and John arrived. Cranston, guarding the doorway with drawn sword, allowed them in. The gate-keeper immediately reported that both he and Hugh had glimpsed intruders garbed like Earthworms near the curtain wall.

'Moving shadows flitting through the dusk,' Hugh said. He gestured at the victims and shook his head. 'May heaven curse whoever did this. Shall we—'

'No, leave them here,' Athelstan instructed.

'Why should Earthworms enter Blackfriars?' Prior Anselm demanded. 'The revolt is over, crushed. Why murder three innocent Dominicans, guests from Italy who have nothing to do with the grievances of the English peasantry?'

Cranston had now joined Athelstan, kneeling on the other side of Fieschi's corpse. 'Perhaps,' he suggested, 'the Earthworms came looking for someone else, slipping like midnight wraiths through the priory. Perhaps they came here by accident and found the three brothers in council. The Earthworms are not known for their love of foreigners, as a number of poor Flemings found to their cost over the last few days.' Cranston's face was now only inches from the death-bearing bolt embedded deep in Fieschi's chest. 'Moreover,' he continued, 'this barb and the others are identical to those used by the Earthworms. Go out into the bailey, you will find similar relics of their attack.' He got to his feet. 'They may be fleeing for their lives, but that doesn't make the Earthworms less bitter or dangerous. They will not have forgotten their defeat here. Who knows, perhaps they thought Thibault's daughter Isabella, even Thibault himself, still sheltered in Blackfriars.'

Athelstan simply nodded his acknowledgement and stared around the death chamber. 'Who found them?' he asked.

'I did.' Paschal stepped forward. 'I noticed none of our Italian guests had joined the brothers in the refectory, so I came over here. I knocked. The door was off the latch. I pushed it open and saw what you did, Brother Athelstan. A heinous abomination here in our own mother house. Father Prior, what are we going to say to the Minister General?'

'We shall deal with that in God's own time,' Athelstan declared. 'And I mean God's own time.' He fought to keep his poise, to betray no hint of the suspicions bubbling deep in his heart. Life was dangerous enough, he did not wish to entice the demons out of the shadows. 'Father Prior,' Athelstan fought to keep his voice strong, 'I beg you to allow me to do what I must, to go where I wish, to speak to whomever I choose.' He indicated that Cranston and Anselm should join him outside. Once they had done so, he crossed the yard to the church. It was now empty and dark, the shadows lengthening, the candle flames guttering out in their last burst of life.

'Brother?'

Athelstan crossed himself. 'I am in mortal danger. I hunt the pernicious, yes, even the diabolic cause of all the wickedness which has erupted here in our mother house. To be honest with you, the assassin is winning, like a ship making headway against the wind.'

'What do you mean, Brother?' Cranston queried.

'So close.' Athelstan held up his forefinger and thumb. 'So close is this demon in human form to ending all this on his terms rather than ours. Believe me, if I am killed and murdered, everything that has happened here will remain the murkiest of mysteries. I recognise that and so does the assassin. Accordingly, Sir John, I need Flaxwith and his burly boys here with me. Father Prior, only you – and I mean only you – will prepare my food and bring it to me. Do you understand?' They both agreed.

'This business of Edward II—'

'Father Prior,' Athelstan interjected, 'that must be left for now. Disappointed though they may be, the Holy Father and His Grace the King must, someday, try another path into that tangled mystery. Sir John, please ask Thibault if I could have the dedicated services of Master John Ferrour; I need him close to me.' Athelstan peered through the gloom. 'Needs must when the devil drives, so it's best to use the children of this world in situations such as this rather than the children of the light.'

Both prior and coroner stared at the little friar standing so close to them, though they could see his mind was far away. Athelstan swiftly grasped each of them by the wrist. 'You are with me on this?'

'We are,' both answered.

'In which case, let us begin. We have much to do.'

Athelstan, as he put it, 'set up camp' in Brother Roger's chamber. The prior had seen to the swift repair of the door, securing it with a sound lock, bolts and clasps. A day later John Ferrour came sauntering into the cell, humming a drinking song. Athelstan continued to write. Ferrour sat on a stool then leaned forward. He snatched up

261

a quill pen and tickled Athelstan's nose as the friar pored over a manuscript listing the names of Dominicans at their house in Oxford. Ferrour noticed that Athelstan had written on the same manuscript, 'Brother Eadred, chaplain of Newgate', 'Brother Eadred at the royal court', 'Brother Eadred, prior in Oxford', 'Brother Eadred, Provincial of the Order'. These titles had been scored time and time again and Athelstan seemed totally absorbed by them. Ferrour leaned forward and tickled the friar's nose for the second time. Athelstan sneezed, glanced up and grinned.

'Some wine, Master Ferrour?'

'No, I had best not,' the sly-eyed clerk replied. 'God knows what is tainted in this place and what is not.'

'And does that judgement include the human souls who lodge here?'

'We are all sinners before the Lord, Brother Athelstan.'

'And some more than others, Master Ferrour, but, as Aristotle said, what is good for the body is good for the soul, especially exercise.' Athelstan got to his feet and continued, 'I was educated here. I came as a scholar, as a postulant, then as a novice, an eager, bright-eyed young friar, and eventually a priest. Blackfriars is my home, but now I have to see it through different eyes. As you know, hideous murders have been perpetrated here by an assassin skilled in swift and silent killing.'

'You think I am a killer, don't you?' Ferrour retorted, staring at Athelstan out of the corner of his eye. 'I can see that. You hunt murderers,

262

assassins. Sometimes I catch you watching me, Brother, as if you are weighing me in the balance. You suspect I am a dagger man?'

'If the cowl fits, Master Ferrour, wear it. To be honest, I don't know who you really are or what you might be. You are a changeling, aren't you? You are all things to all men.' Athelstan leaned closer and peered into this cunning man's eyes. 'I wager you kill because you are paid to. You see yourself as a retainer, your masters' servant. In this case, John of Gaunt and his henchman Master Thibault.'

'*Voluntas Principis habet vigorem legis,*' Ferrour replied. 'The will of the Prince has force of law, is that not so?'

'Whatever your masters want?' Athelstan queried. 'Thibault wanted you here and at the Tower during the revolt, didn't he?'

'Of course, Brother.'

'Gaunt and Thibault were not averse to certain members of the council being purged, carted off and executed, slaughtered like cattle. You and your masters did nothing to prevent that.'

'Master Thibault mourns their deaths but he is no hypocrite. In a way men like Legge and Hailes deserved to die: their insistence on the poll tax led to these present troubles.'

'Ah!' Athelstan replied. 'I was correct when we spoke before. I truly see which way this is proceeding. The revolt is crushed. Thibault and his master are now returning to London. They will cast themselves as leaders of reform. Very, very good.' Athelstan shook his head in mock wonder. 'You watched all that develop and, of

263

course, you had to keep a sharp eye on young Isabella, not to mention Henry of Derby. Tell me, how did you gain such influence amongst the Upright Men? Of course,' Athelstan tapped the side of his head, 'you posed as their champion – Thibault's creature, but the spy who really worked for them. You have a talent for intrigue, Master Ferrour.'

'I love it more than any game of hazard, Brother.'

'Beware of mistakes! The devious throw of a loaded dice.'

'It's all part of the game, Brother, the sheer thrill of living by your wits and yet, at the same time, controlling matters. You are no different. You love danger, don't you? The hunt, the satisfaction of reaching a logical conclusion.'

'True, but most importantly, of seeing justice done. Well,' Athelstan gestured around, 'as I said, this is my house, it's as if I have forgotten it. I want to walk Blackfriars again but I need you to guard my back.'

He led Ferrour into the great priory kitchen, a hive of activity with servants busy at oven, chopping board, spit and churn. Athelstan opened the cellarer's door and led Ferrour down the steep, slippery steps into the catacomb of cellars, dungeons and passageways which ran beneath Blackfriars.

'A relic of earlier years,' Athelstan declared, glancing over his shoulder at Ferrour trailing behind him. The friar took a tinder out of his belt wallet and lit two pitch torches. He watched the flames greedily take hold before handing one of the sconces to Ferrour, then led him deeper into the darkness. Athelstan felt comfortable. Ferrour was a street fighter, a man of war skilled in combat. Ferrour was the best protection, Athelstan quietly reassured himself, against the murderous spirit which haunted Blackfriars and would strike at Athelstan if given the opportunity. They went deep into the labyrinth of tunnels, Athelstan explaining that these rooms and caverns had now been abandoned and lay unused due to the constant encroachment of river water and development of buildings above ground.

'Like a walk through the underworld,' Ferrour declared, his voice echoing eerily along the groined, vaulted passageway where cobwebs stretched like nets and all kinds of vermin scurried underfoot. If he was honest with himself, Athelstan found it a truly soul-chilling place. They passed caverns lit by the dancing flames of the torches, strange sounds echoing as if ghosts flocked behind them, watching their every move, and enclaves where goods and purveyance had once been stored, now full of broken, rotting items. Athelstan passed one opening and hurriedly stepped back.

'Did you see that?' he whispered.

'I certainly did, like a chantry chapel!'

They went back and entered the enclave. The floor was cleanly swept. An altar table stood against the far wall, the plaster above it decorated with insignia: a crown in chains and a double-headed eagle.

'All this has recently been cleaned,' Athelstan

murmured. He pointed to an engraving on the wall. 'Master Ferrour, can you tell me, the double-headed eagle, what does it mean?'

'It relates to Peter Gaveston, the king's lover, his so-called brother. When he was created Earl of Cornwall, Gaveston adopted the double-headed eagle as his escutcheon, his coat of arms. I suspect the crown in chains is a reference to the imprisoned Edward II.'

'How do you know all this?'

'I work for Master Thibault. I am well versed in heraldry. I advise him on who is present at court, which retinue has ridden into the Tower or Westminster.'

Athelstan raised a hand in acknowledgement and stared round the strange little chapel, crudely decorated to the memory of a long-dead king: the shrine was clean, swept and recently tended by some adherent of Edward II. Prior Anselm had declared that Blackfriars had once been a hotbed of intrigue for the deposed king. It was inevitable that this would be reflected in the life and buildings of the mother house, through inscriptions in secret shrines such as this. Nevertheless, Dominican support for Edward II was at least two generations away. Over fifty years had passed, causes were forgotten as memories dimmed. This was different, clear evidence that somebody at Blackfriars still nourished allegiance to Edward II and his memory. Ferrour moved restlessly. 'Brother Athelstan, what are we doing here? This is a hall of ghosts, a chamber full of the seething past.'

'And one which has spilled out into murderous

activity, Master Ferrour. I agree, it's time to go, though I now need you in the guesthouse.'

They left the labyrinth and made their way across to the chamber where Alberic had been murdered. At Athelstan's request a servant brought the concave looking glass wrapped in a velvet cloth from the Prior's strong box. Athelstan inspected the device, moving it around until he became accustomed to it before peering through the glass, scrutinising the chamber door. The lock and bolts had been replaced, but even so, Athelstan could detect spots of blood, small drops in the grooves of the oaken door.

'What are you looking for, Brother?'

'What I've found,' Athelstan replied enigmatically. 'Master Ferrour, you are a fighting man, yes?' He edged closer. 'You are swift in parry and thrust?' Ferrour, eyes watchful, visibly tensed. 'So even a thrust like this . . .' Athelstan abruptly lunged at Ferrour's chest. Ferrour blocked the intended blow with one hand, the other immediately falling to the hilt of his dagger.

'*Pax et bonum.*' Athelstan lifted his hands in a gesture of peace. 'No harm, my friend. You have just proved something I deeply suspect. Anyway, it's a busy day for you, Master Ferrour. I want you and Flaxwith to escort me to Whitefriars, just a short walk, but,' Athelstan shrugged, 'still dangerous.'

They left Blackfriars within the hour and entered the deserted, filthy lanes which wound across the ward to the house of the Carmelites. Cranston was correct, Athelstan reflected. A great silence had descended on the city. Windows and doors were firmly locked and shuttered. Men-at-arms and mounted archers patrolled everywhere. Chains had been raised across the entrances to different streets. They passed two crossroads where at least fifteen scaffolds had been erected and from each arm hung a tarred corpse whilst severed heads decorated the nearby signposts.

'The moths of menace devour all words,' Ferrour quoted the lines of a poem, 'and worms have swallowed the song of man.' As if to challenge such a doleful description, an audacious itinerant leech, garbed in a red and gold spangled gown, a conical hat of the same colour on his head, climbed on to a barrel which blocked the lane to proudly proclaim: 'Bloodletting is to be avoided for a fortnight before Lammas and for thirty-five days afterwards, because then all poisonous things fly and injure man greatly. This includes poisonous spiders. Now, black snails fried in a hot pan are a great cure, along with this elixir I offer you . . .'

Flaxwith, frustrated at the wait, pushed his way through the gawping soldiers, kicked the barrel over and attempted to punch the leech. This self-proclaimed miracle worker, however, was as swift as any lurcher. He dodged Flaxwith's blow and fled up an alleyway.

'London will soon recover its soul and voice,' Athelstan murmured. 'Ah well, gentlemen,' he indicated with his hands, 'Whitefriars awaits.'

They crossed the grey cobbled square which stretched in front of the imposing entrance to the priory of the Carmelites. Usually this concourse was the haunt of malefactors, their age-old meeting place which dated back to a legend about three pilgrims who, many years ago, arrived on the site in great poverty and distress and, being about to perish out of sheer want, killed each other. The last survivor buried his fellows and then thrust himself into one of the graves they had prepared. He pulled the tombstone over himself but left it as it still was, ill-adjusted and slightly twisted. All three headstones had been absorbed into the curtain wall of Whitefriars. Legend had it that those who touched these three tombstones would never hang, which was why the place was frequently visited by London's tribes of malefactors. As customary with every visitor to Whitefriars, Athelstan touched the tombstones for good luck then pulled on the calling bell and waited for the postern door to be opened.

A lay brother welcomed them and assured Athelstan that the guardian, Prior Henry Catesby, was waiting to see him in the Exchequer chamber, a long, low-beamed room not far from the main entrance.

'Brother Athelstan?' Prior Catesby extended his hand in welcome. 'How can I assist?'

'First, Father Prior, I need to speak to two of your brethren. Secondly, I must meet your apothecary, who I understand is most skilled.'

'As is yours in Blackfriars.'

'I need a second opinion, a true judgement,' Athelstan replied quickly. 'And thirdly . . .' He took a scroll out of the deep pocket of his mantle and handed it to Ferrour. 'If Father Prior here provided you with two sturdy coursers, how swiftly could you be in Oxford before travelling on to Berkeley and then returning here?'

Ferrour pulled a face. 'A day here, a day there, then journeying back. It depends on whatever business you wish to pursue, but it should not be long. After all, the weather is good and dry, the lanes and roads will be sound underfoot. The sun rises early and sets late, whilst the roadside taverns are ready for the pilgrim trade. In all, five days, but,' Ferrour leaned closer, 'why from here,' he whispered, 'why not from Blackfriars?'

'Because, my friend, that would be highly dangerous to me, to you and the business in hand. Believe me, Father Prior, Master Ferrour, I speak with the full authority of the Crown and Holy Mother Church. What I intend to do with your help is resolve a very grave matter, an issue of life or death. So, Father Prior, if you could furnish Master Ferrour here with provender, two saddled horses and some coins that would be helpful. Rest assured, Sir John Cranston, the Lord High Coroner of London, will reimburse all expense. Master Ferrour, now you truly do become a courier, but you must be back within at least six days.'

A week later on the feast of St Peter and St Paul, founders of the Universal Church in Rome, Athelstan asked for a formal colloquium to be held in Prior Anselm's parlour in Blackfriars. He had taken both his superior and Sir John into his confidence, even though his revelations had cut the Prior to his heart, so gravely, Athelstan wondered if Anselm would suffer a seizure. But the moment passed and the prior gave his consent for matters to proceed. Certain people were to be secretly brought into the Dominican house and kept waiting in a nearby chamber. Flaxwith and all his bailiffs would be in attendance, as would John Ferrour. Thibault's man had visited the Dominican house in Oxford before riding on to the beautiful nunnery of St Monica, which lay in the lush countryside only a few miles from Berkeley. Ferrour had brought back the information Athelstan needed. The friar now believed it was time to move the pieces on the board and so trap his adversaries. He had ensured throughout all his preparations that he'd remained well protected. At the same time, he had publicly peddled the tale that he could not resolve the mayhem at Blackfriars and was only waiting to return to St Erconwald's once his parishioners considered it safe for him to do so.

Athelstan was now determined to shed all such mummery and move resolutely to a conclusion. He had risen early that morning, washed, shaved, donned fresh robes and celebrated his Jesus mass in the same chantry chapel where he had been attacked. During the consecration he had invoked all the power of the Holy Spirit and lit three tapers in the Lady Chapel. He had then gone to the refectory and, after breaking his fast, had come to the parlour to prepare for the coming confrontation. He laid out the contents of his chancery satchel on the council table.

As the others joined him, Athelstan deliberately avoided either catching anyone's gaze or greeting them directly. He did not wish to betray himself.

All those summoned came in and took their seats: Prior Anselm, Cranston and Ferrour, as well as Hugh the infirmarian, Matthias and John the gatekeeper. At last all was ready. Flaxwith, standing on guard, closed the door. Athelstan rapped the table top and took away a linen cloth which covered a platter with the remains of the 'St Dominic's Blessing' found in the pocket of Pernel's gown.

'You,' Athelstan began, pointing at Brother John, 'are the gatekeeper here at Blackfriars. You informed me that the old woman found drowned, floating near the water-gate, never entered Blackfriars. Now that old woman was Pernel the Fleming; well, that's what she called herself. You, Brother John, however, knew her true identity, which is why you and your accomplices here drowned her.' Athelstan paused for effect. 'You are all about to earn the wages of wickedness. You are men who are springs without water, murderous mists driven by a storm. Believe me, the blackest darkness is reserved for you. You are assassins to the bone. You will kill and kill again to protect yourselves and your secrets. Nothing can change you. About the likes of you the Book of Proverbs is true: you are dogs who return to their vomit, hogs washed clean which go back to wallow in your murderous mud.'

Brother John just sat gaping in astonishment at Athelstan's passionate outburst. He swallowed hard and raised his hands, fingers fluttering.

'Accomplices!' Hugh exclaimed. 'Athelstan, have you taken leave of your senses?'

'Pernel was not Pernel,' Athelstan intoned.

'Brother John is not Brother John. You are not Hugh the infirmarian, nor you Matthias the secretarius. Brother John,' Athelstan talked swiftly, taking advantage of the stunned silence, 'you are Giles Daventry, lay brother in the Dominican order, and you,' he pointed at the infirmarian, 'are no less a person than Thomas Dunheved, whilst Matthias here is your blood brother Stephen.'

'This is ridiculous!' the infirmarian shouted.

'Preposterous!' Matthias echoed. Both men made to rise. Athelstan noticed that Brother John the gatekeeper remained shocked in silence as the pretence and masks, assumed so cleverly decades ago, abruptly and swiftly crumbled.

'The Dunheveds,' said Hugh, his face creased in anger, 'are buried in God's Acre.'

'You know that's a lie. Two prisoners who died in Newgate lie beneath those headstones.'

'In God's name,' Hugh shouted, 'must we listen to this farrago of lies?'

'Silence!' Prior Anselm shouted. 'Silence,' he repeated. 'Brother Athelstan, lay your charge, then we will listen to any reply. Until then, all three of you,' the prior's gaze swept the accused, 'will remain silent.'

'Oh, by the way,' Cranston intervened, 'let us deal with the pretence.' The coroner tapped his own war-belt lying on the table before him. 'Those games you indulged in before the rebels attacked Blackfriars, you portrayed yourselves as unskilled and unaccustomed with weapons, be it the crossbow or a sword.' Cranston smiled grimly. 'You are experienced enough. You are

273

knowledgeable about sieges: you heard the Earthworms bring in carts and, like any seasoned campaigner, you recognised that these would be converted into battering rams. You said so yourself.' Cranston pointed at the accused. 'You are men of war. For the moment, I will not search you for any concealed dagger or hidden knife. However, Flaxwith, myself, and not to forget Master Ferrour here, will strike if violence is offered.'

The three accused refused to meet Athelstan's gaze but moved restlessly on their chairs. Athelstan realised that all three were in shock. For the first time in years, decades, they were being confronted with who they really were.

'Athelstan,' Anselm ordered quietly, 'proceed with your indictment.'

'Yes, do so,' the infirmarian retorted, ignoring Prior Anselm's objection. 'Let's hear this tattle and tale, this legion of lies.'

'Thomas and Stephen Dunheved, you were born in Warwickshire,' Athelstan began. 'You come of good yeoman stock and were selected to serve as pages in the household of Peter Gaveston. You, like your master, were greatly influenced by the Dominican order, a passion shared by Edward of Caernarvon, both as Prince of Wales and as King of England. Indeed, as you may well know,' Athelstan sifted the documents on the table before him, 'on one occasion Edward warned an opponent of the Dominican order that if he did not desist in his actions, he would rue it all the days of his life. Anyway,' Athelstan continued briskly, 'Gaveston was executed, but

274

you remained firmly locked in your loyalty and allegiance to both the memory of the dead favourite and Edward II. Indeed, Thomas, you were and you are fanatical in such loyalty. This is stronger than any sense of duty to your fellow man, to your order, to your church or to your God. I've heard about assassins who live in Outremer, in the mountains of Syria. They owe complete loyalty to their master, the Old Man of the Mountain. Thomas, you are of the same ilk, the same heart, mind and soul.'

Athelstan stared at the infirmarian. Only then did he notice a shift in those clever eyes, as if the real soul of this fanatic was on the verge of breaking through.

'Indeed, in many ways, what a waste! I recognise that. You were once my master, my teacher. Thomas Dunheved, I will not insult you. You are highly intelligent, deeply gifted and most resourceful. Little wonder you won the attention of a king. You entered the Dominican order and excelled yourself in both philosophy and logic. A master of the schools, you were ordained as a Dominican priest and immediately selected and confirmed as King Edward II's confessor and spiritual advisor. Despite your youth, you advanced rapidly in royal favour. I reckon that when your master was deposed, you had barely reached your twenty-first summer, a young, very vigorous man totally devoted to your king. You were, of course, joined by your brother Stephen as well as your faithful shadow, the lay brother Giles Daventry, known to us now as Brother John the gatekeeper.'

'You are very much mistaken,' the secretarius protested.

'Silence!' Anselm warned.

'I shall cut to the quick,' Athelstan explained, 'and proceed swiftly to the heart of this matter. Thomas Dunheved, you were absent from this country in 1326 when Mortimer and Isabella toppled your master. However, you returned with a vengeance and organised a coven deep in the woods around Berkeley. You received support and sympathy from others, and from one place in particular, the nunnery of St Monica deep in the Vale of Berkeley.' Athelstan gestured at Ferrour. 'I made simple enquiries there, and yes, stories and legends abound about how the infamous Dunheved brothers sheltered there in 1327. Apparently, a young novice Agnes Tyrell fell in love with you and fled the nunnery in your company.' Athelstan sighed. 'She received little in return, didn't she?' The infirmarian simply blinked and glanced away, yet, for a few heartbeats, Athelstan caught a glimmer of sadness in his opponent's eyes. 'To return to the mystery of Berkeley, in a word, you three knew the truth of the situation. Edward II did escape that fortress. However, that does not really concern us now. What is relevant, in the most deadly fashion, is your ruthless opposition to the fate of Edward II being open even to discussion.'

'Why? Why should I object to it? Why should anybody object to it?'

'Because, Brother Thomas, and that's who you really are, you and your companions see yourselves as the keeper of the secret. You cherish it

276

as you would a shrine. You also cherish the true whereabouts of Edward II's burial place. Do you know what I suspect?' Athelstan pointed to all three of them. 'That you find it rather amusing that people visit St Peter's Abbey in Gloucester, go on pilgrimages there, and yet it is all a sham, a charade.'

'And where is he buried?'

'Oh, don't worry, Brother, I shall come to that by and by.' Athelstan glanced around. Everyone in the room was now listening intently to this twisting, tortuous tale which had brought about the violent deaths of so many people. 'Edward II definitely escaped. You took him from his captors, Isabella and Mortimer, and buried a look-alike in his stead, which accounts for why no royal official or physician was allowed near the corpse, and why the dead king's remains were not transferred to the royal mausoleum at Westminster.'

'But there was speculation,' Ferrour intervened, 'there *is* speculation, even I know that, about the true whereabouts of Edward II.'

'Ah yes,' Athelstan replied, 'but only as a tanta-lising mystery. What the Dunheveds would regard as unacceptable is the King's escape being proved to be a matter of fact.'

'It would only be a matter of time,' Cranston intervened, 'before people began to ask: if Edward II is not buried in Gloucester and there is no tomb to him in Sancto Alberto di Butrio, where is he actually buried?'

'Precisely,' Athelstan agreed. 'Anyway, in 1327 you freed Edward II and took him out of this

277

kingdom. You wandered Europe but eventually settled in or around the abbey of Sancto Alberto di Butrio in the diocese of Vercelli in northern Italy.' Athelstan shrugged. 'We know the details about that, the meeting with Fieschi's uncle and the constant rumours that Edward had escaped there. Now, Brother Thomas, for reasons best known to yourselves, you came back to England in 1330. I suspect the reason for this was money.

'When Edward and Despenser fled to Wales after Isabella and Mortimer landed in Essex, they took a great treasure hoard with them, and according to Brother Roger, this has never been recovered. Of course the deposed king would know where it had been hidden. I admit that is just speculation. What is a fact is that you were betrayed, arrested and lodged in Newgate prison, though that proved to be no real danger. You would refuse to talk. You are both priests who could plead benefit of clergy and so invoke the full protection of both Holy Mother Church and, just as importantly, the power of the Dominican order. Prior Anselm here will bear witness to the fact that in those years Blackfriars, indeed the entire Dominican order in this kingdom, fervently supported Edward II and nourished a deep antagonism towards Isabella and Mortimer.

'There is a chantry chapel here which boasts the insignia of a crown in chains, a reference to the captured Edward II, as well as the two-headed eagle of that king's lover, Gaveston of Cornwall, which may well be your work, Thomas, or some other adherent of your coven. We wandered the cellars beneath Blackfriars,' Athelstan smiled,

'Master Ferrour and I. We found your secret shrine.' He paused. He just wished he could provoke his adversaries into some sort of outburst. 'Thomas, Thomas, Thomas,' he murmured. 'You taught me so well! To observe, to list, to analyse, to search for what is possible, to determine what is probable and so reach a conclusion.'

'Little Brother Athelstan,' the infirmarian retorted, 'who would have thought . . .'

'Yes,' Athelstan replied. 'Who would have thought years ago that I would confront you like this, yet, and I am not being arrogant, you feared me, didn't you? That's why all three of you tried to kill me. But, I hurry on. Let us return to Newgate, Blackfriars and, above all, Brother Eadred, who plays a prominent role in all of this, though he has now gone to God.' Athelstan glanced swiftly at the secretarius, who was not as calm as his brother, whilst Brother John also was becoming visibly agitated.

'Brother Eadred,' Athelstan continued, 'was a member of the community here. A fervent supporter, I am sure, of Edward II. He was also chaplain in Newgate. I have held a similar post, as have others. Anyway, you were lodged there, but Eadred arranged for your escape and sent the corpses of two strangers – and God knows there would be enough of those in Newgate – garbed in Dominican robes, to be buried in God's Acre here at Blackfriars. The published cause of death being what many die of in Newgate: jail fever, the sweating sickness. Anyway, the two corpses were brought back and swiftly disposed of. For all I know, in 1330 there were other Dominicans

279

only too willing to cooperate with Eadred. Oh, and of course,' Athelstan tapped the manuscripts before him, 'Eadred will reappear in our story, but not for another twenty-eight years, when he became prior of our house in Oxford, and indeed, provincial of the entire Dominican order in this kingdom.'

'You discovered all this?' Ferrour asked, pouring himself a goblet of white wine. 'Is that why you have been closeted . . .'

'No,' Athelstan replied. 'Some of this work was begun by Alberic and developed by Brother Roger, who researched the secret life of the Dunheveds – and after 1330, it certainly did become very secret.' Athelstan paused. 'Eadred!' He pointed to Ferrour, 'You eavesdropped on Alberic the night he was murdered. He referred to St Alberto di Butrio, but what else did you hear?'

'I thought he said "I dread."' Ferrour's face creased into a smile. 'It's not that, it's Eadred! Alberic was talking about the Dominican who helped the Dunheveds . . .'

'Of course he was,' Athelstan agreed. 'Anyway, Brother Thomas, after your escape from Newgate you rejoined your master. I suspect you spent a great deal of your time in Northern Italy. The years rolled by. Members of your group died. I am sure you dealt ruthlessly with any dissent or opposition. Now one member of your coven was the novice Agnes Tyrell from the nunnery of St Monica. She was probably infatuated with Thomas Dunheved, the passionate Dominican priest. You eventually rejected her. Agnes was left to her own devices. She slid, as so many poor women do, out of the light and into the shadows. I suspect you deserted her in Ghent or some other Flemish town, which turned her wits and seriously disturbed the humours of her mind. She eventually became the woman I knew, Pernel the Fleming, who chattered on about former days and tried to restore her youthful looks by constantly dyeing her hair. Eventually she took ship to London and settled in Southwark.'

'I did not know her,' the infirmarian retorted.

'Yes, you did, and you killed her,' Athelstan declared. 'Now, poor Agnes' life and the truth behind it does not concern us, but her death certainly does, I shall come back to that by and by. After 1330,' he continued remorselessly, 'you, your brother and this man,' he gestured at the gatekeeper, 'stayed abroad with the deposed king. God knows the actual details of your lives. But, Thomas Dunheved, I suggest you honed your skills as an apothecary, a herbalist and a leech, whilst your brother became a most experienced clerk. Of course your main concern was Edward of Caernarvon.'

'Brother Athelstan,' Ferrour interrupted, 'if, as you allege, these three men spent decades in the company of a deposed king they so fervently supported, why did they not try to restore him to his dignity?'

'First,' Athelstan replied, 'only these three men knew the true physical, mental and spiritual state of Edward of Caernarvon after he had been deposed and imprisoned for at least a year. Was he injured, maimed, seriously hurt in mind and body? Secondly, did he want to be restored? I don't think so. He had been rejected by his wife and his elder son. Thirdly, do you really believe that the English crown would welcome him back with open arms? We all know that would not have happened. Thunder rages around the throne, and the Crown of England is fraught with all forms of danger. What reception would Edward of Caernarvon truly receive if he re-emerged at Westminster? Would he be dismissed as an imposter to be tried and executed? Would he be depicted as a madcap, fey-witted and moonstruck like Pernel? Would he be locked up in some hospital as a madman baying at the moon, where he would soon suffer some form of accident? Let us suppose that Edward of Caernarvon returned and was accepted for what he claimed to be. What then? England has its crowned king. Edward of Caernarvon would be rejected as a relict of the past. I suggest he would have gone back to prison where, I am sure, he would not have lived for long but would die suddenly of some fatal accident.'

'True enough,' Ferrour gestured. 'I accept what you say.'

'In 1357 matters changed. First,' Athelstan emphasised the points on his fingers, 'you had been absent from England for a long time, the reign of Mortimer was now dusty history. Secondly, Queen Isabella, the cause of Edward II's downfall, was ageing. I am sure you and your master wanted to confront her for one last time. Thirdly, perhaps Edward of Caernarvon himself was sickly: by 1358 the deposed king would be past his seventieth year and must have been readying himself for death. Fourthly, in England, Brother Eadred, formerly chaplain in Newgate and secret ally of the Dunheveds, had become provincial of the entire Dominican order in this kingdom as well as prior of our house in Oxford, where Gaveston, Edward II's great love, lies buried. It was time to return to England, and so you did.

'You visited Castle Rising in Norfolk, where Isabella and Edward met for the last time. A truly chilling meeting. Two souls who, thirty years earlier, had set the kingdom alight with civil war. Isabella must have always, and secretly with great dread, anticipated that such a meeting might take place. She knew the truth about the burial at Gloucester, about what lay in that lead-lined coffin and the true ownership of the heart she carried in her silver casket. Now what happened in the solar at Castle Rising on that freezing cold night does not concern us, though I suspect you,' Athelstan pointed at the infirmarian, 'fed the Queen secret poison which later bore fruit in a prolonged illness which ended in her death.

'After Castle Rising, you travelled to Oxford, where Prior Eadred welcomed you. Through subterfuge and trickery, you were admitted back into the Dominican order as Brothers Hugh, Matthias and John, who had been "journeying abroad", or so the entry reads. This was in the autumn of 1358. You settled down. No one would think it strange. Our order has houses all over Europe, its members travel, study, come and go . . .'

'True, true,' Prior Anselm murmured. 'You, Brother Athelstan, are a case in point. You belong to Blackfriars but you live in Southwark and, as you know, people come and go – some you know, some you do not – and, of course,' Anselm crossed himself, 'Brother Eadred, as prior and provincial, had the authority and the means to ensure no questions were asked.'

'No one,' Athelstan declared, 'would give you a second thought, nor about the poor man you lodged in the infirmary. Edward of Caernarvon had sickened. An old man, he died of his illness. Again, through the good offices of Prior Eadred, you had Edward's corpse buried beneath the same flagstone which cover the mortal remains of Peter Gaveston, the one and only love of that most unfortunate king.' Athelstan thumbed the manuscript before him. 'It is all here. How the community at Oxford welcomed these three friars from abroad. How they admitted a dying man, a fourth member of the group, into the infirmary there. Little did people realise that, after all the hurling days, Edward II's true last resting place was a Dominican friary in Oxfordshire.'

'But if their shrine is in Oxford,' Ferrour asked, 'why not stay there?'

'Because,' Prior Anselm replied, jabbing a finger at the infirmarian, 'they wanted to ensure no one became suspicious. They wanted to put some distance between themselves and their actual return to England, and again Eadred facilitated this. According to our records, all three came to Blackfriars in 1361 some twenty years ago. Such a move embedded them deeper back into our order. Moreover, Oxford is not far. A pleasant enough journey and again, if you scrutinise the records, the accused have made many return visits to Oxford.'

'Oh, the beauty of it!' Cranston intervened. 'The Dunheveds were last seen publicly in 1326; true, they were detained for a very short while in 1330, but then disappeared again for almost thirty years. Appearances change, memories die . . .'

The prior snapped his fingers. 'Continue, Athelstan.'

'So all is settled. Edward II disappears into history. A period of time best forgotten. Many of those involved in that hurling time are dead. Old causes vanish and new ones emerge. You have nothing to fear. All your secrets are safe until Procurator Fieschi and his delegation arrive in England and journey to London. For you, Fieschi and everyone and everything associated with him is anathema. You considered yourselves safe and secure. No one would either recognise or remember you for who you really are and what you were. After all, you had been absent from England for almost thirty years. Fifty-four years since the stirring times of Edward II's possible escape. No one could pose any real danger to you. Even before 1326 the Dunheveds had really been courtiers, cut off from the mainstream of Dominican life. The passage of time, the death of contemporaries and, above all, the manifest certainty that the Dunheveds had died in Newgate and were buried in Blackfriars along with all the help and assistance provided by Eadred, more than sealed your secret, except,' Athelstan held up a warning hand, 'there was always the terrible danger of someone investigating the mysterious circumstances of Edward II's death.'

Athelstan fingered the cuff of his robe. 'If you pluck the right loose thread and pull it hard enough the consequences can be very unexpected. Fieschi provoked the nightmare you always feared, of someone concentrating not so much on Edward II but on the men who freed him, especially the Dunheveds. I believe this was the path Alberic was pursuing with the help of Brother Roger. They found their loose thread: Brother Eadred. He was chaplain in Newgate at the time of the Dunheveds' imprisonment there. He was also a member of Blackfriars and an adherent of Edward II. So what do we have, this friend of the Dunheveds, chaplain of Newgate, being responsible for sending back the corpses of the Dunheved brothers who, despite their youth and vigour, had died so suddenly in prison? We move on in years to discover that same Eadred becomes prior of the Dominican house in Oxford and provincial of our entire order in this kingdom. Another coincidence. A study of the records of our house in Oxford reveals the arrival of "three Dominicans from abroad", as well as a fourth individual, who was part of their company, and who was placed in the infirmary there. The records describe how he sickened further, died and was buried beneath a particular flagstone in the friary church at Oxford.'

Athelstan spread his hands. 'At first, even second glance, there is little noteworthy here.

However, if you look a little closer, if you try to map a way through the problem, if you have the knowledge to connect the Eadred of Newgate in 1327 to the Eadred of Oxford in 1358, then perhaps you begin to wonder. Did the Dunheveds really die in Newgate? Did Eadred arrange that, as he arranged it so many years later when he admitted people back into the order at our house in Oxford?' Athelstan paused. 'Strange,' he mused.

'What is?' the infirmarian snapped.

'I mentioned Castle Rising and your murderous midnight pilgrimage there. You never challenged or contradicted me. You never questioned me or showed any interest in how I knew of that incident.'

'What does it matter? Just one more fable amongst many.'

'Was that your reply to Brother Alberic? He stumbled on something, didn't he, about the Dunheveds and their possible survival? He and Brother Roger truly believed Fieschi was looking in the wrong direction, the fate of Edward II, when they should have concentrated on the men who freed him. Did Alberic trap you, speak to you in Italian and elicit a response? All of you must be more than skilled in that tongue. All three of you visited him that fateful evening. You conversed in Italian, didn't you? Not that it would matter, because you intended to kill Alberic and, in doing so, terrify Fieschi away from his constant and unnecessary prying.

'In the end Alberic and his colleagues did not know who they were dealing with. They totally

287

underestimated you and your fanatical loyalty, your sheer ruthlessness. They thought they were in the company of fellow Dominicans, when in fact they were in a pack of ravenous wolves. However, to go back to the charge, you visited Brother Alberic. God knows what was discussed but I wager Alberic was suspicious. The confrontation with him would not have taken long. Master Ferrour here attempted to visit Alberic but heard voices speaking in Italian as well as a reference to the abbey of Sancto Alberto di Butrio and Eadred. He then decided to leave.'

'Alberic was young, strong, a former soldier,' the Gatekeeper declared, seemingly recovering from his shock. Athelstan noticed the change, as if the true soul of this man was emerging to confront the deadly challenge he faced. He was no longer the jovial old lay brother; his eyes now blazed with anger, his face was red, lips curled, mouth snarling. Athelstan quietly wondered if the gatekeeper was the one he could break first. 'Moreover,' the gatekeeper snarled, 'Alberic's chamber was locked and barred. Are you saying we now possess miraculous powers to pass through wood and stone?'

'No, but you do have a murderous energy. True, the problem you pose is twofold. First, how can a man like Alberic be so easily overcome without any sign of resistance on his part? Secondly, how could his assassins leave a chamber locked and barred from within? The solution depends on speed and, in this case, a fortuitous accident which only deepened the mystery.'

Athelstan rose. 'Master Ferrour, could you help

me, please?' Thibault's man got to his feet. Athelstan asked him to step away from the table, which he did. 'If I lunge like this,' Athelstan demonstrated, thrusting his hand towards Ferrour's chest, which the man blocked as he had before, 'I am checked, I am hindered but,' Athelstan beckoned Flaxwith and Cranston to join him, 'if Sir John and his noble bailiff seize Master Ferrour's arms swiftly, suddenly, then I lunge, driving a dagger deep into his chest, that is a different matter. Sir John, Master Flaxwith, please.' Each man seized a wrist. Ferrour struggled but Athelstan quickly proved how he could easily stab his victim.

'Remember,' Athelstan stepped back, gesturing at Ferrour to be released, 'our good friend here expected to be seized. Even so, I was successful. Brother Alberic, however, never did, which is how he was murdered. Each wrist was seized by one of you whilst a third struck swiftly with a dagger. I gather from Sir John that in the twilight world of London's wolfsheads, sudden murders are often carried out in such a fashion, two accomplices seizing the victim's arms, making him vulnerable to an abrupt thrust to the heart by a third.'

'And I suppose we left, leaving the door bolted and barred from within,' the infirmarian scoffed.

'For you that was most fortuitous. You stab your victim, you withdraw the dagger, it drops to the floor and you immediately leave the chamber. Your main concern is to get out without being seen. You do so leaving your victim. Alberic is in shock, swaying on his feet, not yet

289

fully aware that he has received his death wound. I saw Sudbury on Tower Hill trying to rise even though he had received the cruellest blow from a cleaver to the back of his head. Sir John, Master Ferrour, I appeal to you and others, haven't you seen men in battle who continue to walk, to fight, even though mortally wounded?'

'Certainly,' Cranston agreed. 'I have seen and heard of men losing a hand or arm, receiving a death thrust to the chest or belly, and still fighting on until they collapse.'

Ferrour and Flaxwith murmured their agreement.

'So it was here,' Athelstan declared. 'Remember, Alberic was once a soldier. Inside that chamber he stands shocked and fearful, doing the only thing he can, or thinks he can do, to protect himself. He turns the key and pulls across the bolts. Behind that door your victim is dying. He turns away, staggers forward and collapses. He has been silenced. The murderous mystery deepens and you are set on your path of destruction.'

Athelstan stared at the infirmarian, recalling earlier happier days, and wondered at the hidden depths, the twisting paths of the human soul. 'I thought,' Athelstan murmured softly, 'I really did, that you were my teacher, my friend. Indeed,' he gestured at the others, 'all three of you, but that did not count here. Only your secrets did. You had trained me well. You may have heard of my reputation elsewhere. It was difficult enough to have Fieschi prying and probing, but when it was your favourite scholar. I am not being arrogant but truthful. You viewed me as a real threat. So what were you trying to do in the beacon tower and then again in the church when you attacked me? Was that a warning? Or did you want to injure, kill me, silence me forever as you did poor Pernel?'

Athelstan did not wait for an answer; in fact, he did not care for it. The past was dead. Friendship did not exist. Memories had shrivelled: these three men were his implacable opponents. 'Yes, let us now deal with poor Pernel,' he continued. 'Her previous life is, as I described it, and like ours, full of coincidences. Time, as the great philosopher argued, also has its crossroads, a point where the past, present and future cross. Pernel had heard about the arrival of Fieschi and his party at Blackfriars. Naturally the name Fieschi evoked sharp memories from her own colourful past. She was confused but her desire to visit Blackfriars and meet this Fieschi was whetted first by my presence here and secondly Pernel's determination to inform me about the men of my parish being mysteriously abducted.

'She hurried across the river. She was welcomed by our gatekeeper and given a St Dominic Blessing, the usual token bestowed on any visitor or guest. Now, the Pernel who presented herself was not the lovely young novice Agnes who once fled from the nunnery of St Monica an eternity ago. Nevertheless, curiosity was stirred by Pernel's demand to see me as well as her enquiries about Fieschi. I suspect she was kept by herself whilst Brother John hurried away to inform his friends, Brother Hugh and Matthias his shadow. They arrived. Pernel, perhaps as would any woman once deeply in love and possibly still having the same feelings, recognised our infirmarian for who he truly really is, the great love of her life, the Dominican Thomas Dunheved.'

Athelstan paused. The accused had now become restless, heavy-lidded eyes half-closed, proof perhaps that the level of evidence rising against him and his confederates was becoming conclusive. 'All three of you met Pernel. All three of you decided on that poor, witless woman's murder, an easy enough task. Hapless and weak, you coaxed her down to a deserted part of the quayside near the water-gate. She is so overcome, Pernel proves to be extremely pliable. Once there it was so easy to tip her into the swirling river where she would have little or no chance of survival. The water would clog her face and weigh her down.'

'We could have been seen, I mean,' the gatekeeper stammered, 'if we were responsible. The old woman could have been a previous visitor, one we never met.' Athelstan glanced at the infirmarian and glimpsed his fleeting expression of anger: the gatekeeper had been stupid, he had foolishly responded to an allegation instead of just dismissing it.

'That old woman was a visitor to Blackfriars,' Athelstan insisted. 'She had received the usual token. Yet all of you maintained that you had never seen her before, which was a lie. You knew her very well. Pernel proved to be a true shock for you. You killed her. Later one of you, probably the gatekeeper, slipped across to Southwark to burn her cottage and so destroy any evidence of her past or possible links to the Dunheveds.'

Athelstan drummed his fingers on the table top. 'Oh, by the way, as I speak, your own chambers and possessions are being thoroughly searched by senior friars—' Athelstan broke off as all three made to rise. They only sat down when Cranston and Flaxwith drew their swords and shouted at them to stay.

'Hush now,' Athelstan mockingly soothed, pleased to see that he had at last ruffled the feathers of his opponents. 'Hush now,' he repeated. 'Pernel has gone to God, so now we must turn to Brother Roger. Let me emphasise. Fieschi's arrival here was the first real investigation into the death of Edward II since the parliament of 1330 over fifty years ago, when Mortimer fell from power and the young Edward III tried to discover what had happened to his father: that came to nothing. This was different. The past was unlocked and all kinds of ghosts jostled for attention. Brother Roger was expert at drawing these out. You knew he was extremely dangerous: his jovial demeanour, his rather pompous, scholarly manner masked a truly sharp mind and very keen wits.

'From the evidence I collected in his chamber, I would say that Brother Roger opened the path I am now following. He had already decided that Brother Eadred, chaplain at Newgate and later prior at Oxford, was an important key to all this mystery. Roger left the fate of Edward II to history. He was more interested in those Dominicans who played an important part in the crisis years of 1327 to 1330. He drew up list after list of individuals. Many of them are dead, in some cases just disappeared. Brother Roger was particularly interested in the Dunheveds. You discovered that. Now,' Athelstan rolled back the sleeves of his gown, 'Roger became very, very busy. He loved what he was doing, but like Brother Alberic he totally underestimated your ruthlessness.

'On the night he died he went to the kitchen for his wine and favourite dish of nuts. Paschal the almoner kindly carried them to our chronicler's chamber. He left and Brother Roger locked and bolted himself in. According to reports, no one visited him that night.' Athelstan smiled grimly. 'Or so Brother John, our so-called honest gatekeeper, reported, for he claimed he was working in the cloisters at the time. Of course that was a lie. You three move as one. Young Isabella was correct when she called you the midnight clover. You are a three-faced demon who enjoy the same murderous soul. On that night our gatekeeper certainly lived up to his title. He watched and guarded whilst his master Thomas Dunheved came tripping like Judas through the cloisters.

'Brother Roger may have had his suspicions, though I am not too sure about that. Perhaps on that particular evening the chronicler was pleased that Brother Hugh the infirmarian was passing by and decided to stop and have a chat. Hugh, or to be truthful, Thomas Dunheved, was invited into Brother Roger's chamber. You act all charming, cordial and friendly. You pick up the bowl of nuts, take a few and eat them, and at the same time you hand a few to Brother Roger. Ordinary actions that don't even deserve a second glance or thought. However,' Athelstan breathed in, 'you are a skilled herbalist, leech and apothecary. You perfected such arts during your years in northern Italy. I have consulted with a similar *peritus*, a colleague who also has extensive knowledge of herbs, shrubs and plants: Brother Hubert, infirmarian and apothecary in the Carmelite house at Whitefriars. He agreed with me: there is a small nut called the abrin seed which is most deadly in its effect once the shell has been broken.

'On that particular evening I suspect you had two or three abrin seeds concealed in the palm of your hand. You sat, you charmed and you gossiped. You pick up the bowl to share its contents with Brother Roger and, as you do so, slip in one or more of those abrin seeds with the rest. Roger, garrulous as ever, chews and swallows. The sin is committed. Murder has been perpetrated as the noxious potion begins its race through the humours of his body. You rise, bid him goodnight and leave. You know that your later scrutiny of his corpse will be equally false and hypocritical. Roger locks and bolts the door behind you but you know he will never live to see it open.'

Athelstan pointed across the room. 'Brother Hubert at Whitefriars is waiting to be called, if necessary, along with two lay brothers from the same house.' Athelstan turned quickly as the gatekeeper moved abruptly. 'Yes, you have it.' Athelstan gestured at him. 'The same two who escorted Odo Brecon here. Prior Anselm thought he had done this most discreetly, asking the widow woman Benedicta to meet Odo Brecon at the gatehouse and escort him in. You, of course, heard about this. You probably watched Brecon arrive. You then immediately hurried after the lay brothers, drew them into conversation and learned the identity of the old man they had brought. Back you hasten to your masters here. They knew full well who Brecon was and again, although you are three, you act as one. It would be easy for you to seize a crossbow and bolt, position yourself, take aim and loose whilst the other two stood on guard. I agree with Sir John, all three of you are as proficient in arms as any hobelar or man-at-arms, be it sword or arbalest. You probably bought such armaments in the city or, as Sir John said, picked up weapons after the rebels had been beaten off.'

Athelstan joined his hands together. 'You are killers. I do wonder, I really do, if you had anything to do with the Earthworms attacking Blackfriars? After all, wouldn't it be appropriate for the rebels of London to do your murderous work for you?' He leaned across the table, jabbing his finger. 'Did you send secret messages to the Earthworms? Did you plot that during their attack, Fieschi and his party, not to mention myself and Sir John, would be barbarously cut down? I am convinced you truly hated Fieschi.

He had turned your world upside down. He threatened to destroy all you had worked on for decades. He would bring everything to nothing, and for what? No one really gives a fig about Edward II. Fieschi arrived here because King Richard is a dreamer and wants to have a saint in his family history whilst the Pope in Rome is desperate for recognition.'

'Your last statement is probably the only true one,' the secretarius murmured, his face twisted in a smirk.

'Fieschi and his companions didn't die in that attack, and you were increasingly alarmed at what was happening. Pernel had suddenly appeared from the murky past; Odo Brecon came hobbling through the doors of history; and you must have wondered how many more there might be. You decided on a course of action which would be brutal and final. You would kill Fieschi and his two companions as an act of revenge as well as to bring the entire matter to an end. If Fieschi and his comrades were massacred it would take years for the Pope to arrange another embassy, select the envoys and despatch them to England to begin the entire process again. Once the brutal murder of Fieschi and his entourage became public knowledge, the Pope would find few willing to assume such a post. You were confident that you would escape. You had committed other murders and walked away unscathed. The murder of Fieschi and his two colleagues would be just as mysterious. Three Dominican friars, strong, vigorous men murdered silently, swiftly in a guesthouse chamber with no sign of resistance and, more importantly, with no evidence for who was responsible. Perhaps you would like us to think the slayings were the work of a wandering band of Earthworms who had broken into the friary to carry out one last desperate act. No one would even think of blaming three Dominicans, old and venerable, who, at least in public, could not handle an arbalest let alone release a bolt.'

Athelstan tapped the table. 'When I saw the murder room it reminded me of what I had seen in Alberic's chamber and my suspicions hardened. Your victims had not expected it, and why should they? Closeted away, discussing the business in hand, there was a knock on the door and three Dominicans, men who they considered to be friends and brothers, entered the room. Fieschi and his comrades paused to greet you; even as they did, each of you chose a victim. You drew close, brought the hand-held arbalest from beneath your cloak, the crossbow already primed, and released the bolt. No longer than it takes to patter an Ave. At such close range death is instantaneous. They may stagger and groan, but you just stand and watch them die. Fieschi has gone and peace can return to your world.'

'You have no proof!' The infirmarian scraped back his chair. 'I appeal to our Minister General in Rome. I demand that all these false, heinous and outrageous allegations made against me and my friends be formally investigated according to the rules of canon law and the decrees of both Popes and councils. I . . .'

He paused at a loud rapping on the parlour

door. Prior Anselm rose and answered. Athelstan heard voices slightly raised. The prior left the parlour, closing the door firmly behind him. The infirmarian sat down, glancing swiftly at his two companions. Athelstan closed his eyes, sick to his heart. Prior Anselm returned.

'Brother Norbert,' he announced, 'and other senior friars have conducted the most thorough search of your chambers. They have found certain items: pouches of documents secreted away, articles of clothing, mementos, weapons which certainly have bearing on what Brother Athelstan has told us.'

'But what does it matter?' The gatekeeper smiled. 'We will make an appeal. We are prepared to journey to Rome. We are Dominicans; we plead benefit of clergy.' The gatekeeper pointed at Cranston, whose hands now rested on his sword in its sheath on the table. 'The King's courts have no authority over me or my companions. We are religious and must be tried by ecclesiastical commission.'

Athelstan stared at the three men. He already anticipated their defence. The gatekeeper was correct, they were clerics. There would be long appeals to Rome followed by even longer journeys there to appear before this tribunal or that. Adjournments, delays and postponements would be the order of the day. The process might take years to complete and these three men would continue to live in relative comfort, even though their hands were soaked in the blood of innocents. Athelstan arose abruptly to his feet.

'Confess!' he demanded.

'Nonsense.' The infirmarian sneered. 'In God's name, little Athelstan, you do not know who you are dealing with.'

'No, I do not and neither do you. So,' Athelstan jabbed a finger in the face of the man whom he'd once regarded as a close friend and master, 'you can prattle on,' Athelstan accused, 'you can jabber, you can twist and turn, but I tell you this, Prior Anselm and I will petition our Minister General on a matter of great urgency.'

'Which is what?'

'Something you have overlooked,' Athelstan retorted. 'I will demand that a certain grave in our house at Oxford, the one beneath the flagstones of the church there, the small crypt which now houses the mortal remains of King Edward II of England as well as those of his lover Peter Gaveston, be opened. I will argue that these remains should not lie buried in hallowed ground. In my view, the lives of both men leave much to judge and even more to condemn. So why should a Dominican church house them? I shall argue, and Prior Anselm here will support me, that the diabolic coven which supported both men have caused the death of at least four Dominicans including the papal envoy, not to mention a host of innocents. I shall insist that the remains from that tomb be removed from consecrated ground and hung in chains from a tree in a common cemetery . . .'

Athelstan paused. He had hit his mark, an arrow to the heart of the target. 'Thomas Dunheved,' he hissed. 'What say you?' Athelstan hid his excitement. For the first time ever his opponent had dropped the mask; he now stared in horror at Athelstan.

'You wouldn't,' he stammered.

'By God's grace we would,' Prior Anselm retorted. 'I would use every single drop of influence I have in both church and court to purge that grave. After all,' Anselm's face creased into a sour smile, 'what does it contain? Gaveston and the other remains?'

'The King would object.'

'No, Brother Thomas,' Cranston swiftly intervened, 'that is where you are truly wrong. The King and his councillors will review what has been discovered. Trust me, discretion is the better part of valour. The royal council will eventually decide that the canonisation of Edward II is not the best path to follow.' Cranston drummed his fingers on the table. 'They will soon put an end to all this nonsense. They will confirm the published and proclaimed story, that Edward II lies buried in splendour at St Peter's Abbey, Gloucester and no other place.'

Athelstan sat down on his chair and hid his surprise as the three accused seemed to forget where they were. They conversed swiftly in Italian, a patois Athelstan could not follow and, from the looks on other people's faces, neither could anyone else in that chamber. Prior Anselm was going to intervene but Athelstan lifted his hand as a sign to let them continue. Thomas Dunheved spoke swiftly, jabbing the air with his fingers. Once he glanced towards Athelstan and the friar flinched at the sheer hatred in Thomas Dunheved's eyes, a malice which could also be seen in the expression of his two companions. Athelstan realised these men were his mortal enemies. He must never be alone with them or, if they requested, meet them without a sure defence and shield. At last the strange conversation ended. Thomas Dunheved placed his hands flat on the table, drawing one deep breath after another. He glanced up, forcing a smile to hide his fury. 'And if we accede to what you want? If my colleagues and I write a true account, the tomb at Oxford will not be disturbed?'

'The tomb at Oxford will not be disturbed,' Athelstan confirmed, 'but you must face the consequences of your actions.'

Dunheved turned and spoke swiftly in Italian to his two companions, who nodded in agreement.

'Knowing you, Athelstan,' Thomas Dunheved's sharp black eyes were unblinking in their gaze, 'we are to be taken to a chancery office. You want our confession in writing?'

'I do. One account will suffice, provided all three confirm it. Brother Paschal and two other friars will be witnesses. I do have questions.'

'Of course you have, little friar.' Thomas Dunheved was now relaxed. He reminded Athelstan of a gambler who'd played a game, put all on one throw and lost; the way he now looked and how he acted was all that mattered. 'I won't beg,' he sneered. 'Nor will Stephen or Giles.'

'I know that,' Athelstan agreed.

'But you have questions?'

'My first question is why?' Athelstan asked.

'You are Dominicans, friars, preachers, priests. Why all this murderous mayhem?'

'You ask me that, little Athelstan, and I taught you. Don't you have a force within you, a dream to follow?'

'But you killed, you murdered.'

'Hasn't Sir John here killed Frenchmen in battle in pursuit of some dream by our war-like Edward III to become king of France and God knows what else? Remember what I told you, young Athelstan, many years ago? Every heart has its hymn, every soul has its song. Edward of Caernarvon was ours. He was our king, our liege lord, our vision. We friars go through life telling people to love each other. Look at them, Athelstan: whom do they love, really love? We loved Edward of Caernarvon who later became Edward II. We loved Peter Gaveston, his beloved. As a boy I was a page in Gaveston's household. We were Edward II's men, body and soul, in peace and war, in life and in death.

'Fieschi was a threat to the secret about what really happened. What good would have come of it? The kings of England have their shrine to Edward, our master. Let them be content with that. Edward II was no saint. He was a man with all the weaknesses of human kind. He was a prince who suffered one misfortune after another. He was a soul who loved wrongly but passionately. And what would Fieschi have achieved? Nothing but a lie, and in doing so, would have only provoked others to lie about our master. Do you think the French would just ignore it?' Dunheved abruptly stretched across, picked up a goblet and filled it with a jug standing on a tray. He drank greedily before slamming it down on the table before him. 'Pope Urban in Rome wants Richard of England's support. You know what would have happened. Urban's rival in Avignon, Pope Clement, would have immediately attacked the canonisation of Edward II in the firm hope, and he would have been correct, that the French and others would support him.'

'I agree,' Prior Anselm interposed. 'Both the public and personal life of Edward II would have been openly aired and discussed throughout the courts of Europe.'

'More than that.' Stephen Dunheved spoke up. 'Every obscene tale, every sordid story about our master would have seen the light of day. He would have been made an object of ridicule, depicted as a demon incarnate. Richard of England should not look to our master to sanctify his own reign; he should leave the dead to peace and stillness.'

'And Fieschi was a threat to you, wasn't he?' Athelstan demanded. 'I mean, it was only a matter of time before the accepted story was seriously questioned. In time, the French too may have stumbled on this. Their secret chancery at the Louvre would burn the candles late into the night as they searched and studied to discredit every conclusion Fieschi reached.' He paused. 'Alberic had his suspicions, didn't he? And so did Brother Roger.'

'Yes,' Dunheved sighed. 'They were beginning to seriously question the alleged deaths of the Dunheved brothers in Newgate. They both thought it a strange coincidence. They also concluded that our good friend Brother Eadred was of one mind and soul with us.' Dunheved sat back in the chair. 'Once you start stirring the pot all sorts of things begin to rise to the top. It's as you say, Athelstan, Alberic asked to see us, said he wanted to talk about Brother Eadred. You now know what happened.'

'And Pernel?'

'Ah, poor Agnes! We always wondered what had happened to her. Yes, Athelstan, she loved me but I did not abduct Agnes from her nunnery, she came of her own accord. She pledged herself to be one of our coven. Yes, she said she loved me with a passion beyond all telling. But that's the way of the world, Athelstan. She loved me, but in time she realised that I did not love her. While we were abroad, the humours of her mind became deeply disturbed. She fled our company. I thought she had died until she arrived here that morning demanding to see you and Fieschi. The gatekeeper brought her to see me and Stephen immediately. I met her secretly in the small physic garden down near the water-gate. I didn't recognise her but she certainly knew me. One glance and she was calling me Thomas. Poor soul. We tricked her, said we would take her to a safe place further down river. We escorted her to the steps and I pushed her, simple and swift, as easy as snuffing out a candle.

'What you say about the rest is true. Odo Brecon was always a chatterbox, garrulous and loose-tongued; I couldn't believe he had survived. We silenced him as we did poor Agnes whom you call Pernel. I sent Stephen here across the river to burn her house and destroy all memories.

'You were also correct that we sent messages to the Earthworms beyond the walls. The attack was a risk, but it would have been good if the priory had fallen. In our message to the Earthworms we warned them not to hurt or injure any English Dominicans. In fact we thought Blackfriars would swiftly surrender and all would be well for us. Fieschi and his companions, however, would have been treated as foreigners. When the attack failed that left us with no other choice. Our great secret was threatened. We were in danger whilst the true burial place of Edward II of England might also be exposed. It is as you say. The death of Fieschi and his colleagues will silence this matter once and for all. It will take years, if ever, for the papacy and the crown of England to begin this process again.'

Athelstan studied Dunheved. He repressed the deep chill this former friend and mentor now provoked: the other two were simply extensions of Thomas Dunheved's soul. He was the real killer, cold and analytical. Dunheved believed he was above all forms of morality and had free licence to do what he wished to protect himself and the vision he pursued.

'And me?' Athelstan asked. Thomas Dunheved's face creased into a smile.

'I taught you, Athelstan. I know how you can ferret out the truth. I did not wish to hurt you. We did not want to harm you, but you were, and you are, very dangerous, as you have so clearly demonstrated. My heart sank when I saw you. We discussed it amongst ourselves. In the end we had no choice. Fieschi was one thing, Brother Athelstan was another. You should be proud; I am.'

Athelstan tried to hide his revulsion by sifting through his papers.

'And Edward II?' Cranston asked.

'I do not wish to talk about him,' Thomas Dunheved retorted. 'He was in our charge, not yours. This kingdom rejected him. We did free him from Berkeley but he had been abused, beaten, crowned with thorns, stripped, starved, thrown into filth. We fled. Agnes helped us, we sheltered in her nunnery. The King grew strong and we continued our flight. We left this kingdom, moving through Flanders and Hainault across the Rhine and southwards towards Italy. I will not provide you with details. We settled down here and there. Our gatekeeper was our guard. Stephen and I earned good silver working as a clerk, herbalist, leech and apothecary. I became very skilled,' he smiled, 'especially with poisons.'

'And Eadred?' Anselm intervened.

'It's as Athelstan says. We needed money. Edward our master, when fleeing his wife and Mortimer, hid a treasure cache in the royal manor of Alversbury to the north-west of the city. We returned, unearthed it and sent it abroad with others we trusted. We delayed a day and were arrested at Queenhithe.' He grimaced. 'We were lodged in Newgate, but, thanks to Eadred, we were free within days. Brother Eadred took care of the rest, obtaining two corpses to place in our

307

cell, which were then sheathed in deerskin, and so on.' He looked at Athelstan. 'Very clever,' he murmured, 'very clever indeed.'

'Did Edward want to return to England?' Athelstan asked.

'As God lives, little Athelstan, Edward of Caernarvon wanted nothing to do with his former kingdom. He was a broken man. He realised what would happen if he emerged from the dark to lay claim to what was rightfully his. No, no, he was quite content. He lived in relative comfort, and the only passion he betrayed was for his former wife, Isabella. Once again, time, place and occasion met. The King fell ill, some growth deep in his belly. There was nothing the physicians could do. He wanted to return to England one final time. He needed to confront his wife before he died, and he also expressed a deep desire to be buried next to the only person he ever really loved, Gaveston. We had been in contact with Brother Eadred, who was not only provincial of the order in this kingdom but prior of our house in Oxford.' He shrugged. 'The rest you know.'

'Did you poison Isabella?'

'Yes. I gave her a special potion,' Dunheved tapped his own stomach, 'which did damage her, an injury that would take months to develop.'

'And the confrontation between the former king and his wife in the solar at Castle Rising?'

'A matter of the confessional, Brother Athelstan. Isabella the She-Wolf learned that her husband had not died. What passed between the two of them is not for anyone but themselves and God.' He drew a deep breath. 'And now, Athelstan, I have said enough. There are things to be done. I have a letter to write.'

Athelstan nodded in agreement. Cranston called Flaxwith and his bailiffs to take the three prisoners to where Prior Anselm instructed. Once they were gone Athelstan felt the deep, brooding silence of the parlour, as if the passionate words exchanged there still hung heavy in the air.

'What will happen to them?' Cranston asked.

'Oh, they will plead benefit of clergy,' Prior Anselm replied. 'They will appear before a church court who will hand them back to us Dominicans to deal with. Their judgement will be harsh. They will be separated one from the other, which will be a grievous blow to men who have lived their lives in each other's pockets. Each of them will be despatched to live on bread and water on some lonely island or rocky outcrop. They will know true isolation. They will hear no sound except the crash of the waves and the strident call of the gulls. They will have no company. They will never taste wine or soft bread again. They will wait for death and, when it comes, they will welcome it.' Prior Anselm rose to his feet. 'Brother Athelstan, my thanks to you. You must submit a report which I can send to our Minister General. In view of what has happened in the city and here, you are welcome to stay.'

'No.' Athelstan got to his feet. 'Every heart has its hymn, every soul has its song and,' he grinned at the coroner and Prior Anselm, 'whether I like it or not, in my case, it is the parish of St Erconwald's in all its glory.'

Author's Note

The fate of Edward II is one of the greatest mysteries in English history. Most of what is written here is based on historical evidence, as investigated in my non-fiction work, *Isabella and the Strange Death of Edward II*. The Dunheveds did exist. They did storm Berkeley Castle. The imprisoned king may well have escaped and he may have wandered Europe and met Manuele Fieschi. The Dunheveds eventually disappeared from history, though their true fate is not known. However, in those stirring days of 1326–7, they played a crucial role in the history of the English crown.

Richard II did attempt to have Edward II canonised, but in the end this came to nothing, as Richard himself became entangled in a bloody and violent conflict with his leading nobles.

As for the Peasants' Revolt in London, I have been guided by primary sources, though I have exercised poetic licence in allocating a major role in the destruction of Wat Tyler and the consequent sudden collapse of the revolt to Sir John Cranston. Nevertheless, the main thrust of my story is based on fact. The Tower was stormed as I have described and those hapless royal officials brutally butchered. In turn, Wat Tyler met his nemesis at Smithfield; probably drunk and overconfident, he allowed himself to

311

be ambushed by the royal party and paid the ultimate price.

Should any reader think that my story is too fanciful, I must refer to a character who appears in the novel, John Ferrour. He was a real person who went under a series of aliases, one of which was John Marshall. Ferrour was a killer, receiving a pardon on 13 March 1380 for the death of Roger Tibrit of Rochester. John Ferrour had business interests in Southwark. He and his wife Joanna were later indicted for stealing a chest containing a thousand marks from the Savoy Palace and taking it across the Thames. They were also accused of stealing two horses and a considerable amount of pure wool from the priory of Clerkenwell. The same indictment also accuses them of participating in the brutal murders of Sudbury and Hailes. Joanna Ferrour was described as 'a chief actor and leader' in the violent events in London during June 1381. She and her husband were arrested but eventually acquitted by juries, John Ferrour being freed at the request of no less a person than Mayor William Walworth. Ferrour certainly seems to have had a nose for mischief. He was in the Tower when young Henry of Derby was seized. Ferrour intervened and saved the boy. Fast forward nineteen years, and that same Henry of Derby is now King Henry IV, having deposed and executed his cousin Richard II. Not everyone in England was happy with this and conspiracies were formed against the new king. One of those indicted for treason was John Ferrour of Southwark, but he was pardoned because he had saved the life of Henry, 'in a wonderful and kind manner', during the Peasants' Revolt of 1381. In the end historical novels often reflect a reality based firmly on fact rather than fiction!

Dr Paul Doherty OBE
www.paulcdoherty.com